THE AFTERLIFE EXPERIMENT

Also by Sam Weiss

The Altered Planes Trilogy

The Afterlife Experiment

In the House of Root and Rot

Beyond Dreams Into Dark*

The Altered Planes In-Betweens

Asylum, Anomalous

The Stages of Decay*

The Other Seven*

**Forthcoming*

THE AFTERLIFE EXPERIMENT

SAM WEISS

WISE CAT

First published by Wise Cat Press 2023. The Afterlife Experiment. Copyright © 2023 by Sam Weiss

All rights reserved.

No part of this book may be reproduced in any form or by any electronic or mechanical means, including information storage and retrieval systems, without written permission from the author, except for the use of brief quotations in a book review.

The story, all names, characters, and incidents portrayed in this production are fictitious. No identification with actual persons (living or deceased), places, buildings, and products is intended or should be inferred.

ISBN 9978-1-7389440-5-7

Book cover and interior illustrations created by Todor Gotchkov (@artworks.by.tag)

Typography created by Faera Lane

Ornamental breaks created by Fred Kroner of Stardust Book Services

SECOND EDITION 2024

For my mom, see I'm finally letting you read it.

Content Warning

The Afterlife Experiment contains themes and topics of violence, death, gore, mental health, abandonment, death of a child, and domestic abuse.

Part One

In Between Black and White

Chapter 1

Meds

Few things in life are certain. For Atra Hart, losing her mind was one of them.

But not today. Not in this place.

She knelt in front of the toilet. Scraping her finger under her tongue, she dislodged the two pills hidden underneath.

Plop! Plop! into the toilet bowl they went.

She spat several times for good measure, her mouth bitter with the taste of partially dissolved medicine.

That was close. If the nurse had loitered any longer, the pills would have turned to mush.

Fifty-two days had passed since she stopped taking her meds. Fifty-two days in which Dread had been tolerable.

They were also fifty-two more wasted days of her life. But today, her brother was coming. Today, she'd find out how much longer she'd be locked away in Vanishing Plains Psychiatric Hospital.

Maybe this time next week she'd be waking up at her brother's house, never having to worry about palming another pill in her life. She'd stroll down his hallway, the carpet plush under her feet, and enter the kitchen where her brother would be sitting, drinking a coffee. At least, that's how she imagined it. She'd never been in Seth's place. She didn't know where he lived.

Atra's fantasy fractured as footsteps approached. She froze, hidden behind the half-open bathroom door, her fingers hovering over the toilet handle. The pills that should've been digesting in her stomach stared at her. She shut the lid as quietly as she could. Who was here? The nurse had already been in to make sure she was up, dispense meds, and give her permission to leave for breakfast.

"Hello?" a man's unctuous voice came from the bedroom doorway.

Not a familiar voice.

She bit her lip; to flush or not to flush? If she did, the evidence would be gone. But it was awfully suspicious timing for a patient who'd just been given her meds. They'd know she was refusing them again.

The footsteps walking to the edge of her bed thumped in time with her heart. Any second, she'd be in full view, crouched over the toilet.

She shot upright. Something flickered in the corner of her vision. She could tell herself it was a wayward lock of her unruly black hair, but that would be a lie. It was her shadow, moving on its own. It was Dread.

The bathroom door banged open, revealing a stocky man in a lab coat.

"Atra?" His words had the same effect on her teeth as styrofoam rubbing together.

"Who's asking?"

"Dr. Creeley." He tapped the plastic name badge clipped to his chest pocket.

More like Dr. Creepsley. His wide-set eyes glistened under gold-rimmed glasses. He reminded her of a deep-sea entity.

Seth didn't like it when she did that. He said it was mean to judge people so quickly. Usually, she agreed with her brother. But she couldn't wait to point this creep out during today's visit and watch Seth shudder.

"May we talk?" Creepsley asked, when she didn't respond.

"Yeah. Sure." Like she had a choice. If he knew she was in a rush to leave, he'd keep her longer.

Against the bathroom wall, her shadow gripped its own neck, half a second behind. Her stomach clenched, but she ignored it. She'd deal with Dread later.

"Have you been sleeping well, Miss Hart?"

Miss Hart? No one in here addressed the patients so formally.

What a stupid fucking question. The ashen-grey bags beneath Atra's sunken eyes matched the colour of her irises. Between the stress of her possessed shadow and her sundowning roommate, sleep had been next to impossible lately.

Creepsley backed toward the bedroom door. He reached for the handle, awaiting her answer.

"Been sleeping"—*Click!* went the self-locking mechanism as Creepsley shut the door tight—"great."

The last word came out in a wheeze as the air left Atra's lungs. The shatterproof light overhead was particularly harsh against the cold, dark world beyond her room. She felt like an animal called to slaughter.

"Where's Dr. Badar?" She failed spectacularly to keep the fear out of her voice as she asked for her doctor of the past seven years.

"I am reviewing your file today. That's all you need to know."

She didn't miss that he dodged the question entirely.

She scrutinized Dr. *Creeley*. The lab coat, the name badge, the polished black shoes. Everything in order, but she couldn't shake the feeling something was wrong.

"What about your medication?" Creepsley continued. "Have you been taking it daily?"

"Every day," she replied, muscles tensing.

She scanned the room for anything to defend herself. Her twin bed, her roommate's identical one, the shared night table between them; all were bolted to the floor. That was the point. They weren't supposed to have anything to defend themselves with.

"And what about Dread?"

Her hands involuntarily closed into fists. She tried to swallow, but her throat had swollen shut. Her reaction didn't go unnoticed.

Creepsley ducked his head, pretending to look at his clipboard while failing to hide his smirk.

"Has Dread been around?"

"It hasn't been around for years." Her voice wavered.

Against the wall, Atra's shadow turned to face her.

Dread.

Her own personal Grim Reaper. At least, that's what she'd thought it was when it appeared on her bedroom wall when she was nine. That Death had finally chased her down.

Every day since, she clung to the hope it would disappear as abruptly as it appeared. But now at twenty years old, Dread remained, invading her mind like a tumour. She'd hoped stopping her meds would stall it, but it still grew. Her greatest fear was that it would consume her one day, and all that would be left was Dread.

"Is that all? I have to get to the common area and eat before visiting hours start."

"Oh, Miss Hart, I hate to be the bearer of bad news, but there will be no visiting hours today."

A bottomless pit replaced Atra's stomach.

"At least, for you. Your stepbrother won't be coming."

The rocky walls of the pit shook, on the verge of collapse.

"Why?"

Now *she* was falling down the bottomless pit, struggling for something to grab onto.

No, no, no.

Seth had to come today. The process was in motion for him to take legal guardianship of her. She'd finally have her life back so it could begin.

"Because you're leaving today. I've been assigned to transfer you to a new facility," Creepsley went on.

New facility? They couldn't transfer her like a piece of meat in a packaging plant.

"You've become withdrawn, isolated. You've stopped showering, you've stopped sleeping, you're not taking care of yourself. We are very concerned for you."

"I want my doctor." Atra found a foothold in the pit, clinging on for dear life. "Not you. *My* doctor!"

She'd make a scene. Get thrown into a padded cell if she had to. Anything to keep her here long enough for Seth to get to her.

Her gaze moved to the long line of tick-marks scratched into the metal frame of her bed. Each one she'd etched represented a day wasted in this hellhole, all the way back to the day her stepmother had locked her in here and thrown away the key. Seth was her lifeline, her single tie back to sanity. And she would not let this slippery little man take that from her.

"Atra—" Creepsley took a step toward her, extending his hand.

"Don't touch me!" She leapt onto her bed, out of his reach.

"Are you *sure* you took your meds today?" He narrowed his eyes.

She didn't reply. It was always *medication* to the doctors. "*Atra, I know you don't want to take your medication, but we're not trying to poison you; we're trying to help you.*"

Only the patients referred to them as *meds*.

He continued to scrutinize, licking the corner of his liver-toned lips.

"Tell me, what were you doing in the bathroom when I came in?"

In that moment, she realized each of them had figured out something about the other. He knew she wasn't medicated. And she knew he wasn't a doctor.

He backed into the bathroom. His eyes never left her. Although he wasn't smart enough to pass as a medical doctor, he was apparently smart enough to never turn his back on a psych patient.

He was going to lift the toilet seat and find those pills. She wished that was still her biggest problem. The pills didn't matter anymore. She was locked in a room with someone pretending to be a doctor. It was so obvious: his lab coat was faded, the edges frayed. The name badge pinned to the pocket was too small, the letters spelling out his name not quite right.

When she was younger, she remembered patients exchanging tales about fake doctors kidnapping those who didn't behave, but that's all they were—ghost stories. Shit like that didn't happen in real life.

Until now.

Over the booming of her heart, she thought she heard a scream.

Creepsley shifted his clipboard. It rested in the crook of his elbow as he reached into his pocket. The fabric rippled as his fingers wrapped around something. The other hand reached for the toilet lid—

The lights went out. The room plunged into darkness, save for the faint band of dawn blooming on the winter horizon.

Click.

The door swung ajar as the automated locks failed.

Atra sprang off the bed, toward the unlocked door and her freedom. The backup generator kicked in, the grinding of it whirring in her ears. The blue light above the bathroom door illuminated Dr. Creepsley as he reached for her.

A shrill bell erupted, echoing down the halls and into the tiny bedroom. Creepsley clamped his hands over his ears, his clipboard clattering to the floor. Something small and made of glass fell next to it. A syringe?

Atra wasn't sticking around to find out.

She bolted, the previously white hallway awash with the same blue lighting as her room. She'd escaped Creepsley because, unlike him, she expected the siren. Every time the emergencies came on, the wail wasn't far behind. It usually signalled a dangerous patient was on the loose.

But the locks had never failed before. The doors had never opened.

Where was everyone?

If all the locks failed, why am I the only one running?

Orange light flickered at the end of the hall, a stark contrast to the blue emergencies. Black mist billowed down the corridor. It pooled around her ankles and stung her eyes. She inhaled a lungful. Her throat seared as she skidded to a stop.

Not mist. Smoke.

Those sirens weren't warning about a patient on the loose.

Tendrils of fire shot around the corner. They originated from the common area, where she would've been picking apart her breakfast of dry toast and oatmeal had Creepsley, the patient-napper, not intervened. She could thank him for something after all.

Did everyone make it out before the fire spread?

Or had no one made it out at all?

The image of her roommate being roasted alive flashed through her mind as Dread danced across the wall, caught in the red-orange light of the blaze.

The warmth of the flames licked her face.

Run, Atra, run.

Her paralysis broke as she doubled back into the sleeping quarters. As she fled, a single thought stabbed at her brain: Vanishing Plains was designed to have one way in and out of the sleeping quarters. And that way no longer existed. She couldn't even break a window in one of the bedrooms. They were reinforced to prevent patients from doing just that.

But wait—yes. There was another way. The doctors and nurses used a back stairwell, its door painted to match the wall. Those whitecoats waved their keycards over it, thinking they were being sneaky and slipping through before anyone noticed.

But Atra noticed. Nothing got by her in here.

She found the door and barrelled forward, smashing her elbow into it. She expected it to be locked, for the unyielding metal to ricochet her back into the hall. Instead, the door flew open.

Down the stairwell she went. She pivoted around the landing, gripping the railing for balance. Something swooped in the top of her vision, reminding her of a giant bird. At first, she thought it was Dread, but the wings were white, not black.

A lab coat.

She didn't glance behind her to see where Creepsley was. Instead, she focused on keeping one foot in front of the other. Her bare toes slapped the metal ridges of the stairs. Were those Creepsley's footfalls intermingling with the siren? How long until he caught her?

Atra burst onto the main floor, finding herself in a mirror image of the long white hall upstairs.

Left or right?

At the end of the hall to her left was a cluster of patients. They were dressed in the same institutional white T-shirt and grey sweatpants, identical to what she wore. A nurse stood in front of them, creating a barricade with her arms so the patients wouldn't run off.

It looked like the breakfast crew made it out after all. Atra scanned the panicked group for her roommate.

Where am I?

Not a single face, a single body type, fit the description ...

Atra started toward the group. She needed to know if her roommate made it out, but Dread took hold, yanking her back.

The hairs on the back of Atra's neck bristled; through the bray of the siren, she sensed the support beams in the ceiling groan.

She surrendered to the tugging sensation as Dread pulled her to the right, away from the crowd. The ceiling let out a deep shudder. An intolerable wave of heat washed over Atra as it caved in.

She didn't know how close the flames were as she veered into a narrow corridor. A sob rose in her throat. Had the ceiling crashed down on the others?

A shape darted in front of her. Dread?

No, too small. It was ... a *cat*?

Animals were forbidden in the asylum.

Then again, so were fake doctors out to snatch patients.

The cat caught her so off guard she almost stopped. Her sweaty feet slid on the linoleum. She pushed forward, smoke and ash following. How long until the inferno caught up to her?

Ducking her head into her shirt, she covered her mouth and nose. The difference was marginal.

No way out.

The words clanged through her head as she became disoriented by the twists of the hall.

Up ahead, she spotted a door barely visible through the black ash. She rushed through, closing it behind her.

Smoke still seeped in, but at least it wasn't suffocating her. A neat row of coats and boots lined the walls. Doctors' and nurses' daywear; she'd entered the staff room.

Into the closest pair of boots her feet went. They were too big but still better than nothing. She then grabbed a thick coat, stuffing her arms through it. She couldn't imagine ever being cold again, but if—no, *when*—she escaped, the unforgiving prairies would make her the poster child for hypothermia.

Her mouth went dry as a bone. How would she move under these suffocating layers?

She snatched a scarf off the rack, the finishing touch to the outfit. But this wasn't for protection against the cold.

She wrapped it around her face as a barrier against the smoke, once, twice—

Darkness. Silence.

Beads of sweat collected at her hairline and dripped down her face and neck. Over the roar of the flames, her breath ran ragged in her ears. She struggled to inhale, the taste of smoke thick on her tongue. Dropping to her knees, she found clearer air, if only just.

She had to get out. Now, before all she could breathe in was noxious ash.

Easier said than done.

The smoke obstructed any light source. She couldn't tell which direction she'd come from. There must be a window in here. She crawled in what she guessed was the opposite direction from the door. Her eyelids clamped shut, but it didn't matter whether they were open or not. She was blinded, trapped in the room that would become her tomb.

You are not dying in here.

She forced her lids open, searching for a sliver of light.

"*Mew.*"

Her head snapped up, eyes meeting nothing but darkness.

Not a human sound. A cat.

"*Mew.*" Again, but this time with an impatient edge.

Atra dragged herself toward it, growing lightheaded. She wanted nothing more than to lie on the floor and take a break. But that was the smoke talking. If she stopped now, she'd never start again.

The dimmest crack of light shone up ahead, the cat silhouetted against it. His tail flicked back and forth as if to say, *Hurry up*.

The scarf slipped off Atra's face and she spluttered, sucking in a mouthful of ash. She secured the fabric, and when she looked back up, the cat had disappeared.

Great, now you're hallucinating animals and *possessed shadows.*

She reached out, grabbing a ledge. The window above it was covered by a plastic frame, unlike the reinforced windows in the flame-engulfed floor above.

She fumbled for the crank handle, the metal hot. She pumped her arm over and over. The window took forever to open.

Where was the fire? She imagined it devouring the hall, about to burst into the room and take her next.

Once the window was open far enough, she stood. She held her breath, squeezing her eyes shut against the acrid air. Raising her foot, she kicked blindly at the window screen, the last remaining obstacle between her tomb and her freedom. It gave way, the flimsy plastic clattering out onto the snow-covered ground.

Gripping the windowsill, she vaulted herself up and over. Her feet crunched on the snow. The crisp air seared her lungs; she doubled over, coughing.

The building crackled like a poisoned campfire. Even in the early morning, the air outside blazed. The snow's surface mottled as it melted in the heat. Atra made a beeline for the electrified fence surrounding the asylum. When the power went out, did it affect the fence as well?

Hooking her fingers around the chain-link, she tensed for the jolt that never came. She scrambled up. Her boots slipped, slick with snow.

The metal vibrated under her fingers.

She almost released her grip, thinking the power to it had been restored.

But it wasn't the fence that was vibrating.

Everything was.

The snowy field in front of her shook. Deep crevasses shuddered across it, resonating through the fence. It reminded her all too vividly of when the ceiling crashed down.

An ear-shattering crack rattled her bones as a blinding light enveloped her. She clung to the fence, waiting for the ground to open and swallow her whole.

But what opened was above, not below.

Atra squinted through the brightness. A long electric-purple fissure blossomed in the sky, green tendrils twisting into the ether.

Before she could make sense of it, something clamped around her ankle. It yanked her down.

Her fingers slipped off the cold metal. She would've tumbled to the ground, save for a button from her coat getting caught in the fencing.

Dr. Creepsley stood below, his fingers wrapped around her leg. Soot covered his sweaty face, his thinning hair singed on one side. Atra tried to squirm her leg out of his grasp, but it might as well have been caught in a vise.

She kicked out with her other leg. Her boot made contact with his face. His grip loosened and she pulled free, scurrying out of his reach. She flung herself over the fence, not checking if he was coming after her.

The barbed wire tore a gash through the coat. It dug into her flesh, but she ignored it.

She was so intent on getting to the other side she didn't contemplate how far the drop was. Her boots smashed through the icy cover of snow. Shocks of pain radiated up her knees. Behind her, flames shot out of the shattered windows.

Creepsley picked himself up off the ground, his nose swollen. He bared his blood-coated teeth at her. The unnatural purple light reflected in his crooked glasses.

Atra turned and fled through the vast snow-bound field. Would he chase her?

The city lights beyond the asylum glowed, muted by the rift dancing in the sky above.

All the times she imagined leaving Vanishing Plains, Atra never thought it would play out quite like this.

Chapter 2

Infrared

"Mr. Henderson."

Tom suppressed a gasp, nearly knocking over his coffee in his haste to exit his email browser.

"Y—yes?"

He cleared his throat. On the other side of his desk, his boss stared daggers at him. Tom's blood pounded through his veins at such a frenetic pace he thought he might vibrate off his ergonomic office chair and straight through the tiled ceiling.

He knows. You were going to be found out eventually, you fucking fake.

Tom wiped at his mouth. The same damp sweat collecting on his upper lip had also soaked through the armpits of his cheap white button-up.

"Are those expense reports ready?" the boss asked, in a no-nonsense tone.

The expense reports didn't matter. The audit didn't matter. Tom was going to jail for life.

"Are you listening? End of the day." The boss made a point of staring at the clock on the wall behind Tom's desk. Twenty to five.

"This is the most important thing you'll ever do for this company."

"Righto, sir." Tom picked up the nearest pen, clicking it. "Will do."

His smile failed to achieve liftoff.

The boss's face screwed up in frustration, veins popping up along his temples. Tom sensed he wanted to unleash a few choice words on him, but—

That's what happens when you're idiotic enough to blackmail me into committing major corporate fraud for you.

As soon as the boss was out of sight, Tom re-opened the window on his computer. He refused to meet his own eyes in the reflection of the monitor—shit brown, like the rest of him. He was filled to the brim with it. The corners of his mouth pulled down from years of stress, making him look older than his forty-four years.

The email had to go. Without glancing at the words on the screen, he deleted it.

There.

Although it didn't change anything—Mr. Unknown Sender still knew his secret—a sense of relief washed over him. Those incriminating words were no longer on display for prying eyes to see.

Tom thought back to ten minutes ago, before the email reared its ugly head, when his biggest problem was a potential prison sentence for fraud.

He tried to turn his attention to the expense reports, but his thoughts pulled him in a thousand directions. This fucking audit was the least of his—

Concentrate, Tom.

He grabbed a fistful of his black hair and tugged on it. How many weeks in a row had the wife nagged at him to get it cut now?

He had to finish this fucking report by five. It took exactly eleven minutes to drive to his apartment complex. He lived on the other side of this pathetic excuse for a city; if he arrived at the apartment any later than 5:15 p.m., the wife would start thinking he was out gambling away the remainder of his paycheque. And the last thing he needed was Naomi up his ass about something he hadn't even done. Yet.

It was 5:02 when he tossed the reports into the metal file sorter on his way out.

Tom was halfway out the door when he remembered his coat and bag still slung around his chair. Cursing under his breath, he doubled back to retrieve them.

The second hand on the clock ticked past 5:04 as he threw on his jacket. Fuck. He was going to be late.

"Are those expense reports done, Tom?" the mousy woman occupying the front desk asked, as he passed her.

"Huh?" He hadn't noticed her. "Yeah."

"Do a good job on them?" she pressed, her question simmering with implications.

He didn't deign to give her a response.

He clomped down the two flights of stairs, bursting through the glass doors to the outside world. Cold mountain air hit his lungs, sobering him. The winter solstice approached; the sun had already dipped behind the white-capped mountains.

As he navigated the icy patches in the parking lot, he fished a pack of smokes out of his jacket pocket.

He started the car and lit a cigarette. The panic snaking through his body dissipated as the nicotine hit his bloodstream. The farther he drove from work, the less the email seemed to exist.

"Whoever sent the email doesn't want you in jail or they would've called the police already," he told himself through the cigarette dangling between his lips. "They want something."

But what? He was a nobody in a dead-end job in a city no one knew existed.

Right?

Tom slowed to a stop at a red light.

He almost didn't notice the figure standing at the crosswalk, unmoving. The glowing lights from the surrounding shapes and cars should have illuminated the person, but instead, they remained silhouetted. Tom didn't like it. The person reminded him of a decomposing corpse stuffed into their Sunday best.

Tom watched, waiting for them to cross the street. His muscles tensed the longer the person remained still. Sweat bloomed under his collar. Why did he care if they crossed or not? Once the light turned green, he'd never see them again.

That damned email did more than fry his nerves; it was making him downright irrational.

The light turned. He accelerated, body relaxing as he left the silhouette behind.

His mind pivoted back to the email. Back to Mr. Anonymous Sender. How had they found him? He had a new name. A new life. Fox's Glew had one pathetic excuse for a mall. One community bus that never seemed to run. Tom chose this city because it was the perfect place to be forgotten.

He thought wrong.

Another red light. As he stopped, he checked the time on the console.

5:12.

He hissed through clenched teeth, picturing Naomi hovering by the apartment door clutching a glass of wine. Cracking the window, he ashed his smoke out of it. That was when he noticed another silhouette at this crosswalk. The person stood so still they could've been made of marble.

He'd almost chalked it up to a coincidence when he realized the suit jacket had the same broad, pointed shoulders as the silhouette at the previous crossing. In fact, everything was the same. Same height, same build, same freaky skeletal arms and legs.

Not possible. Even if they sprinted, that person could not have gotten to this next set of lights before Tom's car. There had to be another explanation.

The panic clutching Tom's chest was ludicrous. It was a person at a crosswalk!

The silhouette turned in his direction. It happened so slowly Tom didn't register it at first.

He glared at the traffic light, which remained stubbornly red. His temples throbbed from clenching his jaw.

Change, you bastard, change!

The silhouette continued to turn, almost revealing their face to him.

The light changed, the green glow like the sun breaking through a stormy day. Tom floored the gas pedal, tires squealing on the asphalt as he flew down the street. He made a point to not look at the crosswalk in his rear-view mirror—if he saw that face, he was certain he'd go mad. His hands were wrapped so tightly around the steering wheel, he'd broken his smoke in two. After picking the halves off the dashboard, he tossed them out the window.

Something darted in his peripheral vision.

His stomach sank, knowing what the movement was before he glanced at it.

That silhouette, tall and gaunt, was on the sidewalk. It moved at an impossible speed, keeping pace with Tom's car. Tom threw an arm up to shield his view of the thing.

He refused to see it. No human could match his vehicle's speed, and yet the silhouette kept pace without effort.

He accelerated, cutting off an SUV as he switched lanes, turning onto the street his apartment complex was on. He sped into the underground parking, pulling into his designated spot beside Naomi's car.

Tom cut the engine and sat in silence, pulse beating erratically in his neck. He didn't see anyone.

But who knew what was lurking behind those pillars, just out of sight.

He opened the car door. The sound echoed across the concrete walls. He told his legs to step out of the vehicle, but they wouldn't comply.

He didn't want to admit it, but that silhouetted—

Ghost, his mind filled in before he could suppress the word

—thing had him scared shitless. No matter how much he willed himself to stand, his ass remained adhered to the seat.

Get the fuck up, Tom, before it finds you.

He finally managed to unglue himself. The space between his car and the elevator stretched out like a vast chasm. Putting his head down, he proceeded forward at just short of a run.

When he reached the elevator, he realized his work bag, and the gum he chewed to disguise his cigarette stench, was still in the car.

Dammit.

Naomi would smell his ashy breath and rag on him about how they couldn't afford a pack of smokes every second day. Money. That's all she cared about. She didn't give a shit if it gave him lung cancer and he croaked. At least he wouldn't be costing her money anymore.

The sweat between his shoulder blades turned clammy. He suppressed a shudder as he hit the call button on the elevator panel. He'd forgotten about the email after the spooky silhouette. But now its weighty implications came crashing back down like the proverbial ton of bricks.

What to tell the wife when she'd inevitably ask why he seemed distracted tonight?

The answer was obvious. Nothing.

It's not like she knew anything about his past. She thought she was married to Thomas Henderson, who'd grown up two towns over and had a bachelor's degree in business. Little did she know that all he had was a bachelor's degree in bullshit. Mr. Big Phony Fake.

He jabbed the call button again. His shoulders tensed, waiting for the silhouette's hand to clamp down.

Stop it. There's nothing there.

The doors slid open. He stepped inside, not turning around until the doors closed. He drummed his fingers against his legs as the elevator ascended.

The second floor appeared no different than usual. The same chipped walls in desperate need of a patch job, the same mouldy carpet that gave off a permanent funk no matter how many times it was deep cleaned. But something was *off*, something he couldn't put his finger on.

He forced himself not to break into a run as he dug his keys out of his jacket pocket. His hands trembled as he attempted to fit the key into the apartment lock, missing once ... twice ...

Get your shit together, Tom.

Behind him, the elevator doors pinged open. He imagined the silhouette flitting toward him with its unnatural speed.

Into the lock the key went. His sweaty palm slipped off the handle. The silhouette was closing in, arms outstretched, ready to take him.

The handle turned. He flung himself inside, slamming the door shut and fastening the chain lock into place.

"Naomi."

The wife's name tumbled out before he thought to say it. At that moment, he needed some form of human comfort. It surprised him he sought it from her. He rarely associated the two things together.

The apartment was dark with no sign of her being home.

Then whose car did I park beside?

Maybe the silhouette stalking him had gotten to her first.

The red light on the corner of the TV pulsed across the living room, revealing the shape of a person sitting on the couch.

So, Naomi was here after all. What had he done to warrant her ignoring him in such a dramatic fashion?

"Naom—" he cut off mid-name as he really took her in. The shape was too tall to be the wife, with broad, pointed shoulders.

A strangled cry rose in the back of his throat. He tore away the chain lock, backpedalling out of the apartment. He raced down the hall. The elevator doors stood open, waiting for him. Skidding to a stop inside, he smashed the main floor button.

The elevator lurched. Instead of descending, he watched the number panel climb from *2* to *3* to *4*.

He punched main floor again with such force he was surprised the plastic didn't crack.

… *5* … *6* …

Impossible. The building had five floors. He pushed the emergency stop, a frantic cry escaping his lips.

At first, Tom thought the whispers were his own panicked thoughts. They slithered into his ears, insidious, swelling to a steady crescendo until the space was filled with a horde of ghostly voices murmuring his name.

"Tom … Liar … Fake …"

… *7* … *8* …

The whispers vibrated his eardrums. He pressed his hands over his ears as the elevator stopped at the nonexistent ninth floor.

The voices ceased. He held his breath, nails biting into the sides of his head. What awaited him on the other side of those doors?

They slid open. He squeezed his eyes shut, shrinking away; any second and the silhouette would be reaching out for him, enveloping him in its sinister embrace …

Nothing happened.

He cracked his eyes open.

The elevator revealed the main lobby. The midnight blue of the outside world stood beyond the glass-front doors. He had to get the fuck out of this building.

But was this a trick?

His cell phone vibrated in his pocket. He didn't want to read the text, but—

> **Unknown Sender**
> Behind you

The elevator might have stopped moving, but his stomach hadn't. It plunged through the floor, the cavity it previously occupied replaced by a chunk of ice.

Everything between tumbling out of the elevator and bursting onto the street was a blur. Tom fled down the sidewalk, not caring where he headed. The only thing he cared about was putting as much distance between himself and the apartment complex as possible.

The bite of the outside air chilled his skin, yet the veins underneath had turned to acid. His teeth chattered. A lump formed in the back of his throat and he swallowed the urge to vomit.

The street appeared fine. *Normal*. The same as it had for the past eleven years, ever since he'd arrived in Fox's Glew. But it no longer felt like the same innocuous street. That silhouette could be lurking behind every bush, every covered patio, every gap between buildings. Tom had descended into a reality where the monsters lurking under his childhood bed were hungry for him again.

His cell phone, still clutched in his hand, vibrated again.

And again.

And again.

He looked.

> **Unknown Sender**
> Polaris

His heart stopped cold.

> Blaire Callisto
>
> Quillon Glasser

He stuffed the phone in his pocket. The urge to vomit returned. His phone continued to vibrate.

> Stella Maris
>
> Magnus Deadmarsh

And then, the same words as in the email that had started it all:

> I know you killed them

The sidewalk greyed out of focus.
Helpless.
Out of control.
Tom simultaneously wanted to curl into a ball on the ground and throw his hands into the air and scream.

He did neither. Instead, he kept walking.

A corner store stood up ahead. The white lights shone out the windows, a beacon of respite. He charged toward it.

He'd thought being outside would be better, but now he wanted back in. Perhaps the four walls of the corner store would keep him safe, contained.

A bell above the door dinged as Tom stepped inside. The clerk didn't bother to look up from the magazine in his hands. No music played overhead, leaving Tom with nothing but his own uneven breathing to listen to. He made his way to the back coolers, pacing in front of them. He read the texts on his phone again, as if doing so would change their meaning.

> **Unknown Sender**
> You killed them

How did Mr. Anonymous know? Everyone who knew of Polaris's existence died inside it. He was the sole survivor. The only one left to suffer.

His phone rang, breaking the suffocating silence. His thumb

declined the call before he had a chance to process it. The clerk at the register tore himself away from his reading to glance at him.

Tom had a moment of clarity, seeing himself through the clerk's eyes: a scrawny man, clammy with sweat, eyes darting around nervously. Probably thought he was some junkie ready to rob the joint.

The walls of the corner store closed in.

"Tom ..."

He jerked around. His strung-out reflection met him in the cooler's glass door.

"Tom ..."

"Tom ..."

The whispers were back.

"We know what you did, Tom."

"You killed them all."

Their breaths fell on his neck, the voices of those long dead at Polaris. They followed as he turned down the aisle.

"Fake."

"Liar."

His phone vibrated. Mr. Anonymous again. Tom wanted to throw his phone at the clerk, who continued staring, and run out of the store with his hands over his ears.

Instead, he accepted the call. He didn't know what made him do it, but the moment he held the phone to his ear, the whispers ceased.

"Hello?" He didn't recognize the guttural growl as his own voice.

No response on the other end.

"Look, asshole—" he began, mustering courage from the depths.

"Where the hell are you?"

"... Naomi?"

He choked her name out. He did a double take at the phone screen. Not Mr. Anonymous, but the wife.

"Dinner's ready, *asshole*." Even though his phone was an arm's length away, Naomi's voice rang through the store.

He cringed, knowing she would not forget his unfortunate choice of words anytime soon.

"What the hell are you doing?" she ragged on. "You ran straight back out of the apartment before I could say hello."

But the apartment was empty when he arrived. Just him and that spooky silhouette.

"Tom, are you drunk?"

He held the phone back up to his ear. "Umm …"

"*Get. Home.*"

Click.

He remained frozen, the phone pressed against his face. The clerk's suspicious expression changed to one of amusement. Yes, Tom was just a schmuck husband in trouble with the old ball-and-chain.

He opened his call history. Nothing from Unknown Sender. But two from Naomi, at 5:35 p.m. and 5:37 p.m., respectively. He scrolled through his texts, the phone heavy in his shaky fingers.

The only recent texts he'd received were from the wife.

> **Naomi**
> Where did you go?
>
> Are you okay??
>
> Answer me!!!!
>
> Where the fuck are you??!!!!

The names, the threats, everything about his dirty little Polaris secret, gone.

He shoved the phone back into his pocket. Straightening himself out, he left the store, avoiding eye contact with the clerk. Had he imagined everything? But how did that explain the original email, back in the office, which led to his downward spiral?

The sensation of being followed disappeared. He was alone as he returned to the apartment, not a silhouette in sight.

Chapter 3

Shadow Play

The door banged shut behind Atra as she entered the diner. She fully expected everyone to drop their utensils and stare at her.

"It's the crazy one!" someone would shriek, as they cowered in terror. *"Call the cops. Put her back where she belongs!"*

A waitress bustled past with an armload of dirty dishes.

"Take a seat where you can find one," she said, with a polite, yet rushed, smile and disappeared through a set of swinging doors behind the counter.

That was it. Because no one out here knew she was nuts.

Atra shuffled down the checkered floor between the tables, keeping her head down. Although she'd washed the soot off her face with melted snow and shaken the ash out of her hair, she reeked of smoke. She crossed her arms over her body in an attempt to feel less exposed.

She took the only available seat at a booth beside a window. Her legs shook, exhaustion setting in. After she'd jumped the fence, she made for the city, putting one foot in front of the other. She never looked over her shoulder to see if Dr. Creepsley had caught up.

Technically, Telos was her home. She'd grown up in this city—

hell she could've eaten at this very diner when she was a kid. But after being locked away for seven years, entering civilization was like landing on another planet. The skyscrapers, the cars whizzing past, the shopfronts—nothing looked familiar. The diner seemed as good a place as any to hunker down while she formed a plan.

The nurse's black peacoat she'd stolen suffocated her in the indoor heat. She shrugged it off, pausing with the coat around her elbows. Her bright white medical bracelet stood out against her pale olive skin. *Atra Hart,* it might as well have said, *if found, please return to VANISHING PLAINS.* Hastily, she put the coat back on.

The gash she'd received from the barbed wire burned. Her shirt, glued to her side by her blood, tugged at the edges of the wound. At least the thick coat had borne the brunt of the damage.

The voices surrounding Atra grew louder. So many people. Too many.

At least she was blending in. At least no one was paying attention to her.

A waitress slapped a menu in front of her.

"And how are we doing today?"

No reply seemed fitting.

"That's good. Coffee?" The waitress reached for the cup, not noticing Atra's lack of response.

"Uh—sure." The waitress had already started to pour. Brown liquid sloshed down the side of the cup, pooling in the saucer.

"I'll be back in a few when you're ready to order."

And with that, she was gone.

Busy, busy, busy. This city was so *busy.*

Atra stared at the coffee cup. Seth always clutched a paper cup of the stuff when he visited. She'd never tried it. Coffee was banned at the asylum.

Through the window, the rift hovered over the skyscrapers. Its purple light dimmed as the day brightened. No one else pointed toward the sky and claimed the heavens had torn open. Even though everyone out here seemed unobservant, this was something Atra didn't think would go unnoticed.

She had to be the only one seeing it. Just like how she was the only one seeing Dread, who hovered between the table and the window.

She focused on the menu, the laminated cover tacky under her fingers. Too many choices. She flipped the page. More choices. And on the next page, even *more* choices.

The never-ending menu.

She couldn't decide.

Everyone in here, making choices. What time they wanted to eat, what they wanted to eat, what they wanted to do afterward. And they looked miserable doing it.

A middle-aged woman scowled at her plate of pancakes as if she'd been served dog shit. A man wearing an oversized trucker's hat barely kept his eyes open over his cup of coffee.

They weren't poked and prodded at with a nurse's cold fingers before the sun even came up. *They* weren't told when it was lights out, or when it was time to eat, or when they could see their loved ones. *They* didn't have one shelf containing the same thirteen books and five puzzles as their only source of entertainment for almost a decade.

Hadn't, Atra corrected herself. *It's in the past now.*

"What can I get ya?" The waitress had returned, notepad at the ready.

"Umm ..." She scanned the page. Anything was better than those rubbery, rehydrated eggs in the asylum. "Chocolate chip waffles."

"Want syrup or whipped cream?"

"Yes. Both. Extra syrup." Because why not?

The waitress took the menu, departing once more.

Just like how coffee wasn't allowed in the asylum, sugar was only tolerated in small doses. There was maybe a teaspoon in the bowls of gluey oatmeal they served. Atra had always asked her roommate to grab her a bowl from the food lineup in the common area while she stayed behind to dispose of her meds.

Beryl would give her the stink eye, with her one cloudy cataract boring through her. Beryl wasn't stupid. Blind as a bat? Definitely. Mad as a hatter? Came with the territory. But she knew exactly what Atra was doing in that bathroom.

Beryl hadn't been in the hall with the morning crowd as Atra was escaping the fire. That meant she hadn't been crushed with the rest of the patients when the ceiling collapsed.

Right?

That didn't make it better. It meant Beryl hadn't made it out of the common area at all. Atra chewed on her lip. Why hadn't she done more? She'd ditched on Beryl like her own father had done to her.

"He couldn't do me at least one favour and take you with him." She could almost hear her stepmother's biting words after her father left them. *"Instead, he saddles me with you. Typical."*

Seth quite literally had been the only thing keeping her sane in that house after Dread emerged. But no matter how hard she tried to push her shadow away, she couldn't fool her stepmother. In the end, that woman had gotten her wish, and Atra was gone too.

She shut out the memory as she raised the mug to her lips and took a sip of coffee. Her nostrils flared; she would've been better off licking asphalt. Adults *enjoyed* this stuff? Everyone in here clutched a mug of it as if it contained precious gold.

She placed her mug back, the saucer seeming too far away. She'd dreamed of this moment forever, of being out of the asylum. Now that the time had arrived, it was difficult to believe it was happening.

Picking up a spoon, she stirred the coffee. What to do? The answer was obvious: find Seth. But she didn't know where he lived. Where could she obtain such information? The first place that sprung to mind was a library.

Atra remembered they came with cards, but for what? Did you need the card to enter a library?

No. Even she knew how stupid that sounded.

Her childhood memories were a smattering of islands in a vast ocean, with deep trenches of nothingness in between. She *should* have a memory of going into a library. She *should* have a memory of how they worked.

But she didn't.

Her stomach twisted. She knew so little about the outside world. What if she never found Seth?

The metal spoon clinked against the mug as she swirled her coffee.

No. She'd find him.

She imagined walking up the driveway to his house and knocking on the door. What would Seth do when he discovered her on his doorstep?

He'd be mad.

No—of course he wouldn't be mad. He'd be happy. Stoked, in fact, for her to show up, unannounced, his nutjob of a sister moving in to throw a wrench into his life.

"Maybe I should phone him first," she muttered.

Clink! Clink! went the spoon as it whirled faster and faster.

Great—now she needed to find an address *and* a phone number. Atra had no clue what she was doing out here in the real world. She'd craved this freedom for years, and now that she had it, it was too much. She almost wished she was back in her shared quarters with Beryl.

Almost.

Beryl had a family out here, too. She'd talked about her grandkid, who was never allowed to visit, almost as much as Atra babbled about Seth.

Stop it.

Atra's mind bounced like a ping pong ball, landing on her last visit with her brother.

Seth had asked questions. *A lot* of questions.

They'd sat in the common area, at a table near the back. Seth had peered over his glasses at her as he clutched his mug, filled with the same tar currently swirling in front of her.

"Are you really okay, Attie?"

"I'm fine." The standard response.

He said nothing, still staring. Her answer wasn't good enough.

"I'm not crazy, Seth. They've never been able to pinpoint what's 'wrong'"—she made air-quotes—"with me. First, they thought I had schizophrenia. Then it was paranoid personality disorder. Then, fuck it, I'm bipolar. But nothing sticks. Nothing ever sticks. It's because I'm. Not. Crazy."

Her argument would've sounded more convincing if she really believed it.

By the doorway, the nurses whispered to one another as they glanced in her direction. What were they saying about her?

Atra wanted to tell Seth about how they watched her. Always watching. She couldn't tell him, though. Adding paranoia to her laundry list of symptoms definitely wouldn't help anything.

"What about ... that shadow?" Seth had chosen his words carefully. "Doom, or whatever you call it."

"Dread," she corrected him, her voice soft in juxtaposition to her booming heart. "I haven't seen it in years."

She'd wished it didn't have to be a lie.

At the time it almost wasn't. Dread had been nothing but a whisper of a shadow then. It wasn't until the days leading up to the fire that it had grown prominent enough to worry her.

Atra met her brother's gaze.

Fear. That's what was in his eyes. Fear of what she was capable of. Wondering if he was doing the right thing by setting her loose.

"I want to make sure you're okay before you come home with me." Again, choosing his words carefully. "I want you to have the best life you can."

She tried scooting her chair in, but it was futile; the legs were weighted so they couldn't leave the ground. "That isn't happening here."

Clink! Clink! Clink!

The spoon hitting the mug rattled her out of the memory. The voices around her swelled, like someone had cranked the volume. She clunked the spoon harder, trying to drown them out.

Clink! Clink! Cl—

The cup shattered. She froze, the dark liquid pooling on the table, dripping off the edge of it.

She peered up. The diner had fallen silent. The waitress behind the counter paused while grabbing the coffee pot. A man in a business suit seemed frozen, a forkful of scrambled eggs halfway to his mouth. For a moment, Atra had the crazy notion she'd been suspended in time.

The business suit stood.

"The night the moon bleeds is the night the world will end." He pointed an accusing finger at her. "There's death in the moon. And the moon is you."

Atra tore her gaze away, returning to the broken mug. But the mug was whole again. A small puddle of coffee on the table was the only evidence of her hysterical stirring.

When she looked up again, the man was seated. No one stared at her. The volume was back to normal.

Out. She had to get out.

She stood, hip knocking against the table in her haste to leave. Keeping her head down, she made for the doors. The bell chimed overhead, signalling her exit.

She inhaled deeply, thinking the air outside would be fresher. It wasn't. Just the exhaust and garbage of an overpopulated city. How did Seth live in it? How would she?

Comforting thoughts of the asylum, of her metal-framed bed, of Beryl asking what she wanted for breakfast, crept in.

"Hey!" The diner door flew open behind her. "You have to pay for that coffee!"

Atra recognized the waitress's voice but didn't turn around. No way in hell was she going back in there. Instead, she stuffed her hands in her pockets and picked up her pace.

"Stop! Hey—stop!"

Atra turned a corner, losing herself in the crowd. But even though she'd shaken off the waitress easily enough, that damn split in the sky followed no matter how fast she moved. Why was no one else noticing it? They were too wrapped up in those little glass screens clutched in their hands to see the real world.

The street was busy, people on all sides pressing in, suffocating her.

She collided with someone about her age. She started to apologize, but then he pointed at her.

"What is at the beginning of everything and at the end of time?" He spoke in the same deep monotone as the business suit in the diner as his facial features melted away. "Dread. Dread is."

She recoiled, squeezing her eyes shut. She hoped when she opened them, he'd be gone.

He wasn't. The colour had drained from his skin, leaving him with a featureless grey face.

Atra fled, knocking through the throng on the sidewalk. She hoped if she ran fast enough, she'd outrun her body entirely. A car horn blared. Someone grabbed her coat and pulled her back.

She'd gone right off the sidewalk and into oncoming traffic.

"Whoa, careful there!"

She spun to face her rescuer, eyes bugging out of their sockets.

Another grey featureless face stared back.

"Are you all right?" Atra heard it ask, even though it had no mouth.

Panicked, she tore free.

"*The rift, she's the only one who can see it.*" The whispers started.

"*Freak.*"

She scoured the crowd, looking for someone—anyone—

normal, but the city had become a blur of faceless beings, milling around blindly with no eyes in their heads.

"She left her best friend behind."

"But she still has Dread. Until it ends us all."

Atra sank to the curb, pulling her knees close and pressing the palms of her hands into her eyes. She pushed so hard the redness that erupted under her lids matched the chaos around her. Anything to make it *stop*.

A vehicle slowed beside her, tires crunching on asphalt.

"Do you need help?"

She removed her hands. A beige camper van had stopped in front of her. A woman leaned across the seat, adjusting her navy headscarf as she spoke through the rolled-down window.

"Are you okay?"

A loaded question. Of course, Atra wasn't okay. She was a psych patient thrust too early into this world. How could she even be sure this woman was real?

Seth was right for questioning if she was well enough to live with him.

"Do you need a ride?" the woman persisted.

Atra nodded and stood, blood rushing to her head. She sensed movement out of her peripherals. The black cat from the asylum trotted away with his tail in the air. As if sensing her, he turned and let out a mew.

She opened the passenger door and stepped in. The cat pawed at the ground, tail lashing back and forth. He meowed again, distressed.

Don't do it, Atra, he was saying.

She should've listened. She should've trusted the cat.

The woman in the bandana offered her a bottle of water. Atra took it, guzzling it back, the coffee still bitter on her tongue. Her head cleared. Why did she accept this ride? The van reeked of incense.

"I need to get to the library," she said to the woman.

"Sure. We can do that. The closest one isn't far."

Good. The faster she got out of here, the better.

The woman's knuckles whitened as she gripped the steering wheel. The van accelerated.

The skyscrapers turned into animated trails as they whizzed past. Atra averted her gaze, nauseous, but the trails followed her into the car.

"I'm Evie." The woman's voice came from far away. "The Drove is going to take good care of you, Atra."

How do you know my name? she tried to ask.

Something wasn't right. Her chest was being crushed under a pile of bricks. The trails streamed everywhere, though her head remained still.

"*To the field ... down the left-hand path we go ...*" Evie sang softly.

Atra closed her eyes, the bricks now crushing her throat. The trails didn't stop, spinning beneath her lids.

"*Hand in hand, we will never be alone ...*"

Atra awoke to the rumbling of tires over rough pavement. Her neck ached from having passed out with her chin to her chest, but she couldn't lift her head.

Memories flooded in, a tiny fissure in the hull at first, then bursting forth until the ship was sinking.

But she still couldn't move her damned head. She struggled to open her eyelids. Her body wanted to slide back to that place of darkness and nothing.

She forced them open. Beyond the van window, snow-capped peaks shone under the moonlight.

She'd lost an entire day.

And she wasn't in Telos anymore.

Stop the car, she tried to say, but her tongue was stuck to the roof of her mouth. She rolled over to face Evie. But there wasn't a woman with a blue bandana sitting in the driver's seat.

It was Creepsley.

Where did he come from?!

Atra's first instinct was to open the door and jump out, moving vehicle be damned. She didn't get that far. Creepsley had bound her wrists together, then wound the length of the rope around her thighs.

Shit.

Evie was sprawled out in the back of the camper van, facedown, neck bent at an unnatural angle.

Atra struggled in her restraints. Creepsley finally noticed, turning toward her. His cracked glasses magnified his eyes.

"What do you want with me?" Her words sludged out from the muddy depths of her brain.

"My reward. And I *will* be rewarded greatly, Miss Hart."

She didn't know who had this reward and she sure as hell wasn't sticking around to find out. She yanked at her restraints again. Either Creepsley sucked at tying knots, or he'd bought exceptionally shitty rope, because they snapped so unexpectedly she bonked herself in the head with her freed arms.

Stars exploded in her vision, dazing her all over again. Atra shook her head, trying to orient herself. The car handle. She had to get out of here.

Creepsley was faster, slamming the locks down from his side. She lunged for the handle anyway, but it refused to open.

My reward, Creepsley's words clanged through her head. She didn't want to know the sinister implications of it. She wasn't about to be anyone's reward.

On to Plan B.

She lunged for Creepsley instead.

Atra rammed him, disoriented in the cramped space that was all hard angles. His rough, dry hand snaked its way around her face, pushing her away. Opening her mouth wide, she chomped down on his hand.

Creepsley yanked away, screaming at her, calling her a crazy bitch, and then he was screaming about something else. A light filled the vehicle, too bright to be the moon.

Through the windshield, a pair of headlights barrelled toward them. A horn blared, but from which vehicle she wasn't sure.

Atra reached over and yanked the wheel as sharply as she could. It vibrated under her hands as the other vehicle nearly clipped them. The van drifted back into its own lane, sliding over the icy asphalt—

Uh-oh.

Atra had enough time to contemplate her poor decisions as the wall of trees grew closer.

Then, nothing.

Dark.

Chapter 4

Call of the Void

Tom drummed his fingers against his work desk.

Taptaptaptaptap.

The other hand went up to his mouth, teeth whittling away at his thumbnail. The boss better call him in soon. At this rate, he wouldn't have a thumbnail left.

The idea of his nail bed pulpy and exposed ceased his nibbling. He rested his hand on his bouncing knee instead.

Stop it.

But his leg wouldn't listen. It bobbed up and down.

Up and down.

Up and down.

How long could the boss keep him waiting like this? Out of instinct, Tom reached for his phone, then stopped himself. He'd turned it off and thrust it in his workbag this morning. He wouldn't touch it, no matter what. Mr. Anonymous could text all he wanted into the void.

His tongue went dry, like he had wiped it with cotton. He needed a drink of water.

Screw that—he needed a goddamn cigarette.

No—he needed to get the fuck out of here.

The boss wouldn't have gone through this whole performance of summoning Tom to his office if it was good news. That meant Tom screwed up on the Very Important Expense Report.

He glanced at the time in the top right corner of his computer screen. 9:52 a.m. That bastard had kept him on the hook for twenty minutes. He was doing it on purpose to make Tom squirm.

Tom opened his inbox out of habit. The Very Incriminating Email from yesterday sat at the top, marked *Unread*. No matter how many times he deleted it, it returned.

The fluorescent light over his desk buzzed.

Liar, it said. *Fake. Murderer.*

There had to be a way to get rid of this email. He was going to get called into the boss's office, get fired, and after he collected his belongings, the sucker in charge of wiping his computer would find the email waiting right there.

Then, after Tom had escaped to the bar to get away from a furious Naomi, the cops would come to the apartment. Naomi, three glasses of wine in already, would waste no time giving them a detailed list of his regular haunts.

Then he'd find himself at the cop shop, getting fingerprinted, booked, and thrown in an interrogation room.

Mr. Henderson, the cop would say as he came in and placed his coffee beside the File of Incriminating Evidence, *would you mind explaining yourself, you fucking coward?*

A new email landed in his inbox, pulling Tom out of his tortured daydream. Unlike the previous one, it was not from Unknown Sender.

Sender: Tom Hart
Subject: Good luck

He opened it before the name fully sunk in. Then it hit him: he was looking at his old name. Bile crept up the back of his throat. The room blurred, save for the name on the computer screen.

Tom Hart.

He hadn't seen that name in eleven years. It was dead, buried in the past, alongside all those he killed.

An image in the email loaded. It showed him sitting at his computer desk, leaning forward with an expression of petrified panic.

His exact position now.

Murderer, the fluorescent light accused as its flickering intensified, *Tom Hart.*

"Tom?"

He nearly fell out of his seat.

The receptionist stood in front of his desk, to the left of his computer screen.

"The boss is ready for you. Says he's been trying to page you for the last five minutes."

The blinking orange light on Tom's desk confirmed that. How long had he been staring at that email?

Tom nodded, not trusting himself to speak. Exiting his browser screen, he stood, smoothing his pilling tie and wiping the sweat off his upper lip.

The light overhead flickered off.

Run, Tom. Run.

The gap in time between leaving his desk and running for his car was blank. His next memory was of slipping on ice and banging his knee against the metal bumper of his car. His gasp of pain came out as a billow of white. Fucking cold out here.

Ding! went his phone from inside his workbag. Impossible. He'd shut the thing off this morning.

Ding!

Tom flung open the car door. His bag smacked him in the face as he lifted it off his shoulder. The phone bounced out of it as he chucked it on the seat—

Ding!

His seatbelt jammed as he went to buckle it. He hit his forehead on the sun visor as he flailed about—

Ding! Ding!
Look at me! Look at me!

"Fine! Fine I will!" he roared, picking up his phone.

> **Unknown Sender**
> Take a left
>
> It's time we met

Tom's face screwed up in frustration. He *had* intended to go left. On the edge of Fox's Glew lay a little casino with a nice bar, never busy on a weekday. He planned to hole up in the darkest corner there, slots lever in one hand and a gin and tonic in the other. But he couldn't do that now. He couldn't go *left*.

He threw the car into drive, speeding away from that soul-sucking shithole of an office building for the last time. He took a *right*, heading deeper into the downtown.

"How do you like that?" he told his phone, pushing a sweaty lock of hair off his forehead. A hysterical giggle bubbled in the back of his throat.

Ding!

"Not going to look at you."

Ding!

"Not even going to acknowledge you."

He reached for his phone, intending to set it to vibrate without glancing at the screen. His eyes did not obey.

> If you don't agree to meet, your wife will know your secret

Tom's stomach plunged, as if the road had given way and he was falling down a sinkhole. He slowed to a stop at a set of lights, his foot trembling against the pedal. The left turning lane was clear, pointing the way.

No. He would not let this asshole win.

He continued straight, realizing he was re-routing back to the apartment out of habit.

Ding!

> Do not go home
>
> Take your next left

Wait.

What would happen if he told Naomi his Very Big Secret?

Worst case scenario: She leaves.

And was that *really* the worst thing that could happen?

No more nagging.

No more getting scolded for something he hadn't even done yet.

No more getting bitched out for spending his own money at the casino.

Tom shook a cigarette out of its pack and lit it.

And no more having to sneak packs of smokes.

He imagined staying out all night, stumbling to the apartment at dawn, blackout drunk, and smoking an entire pack of cigarettes inside while waiting for expensive Chinese takeout.

He should have confessed years ago.

Ding!

How long had his phone been going off? Tom took his eyes off the road. A long string of texts set his phone screen alight.

Fuck the anonymous texter. He wouldn't let them have power over him anymore. He'd tell Naomi his Very Big Secret. He'd take his power back.

Grabbing the phone, he opened the screen. His thumb hovered over the F, ready to text back *fuck you*, when his car lurched to a stop with a sickening *thwunk!*

His neck whipped forward, rib cage crunching against the

seatbelt. The cell phone went flying. He blinked, dazed, trying to focus on the scene outside his windshield.

Steam—no, *smoke*—swirled from the crumpled accordion that was his car hood. On the other side of the hood was a rusted blue pickup with a hay bale in the box. Where the fuck had it come from?

The pain in Tom's chest and neck crashed in. Like slicing your finger with a knife; the moment of shock before the blood gushes out. Grimacing, he massaged his chest where the seatbelt dug in. The motion did jack shit for the crushing pain spiderwebbing from between his ribs.

The farmer in the truck hadn't moved. At all. Tom hated the way he was leaning against the wheel.

He fumbled with his car door, ready to rush over to see if the guy was hurt, but his legs wouldn't move. What if he got to the truck and the man wasn't breathing?

The four-way where he crashed remained abandoned, save for the guy in the pickup. No witnesses.

Tom threw his car in reverse, stomping on the pedal. The hood of his car popped as it dislodged itself from the farmer's bumper. Cranking the wheel, he executed a record-breaking three-point-turn and sped in the opposite direction.

Run, Tom. Run.

He glanced into his rear-view mirror. Both the truck and man remained in their respective positions.

Can you even die from a fender bender?

The farmer's airbag had deployed. He was fine, just shocked.

Tom's hands trembled as they gripped the wheel. He was overcome with the urge to spew this morning's coffee out the window, but he couldn't pull over. No time. He had to put as much distance between himself and the truck as possible.

Murderer, the car fan whispered.

He killed the control knob. He could turn around. He could

go back. There was still time to correct yet another Very Big Mistake.

Instead, he continued straight. It was Polaris all over again. Leave them all behind.

What now? Get another new name, new life, new wife?

They say third time's the charm.

He reached into his jacket for his smokes, but the seatbelt had crushed them flat.

Was there anything of vital importance in the apartment? Or could he keep driving, leave this trash bag of a city behind, and start anew again?

Ding!

Tom didn't know where his cell phone had landed in the kerfuffle. The anonymous texter may not be done with him, but he was done with them. It was this asshole's fault he crashed in the first place.

"Shift the blame like you always do. I suppose Polaris wasn't your fault either?" he asked himself.

Coward, the wounded motor muttered, as if in response.

Something butted against his shoe. He glanced down. The cell phone. *Aha!* that's where it went. He fumbled for it, keeping his eyes locked on the road.

He had every intention of rolling down the window and throwing the stupid rectangle of plastic out, incriminating texts be damned, but the newest message wasn't from Mr. Anonymous. It was from the wife. She was home sick with a migraine today. She wanted him to grab some painkillers on his way home from work.

Tom faltered.

Yes, there was something from the apartment he needed. Closure. He'd already ditched one wife without notice. He owed Naomi that much.

He turned up a side street. Was that the wail of a siren in the distance?

His crumpled car hood mocked him. He turned the fan back on to distract from the sirens he was or wasn't hearing.

What to say to Naomi? Confess to all of it? Just the car crash? Or just Polaris? What a luxury to pick and choose.

Liar.

Fake. Tom Hart.

The fan whispered its accusations.

He could say nothing. Get rid of the car, go back to work like nothing had happened.

Only you can't go back. The pesky problem of the obviously flubbed audit still existed. He was locked into this trajectory. Fuck, he needed a cigarette.

He broke off the smushed end of a smoke and lit it. He inhaled deeply. Nothing changed, but he felt better.

He entered the underground parking lot, pulling into his designated spot. He stuffed his cell phone into his pocket. Mr. Anonymous had become uncharacteristically quiet. As Tom headed for the elevator, he threw a glance at his car. It didn't seem too bad from this angle. That might give him a bit more time, but he had to get rid of it, fast.

Focus, Tom.

He still had Naomi to deal with. What to tell her? His stomach worked itself into knots as the elevator ascended.

When he entered the apartment, Naomi was sprawled out on the couch, her bathrobe still on. The TV blared in the background as she held her phone two inches away from her face, scrolling aimlessly.

So much for a migraine.

When she noticed him, her expression changed from shock to anger faster than Tom could blink. He held his hand up before she could speak.

"I have something to tell you."

She opened her mouth, no doubt itching to ask what he was doing home from work and not making money. She gave him the once-over. Did she notice how awful he looked, how sweaty and pale he'd become? No, because she never looked at him properly. It was always how *she* felt, how *she* was doing. He could be tying a noose around his neck and she'd be asking how many hours would be on his final paycheque.

It surprised Tom when she sat up, laid her phone on the table, and asked softly, "How bad?"

The early days of their marriage flashed into focus. Before the squabbling, the pettiness, the controlling. That's when her headaches started. The doctor had ordered a CT scan. When the results came back, Tom asked her how bad it was.

"Bad bad," she'd replied.

The cyst the CT scan unveiled turned out to be benign, but Tom remembered how scared he was for her. How much he cared. Their marriage hadn't always been shit.

He reconsidered. He didn't have to say anything.

But there was still the matter of the farmer, laid out flat against his steering wheel. And those botched work reports. He was in too deep either way.

"Bad bad."

Her brows knitted together. Were her eyes growing misty? Did she actually care enough about him to be *crying*? She probably thought he was dying. He wondered, with morbid curiosity, which illness she thought he might have.

Tom seated himself on the edge of the coffee table. Naomi extended a hand, then retracted it at the last second.

Where to begin? Which incident to choose from? Murder was murder; did it matter which one he confessed to?

"I wasn't always an accountant."

What a stupid thing to say.

Naomi raised her eyebrows. *That's it?*

The next thing would sound even stupider.

"I used to be a test subject for a biotech company called Becopra."

The name, alien after not being spoken aloud for years, opened the floodgates. Tom couldn't carry this burden alone anymore. Naomi agreed to for better or worse when she married Mr. Big Fake Thomas Henderson. And it didn't get much worse than what he was about to say.

"We worked in the fringe sciences. Astral projection, genetic engineering, parallel universes—"

"I know what fringe science means," Naomi snapped, clearly wondering where Tom's imminent demise fit into this.

"Okay, okay. Sorry. One of my colleagues, Dr. Glasser, discovered ..." He paused, resting his forehead against his hands.

Even to himself, it sounded too unbelievable. Tom could never tell her about the portal, the awe that lay beyond, the lengths they went through to get to the other side. Naomi would laugh in his face before he got to the important part.

"You know, it doesn't matter."

Truth was, he didn't fully understand what he and Glasser discovered. Ghosts, spectres, demons ... they shouldn't exist.

"We worked out of an underground bunker. There was an accident in the lab. A discharge of energy. It was my fault. Everyone in the room died. Dropped like flies. Except me. I didn't know what to do. Becopra was a privately-owned company. Probably operating in a legally grey area. I was scared. So, I ran."

Run, Tom. Run.

Always running, the instant life got hard.

"Why?" Naomi cleared her throat. "Are you telling me this now?"

Numbly, he handed over his phone. She accepted it. The silence that followed as she read the texts crushed him flat.

Her eyes darted across the phone screen, taking in every word.

"They can't charge you with anything. If it was an accident. They can't charge you," she repeated, voice filled with resolution. Yes, she'd already figured out how they would deal with this. "What does this person have on you?"

Tom could tell she was ready to sweep this under the rug. Bottle it up with his other thousand fuck-ups and move on with their lives.

"Tom?" She placed his phone on the coffee table when he said nothing. "What do they have on you?"

There it was. The edge of suspicion.

His forehead went back into his hands. He didn't have to say anymore. But he had to. For *her*.

"I ... was ..." The words didn't want to come out. He cleared his throat. He needed to purge this poison. "... married once, before you. You were never supposed to know. That part of me died the day we shut down the experiment. But I had a wife. And I had a daughter."

Naomi inhaled sharply, retracting back to the couch. There was the anger he'd been waiting for.

"She was there with me, my kid, when the accident happened."

Saying it aloud felt surreal. Tom had pushed aside the memory of his daughter for so long it almost felt like it was someone else at Polaris.

"When everyone collapsed, she did too, right beside me. I tried to reach down, to check if she had a pulse, but I couldn't do it. I couldn't do that for her."

The memory slammed into him, sending him tumbling through time. The metallic tang in the air Polaris always had, so thick he could taste it. How small Atra looked lying on the concrete floor among the others.

That's what had been haunting him. Not the accident. Not the others. But the fact that he'd been at the hatch door. Turned. Took one last glance at his daughter. And noticed her chest was moving.

"What did I do? I slammed the hatch door shut. I sealed her in that bunker. I killed her."

Tom's eyes burned. A lump grew in his throat. How had he managed to live with himself for so long? Because he'd shut down those memories as tightly as the hatch door. He had sealed them away with the bodies.

Naomi remained silent. Tom tried to look at her but his forehead was glued to his hands. Everything he'd repressed came up, hitting him like a brick wall. His best action would be to jump off the balcony before he could fuck up anyone else's life.

The couch cushions shifted, accompanied by the scrape of glass as Naomi grabbed her phone back off the coffee table. He managed to catch sight of her face as she shuffled into the kitchen. He could tell by her pinched expression it was too much to bottle away. She didn't say a word as she left the room. Was she deciding to grab a glass of wine or grab her bags? He didn't dare ask.

The front door opened, breaking the drowning quiet. Tom turned. Naomi stood in the doorway, bag in hand. She still wore her bathrobe.

"When I come back tomorrow, I want you gone."

The door slammed hard enough behind her to rattle the photographs on the TV stand. Tom breathed a sigh of relief as the apartment became three sizes bigger without her suffocating presence.

Pulling his smokes out of his pocket, he took one out and put it in his mouth. He flicked his lighter, bringing the flame up. He thought he'd feel satisfaction from finally smoking inside, but instead, it made him sick.

Tom wasn't sorry to see her go. His big, courageous moment was not to atone for his sins, but rather to drive her away for good. The coward's way out, as usual.

He blew the smoke out of his lungs. The idea of throwing himself off the balcony was more appealing than ever.

Chapter 5

The Fallen Interlude

"Help!"

Atra didn't recognize the screams echoing through the trees as her own.

"Somebody help!"

But there was no one to hear.

The image of Creepsley, upside down in the van, busted glasses dangling off one ear, flashed through her mind. The van's roof had crumpled like a tin can when it flipped.

She didn't remember how she got out of the van.

Why was she stomping blindly through the heavy snow, pushing herself farther into the woods? Why hadn't she stayed on the road?

Because she didn't want to be near that van. Her head should have been squished like a grape, yet here she was, unscathed.

IT'S BECAUSE YOU DIED! Her mind screamed the awful truth. *THAT VAN WAS WHERE YOU DIED!*

No, no, no. She couldn't be dead.

The forest closed in. Her flesh crawled, sensing something was lurking in the spaces between the trees, out of sight.

The branches ahead glowed.

The light at the end of the tunnel.

No—it was the moonlight.

But the colour wasn't right. Too orange. Atra pushed through the snow, getting closer.

A house sat in a clearing. Its dark dormer windows stared down at her. The screen door hung askew in its frame, the porch boards in front of it rotten.

The light came from a ground window, spilling out onto the untouched snow.

What were the odds, to come upon a place in the middle of nowhere?

IT'S BECAUSE YOU DIED!

Ignoring the voice, she climbed the decaying steps and entered without knocking. Someone had to be in here. Someone who could see her, tell her she was alive—

"Hello?"

A dusty table and rows of kitchen cabinets greeted her. Through the archway, the orange flames of the fireplace flickered against a paisley-patterned couch.

Atra called out again but received no answer. Someone lived here, though, because *someone* had lit that fire.

MAYBE YOU CAN'T SEE THEM BECAUSE YOU'RE DEAD!

But the voice wasn't so scary anymore.

Everything seemed rational now, away from the wreckage. The camper van crashed. She survived and stumbled upon someone's house. Coincidence.

Her body didn't agree. She rushed for the sink in the corner, making it just in time. Her chest racked with dry heaves, pushing against her sore muscles, nothing left in her stomach to empty.

She grabbed the tap. It emitted a dry, sputtering sound before coughing out a rusty fluid. Ducking her head under, she gulped the water. No sooner had she finished did it come right back up.

Wiping her mouth, Atra leaned against the sink, unable to draw in enough air.

She stared out the window in front of her. The gridded panes should have shown her reflection. Instead, they showed her a perfect view of the silhouetted evergreens outside, puffy with snow.

The metal tea canisters lining the counter were lit up on all sides. Bright, but flat. She waved a hand over the sink, but no shadow mimicked her.

She had gotten her wish. But instead of *her* shadow gone, they were all gone.

Time to get out of this place.

Easier said than done, because the door was gone. It had been replaced by the same grimy wooden walls lining the rest of the house.

Fine, she'd climb out the window.

That too, was gone. Above the sink now sat a kitchen cupboard.

This wasn't happening.

Atra shut her eyes. When she opened them, she'd be in the asylum with Dread by her side. But over her ragged breath, the flames still crackled.

Thump!

Her eyes snapped open.

The fire from the living room had been snuffed out. Her breath came out in faint white puffs, cutting through the steel-blue dim. The silence of the house washed over her.

Something thumped again. The darkness—not from inside the walls, but from beyond—closed in. She bolted for the staircase beyond the table. The claws crept out of the darkness, reaching for her; any moment they would be sinking into her back—

Atra entered the upstairs landing. The noise had come from the bedroom. She craned her neck, seeing only an ancient night table and a bed.

The floorboards creaked as she crept forward. The bedroom was empty. She lingered in the doorway, deciding if she should crouch and peek under the bed. The very idea sent a slimy worm of anxiety down her throat.

"I'm glad you finally found this place."

A cry escaped her as a face emerged from under the bed, the vivid-red pigtails and bright green eyes reminding Atra of a fox.

"What are you doing under there?" she blurted, to the little girl under the bed.

Silence, for three of her heartbeats, then—

"I want to play with my brother."

Atra's head snapped around, expecting another kid behind her, but the dark and empty hallway met her instead.

"He's not here." The kid sounded sulky. "I'm supposed to wait here alone, but I don't wanna."

"And where is here?" Atra almost didn't ask the question, afraid of the answer.

"We're in-between."

"In-between what?"

But the kid had vanished.

"Hey! Where'd you go?"

Atra *should* have bent over. Peered under the bed. But she couldn't. The gap between the floor and the bed scared her more than the darkness downstairs did.

"I'm right here."

Atra jumped. The kid was now behind her. A horrid mustard-yellow corduroy dress clothed her tiny frame.

"Are you ready to play?" The kid's voice rang with a lively edge. "Until my brother gets here."

"I'm not in the mood to play games."

The kid's face collapsed. "You're just like the rest of them. You grown-ups are too serious."

Just like the rest of them. The words stung. That's how Atra thought of the doctors and nurses. All the same.

She wasn't like them.

"Okay, we'll play till your brother gets here." Atra humoured her, knowing she'd get more answers if she went along. "But first, I need to know one thing. What's your name?"

"Lex!" the kid replied jubilantly, bounding down the stairs. "And I already know yours!"

Atra pushed her unease aside, following behind.

"What game are we playing?"

"We're hiding."

Atra's throat constricted.

"Hiding from what?"

Lex didn't reply, grinning impishly as she crept toward a small door underneath the staircase.

"I know a secret plane where they can't find us."

Maybe there had been no car crash. No fire, either. Maybe Atra had never left the asylum. This certainly qualified for a complete break in reality. But why *this* place? If she were going to detach from this plane of existence, she'd at least like to spend some quality time with Seth, not trap herself in some creepy house with some equally creepy kid.

The door beneath the staircase revealed a spacious study that stunk of old leather from the books lining the shelves. A large bay window sat above a cushioned bench opposite the doorway.

A window—

An escape!

Lex paused in the doorway.

"Uh-oh. This isn't the right plane."

But Atra wasn't listening. She brushed past the kid, making a beeline for the window. The moss-green carpet emitted puffs of dust as she ran across it. A lamp glowed in the corner. She was going to grab it, smash the window with it, and crawl out of whatever this place was.

Oof! Down she went as Lex tackled her from behind. They fell into the bookshelf, knocking several volumes off. The gash in Atra's back seared. The kid was stronger than she looked.

"You can't let her see you!" A hysterical edge cut into Lex's voice, all playfulness gone.

"What are you talking about?" Atra got back up. "I have to get out of here!"

Lex grabbed at her legs, but it was futile.

"No, she'll see you!"

"Who?"

Lex ceased pulling at Atra, choosing to cower behind the bench instead. "Please, please, get down!"

"No. Not until you tell me who's out there."

"The one who dwells on the threshold. She calls herself the Queen."

Atra remembered the woods and the feeling of something standing in the spaces between the trees. The skin tightened around the base of her skull.

"She hasn't found you yet. But she hasn't stopped looking."

Who? The question danced on Atra's lips, but a glow through the window distracted her. A gnawing grew in her belly as she turned to the kid. Lex had turned her head toward the glow as well.

"You can see it too?"

Lex's eyes shone with more than the rift's reflection; she was on the verge of tears.

"We have to leave. This room isn't safe. It isn't the right plane."

Atra remembered being that young and that scared and that alone. Trapped in her bedroom with Dread, with no father to comfort her because he'd run away. She almost agreed to leave, but she needed an answer.

"Why can we see the rift when no one else can?"

"People like us are more susceptible to seeing the truth."

"Like us?"

"Those closer to death."

The claws in the darkness reaching for Atra earlier finally sunk in.

So, the van crash *had* killed her.

"Lex, is this house where you go when you die?"

"No. *That* is where you go when you die." Lex pointed to the rift. "But you already knew that."

"Through to the Otherside."

The response came immediately, although Atra didn't know why she'd said it. She didn't know what it meant.

Yet, she did.

"Dread wants to go through the rift," Lex said.

"How do you know about Dread?" Atra choked out the words, Lex's statement sucking the air out of the room.

Lex shrugged as if her shoulders weighed a hundred pounds. Suddenly, she was no longer just a scared kid.

"If Dread goes through the rift it will be the beginning for the Otherside but the end for us."

"I won't let it go through."

"It's not your choice. Dread is a force you don't understand. The Queen lies beyond the rift. During the lunar eclipse on the winter solstice, she'll come through for you. For Dread. She'll use you to end the world."

Lex's skin had taken on the same sickly green as the carpet, a far cry from the spunky kid rushing down the stairs.

"The night the moon bleeds is the night the world will end," the man back in the diner had told Atra.

How had he known?

The man's voice changed to Seth's. *This is what crazy people do, Attie. They jump to wild conclusions like this.*

But there was nothing sane about this place.

"I'm tired," Lex announced, resting her head against the bookshelf. "It's hard to stay in this house for long."

"What the hell is this house?"

"A space in between where the worlds are thin. It's easier to climb the planes from here."

Lex kept speaking in riddles Atra didn't understand and didn't care to. Atra bit her lip to prevent herself from saying something really mean, then asked instead, "How do I get out of here?"

"Not out. Forward. Into the altered planes. It's the only way to stop the Queen."

"I don't want to stop the Queen. I want to get back to my own reality."

Lex shifted, picking up a book that had fallen off the shelf when she and Atra crashed into it. Something pearlescent twinkled on its spine under the light of the rift. She handed it to Atra.

The worn brown leather was soft under Atra's hands. She ran her fingers over the raised symbol on the spine, which resembled a lopsided infinity loop.

"Find Magnus. Find the planes." Lex's chest fluttered with shallow breaths, like she was about to deflate out of existence.

"But—"

"The mind is quicker than the lie."

And then she was gone.

Not just Lex, but the room, the bookshelf—

Atra fell backward, no longer supported by it. She hit a familiar linoleum floor.

The sterile stench of the asylum overwhelmed her after being in the stagnant house.

She was back in her bedroom at Vanishing Plains. The last place she'd been before the flames. The last time anything was normal.

Had everything been a delusion?

It couldn't have been. She still held the book.

But her bedroom wasn't *normal* because the standard white sheets covering her bed were blood red.

What the fuck?

Atra got to her feet and darted into the hallway, expecting to fall back into the house. White walls met her instead.

The place had been a deadly inferno this morning. It was gone, and she was *out*.

"Lex!" The kid's name came out as a half-sob. Atra wanted to pound her fists against those stupid white walls until they broke open and gave her a different reality.

"Excuse me?" A nurse's voice was swallowed by a rushing in her ears.

Atra turned. Sure enough, a nurse strode out of the bedroom, her hands clasped in front of her.

Atra's stomach bottomed out. The nurse was Lex. Grown-up Lex, wearing a set of turquoise scrubs.

"I wasn't finished showing you your sleeping quarters." Not Lex's voice. "You're not allowed to run off."

Her face changed from Lex's youthful one to crusty old Nurse Silvia's. One of the nurses who liked to stand by the doorway and whisper things about her.

"You're not real," the words tumbled out of Atra's mouth.

She spun on her heel, headed for the common area. She had to find Beryl. Maybe Beryl would have some answers.

What if Beryl didn't exist?

An iron fist squeezed Atra's stomach.

Something black and wispy floated out of the corner of her eye. She tried to brush it aside, thinking it was a lock of her hair, but her hand passed through nothing. For a moment, she had the crazy notion it was a curl of smoke and the asylum was still on fire. She faltered, sniffing the air.

No smoke in here. She realized she wasn't wearing the thick coat anymore, nor was she covered in soot. She was back in her regular asylum garb of a white T-shirt and grey sweatpants.

Silvia swooped around the corner like an ancient bird of prey. Atra broke into a run.

The nurse called out again.

"Ater!"

That wasn't right.

"Ater, get back here!"

Atra glanced at her plastic ID bracelet. Not there. On the wrong wrist, the left one instead of the right.

ATER HEART, it read. *VANISHING PLANES.*

She bit back laughter at how absurdly wrong, yet almost right, it was.

"Ater!" Silvia closed the gap.

Atra broke into a run. The *clack! clack! clack!* of Silvia's heels chased her.

She entered the common area, where they were doling out breakfast. She scanned the faces of those milling about. After being here seven years, she knew everyone. But not today. She recognized only a handful of the faces as her search for Beryl became more desperate.

Something hard thunked her on the back of the head. An unexpected crack of pain radiated through her skull. She turned, ready to confront the asshole who smacked her upside the head, but no one was there.

Another crack of pain, this time on her shoulder. She spun on her heel, quicker this time. Still no one behind her. Something flickered out of her line of sight, but this time she was fast enough and—*aha!*

Another patient, maybe a couple years younger than her, rode a tricycle in circles around her, clutching a broom. Her jet-black hair had been hacked off at several lengths with what appeared to have been a pair of blunt scissors.

Atra was positive she'd never seen this person before.

"Hey." The new patient stopped pedalling the tricycle—blood red, like those bedspreads—dark eyes boring into Atra. "They're calling you."

Atra gaped at the scene in front of her.

"Ater!" Silvia's shrill voice pierced through the common area.

"Get back here!"

"You're being summoned." The patient grinned. Her mouth split open, unnervingly wide like someone had jammed a harmonica in it.

Atra was a balloon on the end of a frayed tether, about to float away into the ether.

That's when she spotted the back of Beryl's familiar white afro in the food line. She started forward, forgetting about Harmonica Mouth.

Harmonica Mouth, however, hadn't forgotten about her.

"I *said*"—Harmonica Mouth wheeled her tricycle forward, blocking Atra's path—"you're being called. Idiot."

She swung the broom handle. Atra threw her hands up, dropping the leather-bound book, but was too late. Her cheekbone took the brunt of the blow making her eyes well with tears.

Harmonica Mouth wound up for another swing. Atra lashed out, grabbing the handle before she got smacked again. Their gazes locked, Harmonica Mouth's face screwing up in frustration as she fought to get the broom back.

Atra let go. The inertia caused Harmonica Mouth to go tumbling off her tricycle and crashing into the table behind her. A hush fell over the common area. The broom clattered to the ground between them.

A pair of hands grabbed Atra from behind.

"Break it up, you two," Nurse Silvia addressed them like they were a couple of disobedient dogs. Another nurse restrained Harmonica Mouth.

Atra struggled in Silvia's grip. That infuriating wisp of smoke floated in and out of her vision.

"Beryl!" she called out, in the direction of the food line. "*Beryl!*"

She needed Beryl to see her. She needed to be recognized. But Beryl didn't glance in her direction.

"Catch ya later, newbie." Harmonica Mouth grinned victoriously as Silvia dragged Atra out of the room.

"It's time to meet Dr. Creeley," Silvia said, into her ear.

Atra remembered Creepsley tapping his fake name badge in the real Vanishing Plains.

"No."

She stopped walking, but Silvia pulled her forward.

"Let go of me!" Atra twisted her wrist and stomped her feet into the ground. "None of this is right! Creepsley isn't a doctor, people can't ride around on tricycles, and none of that matters because this place burned down—"

Smack!

Her ears roared as the world spun.

"Pull yourself together." Silvia grabbed her shoulders. "You don't want to know what he does to hysterical patients—"

"No, you don't want to know."

An unctuous voice that was unfortunately familiar. Fear shot through Atra before she saw his face. He no longer suffered a bloody and broken nose from where her foot had connected with it.

"Dr. Creeley." Silvia's grip tightened. "I was just bringing her to you. I'm sorry for the delay, but she—"

"Hello, Miss Heart." Atra could hear the subtle difference in the spelling of her name.

Creepsley was still decked out in his shoddy lab coat with the frayed hem. His fake name badge with the botched lettering read *Vanishing Planes*, like her bracelet. Atra turned to Silvia.

"And how are you liking the new place?" Creepsley drawled on.

Atra zoned in on Silvia's name badge: *VANISHING PLANES*. *What was happening?*

The new place. The new place.

The realization surged forward against her will.

Her name, almost right, but not. Vanishing, but in the wrong plane. Beryl, ignoring her. Harmonica Mouth, calling her the new girl.

"Answer him," Silvia hissed, fingers digging in.

"He is *not* a doctor! This isn't a real place!" The bubble of hysteria swelling inside Atra burst, releasing a deluge of panic.

Creepsley let out a low chuckle, baring his oversized yellowed teeth.

"You won't be thinking that for long, Miss Heart. I run a tight ship around here. We have a strict daily schedule, lights on at—"

"I want my brother!" Atra screamed. She writhed, fighting to break Silvia's grip. "I want to see Seth!"

Creepsley reached out. He wrapped his fingers around her throat, forcing her to look at him.

"Ater, you have no stepbrother."

What the hell did that mean? That Seth didn't exist in this fucked-up reality or that Seth didn't exist at all?

"Fuck you," she spat out. Her throat moved against his hand. "I have a brother and that's NOT MY NAME!"

Creepsley's fingers tightened. Not much, but enough. He leaned closer.

"Like I said"—his sulphuric breath washed over her—"I run a tight ship."

Even though Lex said she wasn't dead, Atra couldn't believe it. Because that meant her other option was the thing she'd been running from her whole life: that she was insane.

She jerked her head back, trying to break Creepsley's unrelenting grip. That wisp of smoke drifted into the corner of her vision again. She recognized it now.

Dread.

Different, like everything here. Different, in a place that no longer existed.

A sharp jab in her upper arm.

"That's strike one. You don't want to get to strike three."

Atra struggled to draw a breath, the air too heavy.

The horror that this was *real* crushed her. The memory of her first time being committed surged forward, as she lived it all over again. The stark horror that these walls would be the only thing she knew for the rest of her life. That she'd never experience freedom again. The wicked smile on her stepmother's face as they dragged her away.

Atra's world went grey. She shook her head, fighting to keep her eyes open. A tingling spread through her body. Would she have fallen over if not for Silvia holding her? She didn't know; her feet had gone numb.

It all boiled down to Dread, didn't it? Her life had gone to shit ever since it appeared.

Through the grey, it floated forward in its new misty form.

I have to get rid of you, was the last thing she remembered thinking. *For good.*

Chapter 6

Polaris

The rock in Tom's hand grew heavy as he stood in front of the snowy embankment. All he had to do was chuck it in his car and make sure it hit the gas pedal. Easier said than done.

He was psyching himself up when he remembered the duffle bag in the backseat. It contained a few changes of clothes, a toothbrush, and the plastic bag of bills Naomi kept squirrelled away in the bottom of the freezer. They'd been there so long he doubted she remembered them, otherwise, she would've grabbed them in her sweeping exit from the apartment.

He couldn't leave a trail if he was skipping town. From here on out, it was cash.

After grabbing the bag, Tom readjusted the rope holding the steering wheel straight, making sure it pointed to the closest pine tree. No sense going through the trouble to stage a car crash if it got stuck in the embankment.

Hurry up before someone drives by, you jackass.

He decided the best place to execute his plan was on an old backroad on the outskirts of Fox's Glew. The odds of someone driving by were slim, but the way his luck was going …

Tom gave the rope a final tug for good measure, then picked up the rock. He tossed it up and down, testing its weight, then held it close to his chest. Closing one eye, he exhaled, steadying himself. He focused on the gas pedal and with a grunt, threw the rock like a shot put.

It bounced off the steering column, rolled to the floor and settled on the gas pedal. Tom narrowly avoided getting clipped by his car as it sped past.

Thwunk!

The same sickening crunch as the fender bender. The image of the farmer in the car, unmoving, came to mind yet again. Tom should've stayed at the scene of the accident. He'd never get away with this.

The car hit the tree head-on, lining up almost exactly where the hood had already crumpled.

Okay—maybe he *would* get away with this.

The car engine revved, loud and angry. He waded across the deep snow to silence the car for good.

The airbag had deployed this time. Punching it aside, he reached down and retrieved the rock. He threw it as far from the car as he could, then went back in, fighting against the deflating bag to untie the rope and reclaim his keys.

Turning, he trudged back to the road. His joints throbbed, the effects of the actual accident setting in. Lying in the fluffy snowbank suddenly became far too appealing.

His foot broke through the snow, plunging into the creek below. Tom let out a cry as the shock of water froze his veins. He lifted his leg, but it was too late; the current had sucked his shoe clean off. He waded back to the road with half the footwear and dignity he'd had before he left it.

"Like you ever had any to begin with," he muttered.

The icy chill of winter seeped through his socked foot. How long until frostbite sunk in?

"You'll survive twenty minutes. You're not in the Arctic." Despite his attempts to reassure himself, the mountain's bitter windchill claimed otherwise.

He fished out his phone—Mr. Anonymous had been silent since Tom's confession to the wife—and dialled the number for a tow truck company.

A few months back, someone had slashed Naomi's tires downtown. According to her version of events, she was the innocent victim, but Tom knew her too well. She probably had parked like an asshole or flipped off the wrong person in traffic.

Regardless, she had to get her car towed. If memory served right, she described the company she used as "completely fucking incompetent."

That same company would be perfect for what Tom needed. Odds were they wouldn't call the cops about some idiot who'd lost control of his car and ran into a tree.

There. All set. In less than an hour, all evidence of his fender bender would disappear into the back of a junkyard.

By then, he'd be out of this shithole city for good.

The bus jerked to a stop, jolting Tom out of his thin sleep. His tongue was a piece of dried coral in his mouth. Of course, it was; he had no water. He was entirely unprepared for this bus ride.

Several decrepit souls shuffled to their assigned seats. The bus must've been at a transfer station.

His neck throbbed as whiplash set in. Probably what woke him. He massaged the back of his neck, grimacing.

The dim yellow lights came on overhead as dusk settled in. Out the window, the claustrophobic mountains gave way to hillier mounds. At least he'd escaped Fox's Glew before it swallowed him whole.

His foot grew too hot from the plastic bag duct taped around it. The fellows at the tow truck place had kindly gifted Tom with his makeshift shoe. He longed to claw the bag open, peel off his sock, and let his skin breathe.

The seat across the aisle remained vacant except for a newspaper lying on top of it. Tom leaned over and grabbed it. Unfolding it, he noted a woman craning her neck over her seat, giving him the once-over. Her puffy under-eyes matched her down-filled coat, which was zipped to her chin. Her gaze lingered on his bagged foot. Tom slid it out of her sight, flashing her a thin smile. She didn't return it.

He threw the paper up, using it as a barrier between himself and the judgemental bitch. He was half-expecting the headline on the front to read "Big Fake Tom Hart Kills Man In Crash."

Yesterday, Tom was on his way to his office-drone duties, never once thinking his life would be anything else. How could it go so wrong so fast?

Get yourself together, Tom.

He flipped through the paper as the pain in his neck worked its way to the base of his skull in throbbing tendrils. The newspaper's tiny print strained his vision.

He reached the last page. Before he could draw in a sigh of relief, there it was—squished into the bottom right quadrant beside an ad for snow removal. A brief notice about a hit and run in Fox's Glow—spelled wrong, that's how insignificant the city was. Some poor guy, left with severe spinal injuries but in stable condition. If anyone has a lead, please contact the authorities.

The newspaper stretched impossibly far away as the surrounding seats shrunk in.

Tom tossed the newspaper back where he found it, headache forgotten. The bad news: the cops were searching for a suspect. The good news: the country bumpkin wasn't lying on a morgue slab.

Fuck, he needed a drink. That wasn't going to happen until he got off this suffocating tin box, so he settled for a cigarette. He felt for his pack of smokes, then stood. He intended to go to the bathroom at the back and sneak a quick drag.

Sitting in the seat adjacent to the bathroom door was a familiar pair of broad, pointed shoulders.

Mr. Anonymous.

Tom's surroundings greyed; his busted neck felt like a trash compactor was crushing it.

He sank back into the seat, tucking his legs in. Trying to conceal himself was useless, but it was the same logic as if you were hiding from the bogeyman: if you were under the covers, he couldn't get you.

Liar.

Fake.

Oh no. Not again. He recognized the voices now. Deadmarsh, Glasser ...

Becopra Corporation. You killed us all.

You killed Atra.

He clasped his hands over his ears, but couldn't shut out the names he pretended didn't exist.

Holding his breath, he dared a peek from behind the seat. Mr. Anonymous, who'd been gazing out the window, turned. Tom imagined him smiling as he waved.

When the bus came to a stop on the cusp of the Prairies, Tom bolted. Shoved everyone aside, ignoring the huffy shouts of the bus driver. Dove down an alley, putting Mr. Anonymous behind him. Ran straight into a shitty bar.

The music deafened him the second he entered. The dingy space was hopping for a Thursday night in buttfuck nowhere. His single shoe stuck to the concrete floor as he crossed it. Adjusting the duffle bag over his shoulder, Tom weaved and bobbed around the locals. No one looked at him. No one noticed him.

"Two beers." He pushed his way to the front of the bar.

"What kind?"

"The cheapest you have." He noticed a laminated menu, covered in fingerprints, on the counter. "And a burger."

He glanced over his shoulder, expecting Mr. Anonymous to be waiting in the shadows.

The bartender held out her hand, palm up. She made a gesture. I don't have all day, pal.

Unzipping his duffle bag, Tom produced his diminishing wad of bills. Reluctantly, he peeled a couple off. The tow truck and bus ticket set him further back than expected. He should be saving his precious cash for a motel room, but where could you get one in this day and age without a credit card anyway?

Gripping his two glasses of piss-yellow beer, he searched for the darkest corner. The neon lights made it difficult to see anything beyond the tragic dance floor. He seated himself in an empty booth, the black vinyl duct taped in several spots. He set one glass of beer on the ring-stained surface and brought the other to his mouth. His stomach—shrunken from lack of sustenance—swelled as he chugged it back.

Setting the empty glass down, Tom waited for the familiar buzz that would take away the aches and pains in his body and mind. He thumbed a hole in his shirt collar. Naomi was nagging him to get a new work wardrobe— *"You'll never get a promotion looking like that."* Odd, how he still thought of her in the present tense.

Someone cleared their throat beside him. He jerked his hand away, startled to find the bartender standing at his table. On her tray sat a single shot of some clear spirit. He wondered how long she'd been there, surprised he'd heard her over the pounding music.

She placed the shot beside his empty beer glass, along with a folded napkin.

"From the gentleman at the bar." She gestured half-heartedly before leaving.

He pursed his lips, unfolding the note. Being propositioned was the last thing he needed right—

Hi, Tom.

He dropped the paper, eyes darting to the bar. People crammed around it like sardines in a can, but none of them were *him*.

Tom picked up the shot and held it under his nose. The familiar piney scent of gin burned his nostrils.

His spirit of choice.

"I thought it was time we met."

A voice behind him rang clearly over the cacophony of the bar. He splashed the gin down his front, snapping his neck around so fast he nearly gave himself whiplash a second time.

No one behind him, save for the locals, who were too wrapped up in their drunken, small-town gossip for anything else.

He turned back around, grabbing for his duffle bag, ready to bolt.

Someone sat in the booth across from him.

For the first time, Mr. Anonymous's face was visible. The lighting overhead made his eyes appear as two hollow sockets in a ghostly face.

Immediately, Tom recognized the features. The last time he saw that face was his fateful day at Polaris.

He was out of his seat and exiting the bar before he even considered it.

"Tom, we need to talk."

Again, right behind him, but when he looked back, his booth stood vacant.

What's happening to me?

Tom recognized the voice now that he had put a face to it. Dr. Glasser, lead scientist for the Becopra Corporation. The one he'd opened the portal with. The one he'd closed it with.

Am I going insane?

Glasser was dead. One hundred percent without a doubt, dead and still in that bunker.

The years of guilt were finally catching up to Tom. Who from Becopra would show up next?

The bar lights swivelled, basking him in a bright spotlight. The dull thump of the music, the chattering of voices, swelled as if echoing through an amphitheatre. The light chased him, like the one that surged through the portal. Returning, at last, to finish him off.

Tom wasn't sure, but he thought he might be screaming.

He fumbled for the back door in the chaos, stumbling outside before the light devoured him.

The crisp air shocked his clammy skin. He crossed the narrow alley in three steps, braced himself against the wall, and puked up his beer. Most of it splashed onto his plastic-bag shoe, unpleasantly warm. The bitter taste of bile burned his throat.

Footsteps approached. Tom held a hand in the air.

"I'm fine," he said, head still hanging. The last thing he needed was someone thinking he was too drunk and calling the cops. "Food isn't agreeing with me."

"You can't run forever, Tom."

He spun around.

Quillon Glasser. The silhouette who'd been haunting him. How did Tom not recognize him before? Maybe he had, burying the truth alongside everything else.

"You're dead." The words came out as a croak, as Tom wiped the vomit from his mouth.

Glasser's knobbly fingers gestured to his plum business suit.

"Evidently not."

His amber eyes probed Tom. Glasser's mouth cracked open in a grin, pearly white against his deep-brown skin. A chuckle escaped his lips.

Tom mirrored the grin and laughed himself, not because he

wanted to, but because he had to expel the insanity the same way his body had expelled the beer.

"How did you survive?" The questions began to flow as the laughing spell passed.

"How did you?" Glasser deflected.

Touché.

Tom opened his mouth, so close to asking if his daughter survived as well. But did he really want to know?

Did everyone at Polaris survive? Had he shed his old life in haste, needlessly shouldering the burden of murdering them all these years?

"Let's go for a walk," Glasser suggested, stuffing his hands in his suit pockets and turning around.

Wordlessly, Tom obliged. Though he wore a jacket, the biting cold cut through his makeshift shoe, rough gravel and ice digging into his heel.

Shit. He'd left the duffle bag in the bar. All the cash to his name, gone. It didn't seem to matter. Glasser always had that mesmerizing effect. Otherwise, Tom would've never let him shoot him full of experimental drugs and start prying open the puzzle-box of his shadow DNA.

Glasser pulled a pack of cigarettes from his pocket, the lettering a familiar vermillion red. Tom's brand of choice. Glasser popped the top and held them out.

It was a fresh pack, cancer sticks lined up in neat rows. Tom plucked one out and stuck it in his mouth.

"Light?" Glasser offered.

"I have my own."

Tom fumbled in his jacket pocket, his movements clumsy and awkward compared to Glasser's. He lit his smoke, taking a long drag. It helped calm the angry buzz in his head.

"Do you see that?" Glasser gestured to something in the distance. Beyond the power lines, a purple-green glow, so faint it could have been a trick of the eye. "Not everyone can."

"It's the portal, isn't it?" Tom asked, before he could stop himself. "Or whatever is left of it."

Glasser nodded.

They turned a corner. The street opened, allowing a better view of the glow. It resembled nothing more than light pollution clinging to the skyline of a distant city. But Tom could tell it wasn't of this world.

Their footsteps echoed on the icy sidewalk.

"The worlds should have never touched," Glasser went on. "They didn't separate after the portal closed, as we'd hoped. The thin spots never healed. The shear stress between our world and the Otherside caused a rift to form in one of the thin spots. It will spread as the worlds buckle against one another."

"And then what?"

"I don't know."

The two of them hadn't passed a single person on their stroll. No cars drove past. Tom was walking with a ghost in a ghost town.

"We meddled in a place no living being should be able to go," Glasser continued. "Now, we are paying the price. Life cannot survive without death's counterpart and vice versa. We've tipped that balance, and we must fix it." Glasser's voice shook on his last words, betraying his placid expression.

Tom ceased walking, taking another drag of his cigarette. He exhaled, smoke swirling around his head.

Glasser would've had this problem neatly wrapped up already, save for one snag; the portal only responded to one person.

And that person was Tom.

"I know what you're about to ask next."

A smile danced in Glasser's stare in response. Of course. He'd staged everything up to this conversation, meticulously calculating each step to strip every little thing away from Tom until he had nothing left.

"And my answer is no. I won't seal it for you." This was old Tom's problem. Thomas Henderson didn't care anymore. "That part of my life died the day everyone else did. You can find someone else to fix your mistakes because *you* decided to play God. I won't be your lab rat again."

"Your life is empty, Tom. Hollow. Meaningless."

Glasser didn't miss a beat. How many steps ahead was he already? How close until the inevitable checkmate?

"You had a marriage where your wife treated you like an untrainable dog. You worked at an accounting firm where your boss forced you to embezzle money."

"But it was *my* life." Tom's hand shook, his cigarette breaking in two.

"One you cannot go back to. The audit was flubbed. A man is in a coma, clinging to his life. Your wife is gone. There is nothing left for you in Fox's Glew."

"You could have asked for my help." Tom's hackles raised. "But the esteemed Dr. Quillon Glasser was too proud for that. Instead, you decided to sabotage my life."

The single frayed thread keeping him together snapped. His stable, albeit suffocating, life under Naomi's thumb was gone. Now, it would be one cold bar and hotel room after another until the law caught up with him.

The deep-purple bruises under his eyes begged for sleep. He should be climbing onto his memory foam mattress, tuning out Naomi as she found something to natter about.

Tom missed her. Or rather, he missed what she symbolized. Safety. Certainty if he put in his years with the other sheep, he'd be handed his pension and watch before being sent to slaughter.

"I needed to make it happen." Glasser probed Tom with his unsettling eyes. "You won't take action until all is lost."

Tom rubbed his forehead with a shaking hand.

"So, you're telling me the voices I heard, the texts on my phone, there one minute, and gone the next. That ... fucking silhouette that looked like you, stalking my car. *You* made me imagine all that? Do I want to know how?"

"The mind is quicker than the lie." Glasser stood there, so *smug* and put together.

Tom hated him.

He hated Glasser for ruining his life then, and he hated Glasser for ruining his life now. Fuck him for taking him under his wing, for introducing him to the hidden wonders of Becopra.

What Glasser said was true, though. Tom didn't tell his wife about his past until he was forced to. Until he'd left a man for dead.

He hated himself.

He turned on his plastic-bagged heel and stormed off. Hopefully, his duffle bag was still in the dive bar; he needed the cash in it if he planned on getting so shitfaced tonight he forgot his own name.

But his attention kept getting pulled to the light over the hills.

The rift to the Otherside.

Tom had the same gut reaction when he first opened the portal; that he was no longer looking at this plane of existence.

This is my fault.

No, it's not. I didn't know what the portal was. No one at Becopra did.

"Atra survived."

Tom halted, his skin turning to lace as the night air fluttered through, penetrating him to the bone.

"She survived the accident. Just like you. Just like me."

Tom wanted to rain blows upon Glasser until there was nothing left of him to fill his mind with lies.

Did she grow up?

Did the seven-year-old he left for dead continue to thrive instead of rotting in Polaris?

"I want proof." Tom's voice trembled along with the rest of his body.

"I have it. And I'll give it to you if you agree to help me."

"No. I'm not playing your games. Proof first, or I walk."

Glasser gave him nothing but that infuriatingly arrogant look.

Tom stomped away, grinding his teeth. He neared the corner when Glasser called out. "Knowing Atra is out there will eat you alive."

Tom stumbled, forcing himself not to pause.

"You won't last long before you come searching for me."

Tom picked up his pace, desperate for another drink.

"I have the proof in my motel room. But I want your word you'll agree to seal the rift first."

Tom rubbed at the stubble sprouting on his chin. The bastard was right. This revelation would consume him from the inside out.

Letting out a grunt of defeat, he turned around. Glasser might as well have become a statue. He expected Tom to come crawling back.

But observing Glasser at a distance made Tom realize how bony he was under his clothes. How his cheekbones protruded from the hollows of his face. He was a man who reeked of death, covering it up with polished suits and neat haircuts.

"I'll make *you* a deal," Tom proposed. "We go to the bar. We go back to the booth I was sitting in before you showed up. If my duffel bag is there, I leave. You never contact me again. You find someone else to help fix your mess.

"If the bag is gone, I'll come with you. But I'm not agreeing to anything until you give me proof Atra is still alive. And if I'm not satisfied, I walk."

Even though Tom hoped this came across as an attempt to gain the upper hand, he had an ulterior motive. If his duffel bag was gone, so was his cash. And damned if he'd be forced to go searching for Glasser in the middle of the night begging for somewhere to sleep.

Glasser spread his palms out and nodded.

"Lead the way."

They returned to the dark corner booth of the bar. Someone had cleared the empty glasses, leaving Tom's untouched burger in their place. Holding his breath, knowing his future hung in the balance, he neared the duct-taped seat.

Empty. The duffle bag was gone.

A macabre smile spread across Glasser's face, the creases around his eyes travelling down and across his cheeks like intricately-woven spiderwebs.

"It's not far to my motel. Come, Tom, I'll give you the proof you need."

Part Two
Chthonic

Chapter 7

As Above, so Below

December 10
Five days before the Vanishing Plains Fire

"You don't have to talk." Ophelia resisted the urge to tug at the tassels on her scarf. "You don't have to do anything you don't want."

The woman sitting across from her had introduced herself as Madia. Ophelia had no way of knowing if that was her real name.

Ophelia noted how Madia styled her salt and pepper bangs over her temples to cover the bruised skin underneath. How she hunched over to subconsciously make herself as small as possible. How she flinched every time Ophelia spoke.

Would Madia unleash the howl she held under the surface, or would she remain quiet like the countless others before her?

"I shouldn't be here." Madia broke the silence when Ophelia thought she wouldn't.

Ophelia ground her teeth. She'd heard it a thousand times.

"No one will find out. This is a safe place." The response

Ophelia had given a thousand times. Her words flowed out, serene like the lavender walls of her office. If only she felt that way. Bubbling underneath, she was a lake of molten lava. The insatiable hunger gnawed at her. It had reared its head again sooner than anticipated.

"I don't *need* a safe place." Madia's wide eyes shone. "I have a home."

Ophelia pursed her lips, the fine lines creasing around them. It would never stop. Here was a beautiful woman filled with potential, the universe in front of her, and *her husband* was crushing it into a black hole. She wondered how many times he had told Madia she was ugly, she was worthless, she was nothing without him.

Ophelia wanted to find him and snap his neck.

The hunger surged. The Queen had to be fed soon. As the bond between them strengthened, the void within her grew. She needed to do her job properly; it was her mission to get women away from scum men. But she couldn't do that when she was starving to death.

Madia grabbed the purse lying at her feet.

"I shouldn't be here." It came out in a rush.

Don't go back to him, Ophelia tried to tell her, but her tongue had twisted itself into a knot.

"Wait." The knot in Ophelia's tongue loosened.

Madia paused, hovering half-crouched over the chair. Something in her face changed. Her eyes begged for an excuse to stay.

"I've been there," Ophelia went on. "I know what it's like walking over that field of landmines, never knowing when you'll set one off. But it is *never* your fault. If you believe one thing, believe that."

Madia was Ophelia from three decades ago; barely twenty, buried alive in a grave so deep she couldn't climb out if she tried.

Ophelia unearthed a tiny brass key hanging from a long chain tucked under her blouse. Leaning over, she unlocked the top drawer of her desk. The deep pain in her lower back—which had settled in long before middle age did—the pain that should've throbbed with the movement never came. The Queen had healed it. She grabbed a pamphlet from the stack that lay within, then promptly locked it again.

"When I was at my lowest, this saved me." She held the pamphlet out.

Madia accepted it.

"This is a takeaway menu." She scanned the front, dubious.

"Call the number on it. From a phone he doesn't know about."

Always the same. Make one life better, save one woman, then another, and another, the cycle never satisfied …

"Ask for Evie. Discard the pamphlet before you get home."

Madia nodded, her gaze never leaving the paper in her hands as she walked to the door.

"And Madia?"

The woman paused in the doorway.

"It *will* get better if you let it."

Ophelia knew The Drove would be hearing from Madia as the door clicked shut.

She couldn't wait that long, though. The hunger had to be dealt with now.

Ophelia locked the heavy steel door behind her, walking down the alley to where she'd parked her car. Not even four o'clock. The Women's Resource Centre was so understaffed she had to shut it down two hours early. Another budget slash like this and they'd be forced to shutter the doors for good.

She'd forgotten it wouldn't matter soon. To her, at least. The solstice was only eleven days away.

The sun had already dipped behind the skyline of Telos. Although Ophelia couldn't see it, she knew on the edge of the city stood an asylum.

Vanishing Plains Psychiatric Hospital.

She'd driven past it not hours before on her commute to work. Four stories tall, reinforced windows reflecting the mid-morning sun. Who knew, after all these years passing by it, that the thing she needed to sate this hunger forever was one of the patients inside.

She shifted her canvas bag to her other shoulder, rummaging for her car keys. As she put the key in the car lock, she heard *him*. She might as well have hung a bullseye on her back, walking out of the resource centre alone.

"Ophelia Lampard."

Footsteps approached from the entrance to the alley. She turned, finding herself eye level with a dishevelled beard coated in spittle.

"You piece of work." He slurred his words as his malty beer breath washed over her.

The fucking coward could only face her with the help of his best bud, alcohol. Ophelia didn't recognize the quilted plaid or the ripped jeans, but they all looked the same. She knew what he was here for.

"Do you know how lonely it gets at night since you robbed me of my wife?"

She narrowed her eyes. Of course, this chauvinistic filth would consider her job robbery.

"I have nothing." Beer Breath closed the already-narrow gap between them. "She took my son away. A boy needs his father to become a man."

Beer Breath grabbed the front of her jacket, yanking her toward him.

His mistake.

She slipped her free hand around his neck and slammed his head into her car's trunk. It bounced off with a sickening *thunk!* before he crumpled to the ground.

Ophelia straightened herself out, smoothing a lock of auburn hair that had fallen out of its twist. Beer Breath gripped the top of her rear tire, bleeding freely from the gash in his head, unable to lift himself up. He didn't notice as her boot came down on his knuckles.

But his scream assured her he sure felt it as she pivoted her foot. She was famished, and her meal had been delivered.

She eased the pressure. He snatched his hand away, holding it close to his chest. He half-shuffled, half-crawled away, ass never leaving the pavement. Although his eyes shone with panic, the lids covering them drooped. The blood from the gash glistened across his forehead and down his face.

Ophelia stepped toward him, heels clacking on the pavement. He struggled to stand, but his body wouldn't obey. A smile spread across her face as she watched him flail.

"Don't hurt me," he blubbered, dripping snot mixing with his blood.

She paused, towering over him, then placed her foot between his legs and stomped down as if revving a gas pedal.

His shrieks echoed beneath the dusky twilight. Ophelia's mouth twisted as she drove her boot down harder. She never wanted to stop. She'd make him hurt a thousand times more than he ever hurt his wife.

But another part of her knew his screams would attract attention if she didn't cease. She eased off. He curled into a fetal position, helpless.

She took two steps forward and lobbed him over the head with her bag. Not enough brains to get knocked out by one blow, but two did the trick.

He would do. The Queen demanded her sustenance.

Ophelia exhaled loudly. Still so much work to do. She went

back to her car, finally unlocking it. She then grabbed Beer Breath by the legs and dragged him over. After opening the backdoor, she heaved him inside. His stench—a combination of sweat, hops, and rage—filled her nostrils. She gagged.

As soon as he was inside, she brushed herself off, as if doing so would rid her of the odour. But nothing would get it out.

It didn't matter; she'd have to burn these clothes later.

A rush coursed through her, beginning in her stomach and spreading to her extremities. She clutched the side of her rusted car as the alley swam in and out of focus. The confrontation weakened her to almost past the point of no return.

Soon. We'll feed soon, she told the Queen.

Steadying herself, Ophelia climbed into the driver's seat. As she went to close the door, her shoulders tensed.

Sitting by the back door of the resource centre was a black cat. His orange-tipped tail flicked back and forth.

I saw that, his judgemental stare said.

"Oh, fuck off," Ophelia muttered, slamming the door shut between them.

She let the warmth of the flames lick her face. Her flesh grew so hot it almost burned, yet it did nothing to heat her insides. She gripped the hardwood mantel above the fireplace. Her russet eyes flicked over the objects sitting on it. A vase, an iron candle holder, a set of keys. She chose a small silver dagger in a sheath, resembling an antiquated letter opener. She ran a hand over its tarnished engravings.

A muffled moan from behind. Beer Breath must be awake.

In the middle of her tiny living room, he struggled in his restraints. She'd trussed him like a calf in a roping competition, then wound a gag around his mouth. The whites of his eyes reflected orange from the fire. Ophelia wondered what this scene looked like to him. Waking up on a tarp covering a woven rug. The heavy curtains pulled shut. Had he accepted this was the end? Or did he have hope he'd be saved at the eleventh hour?

She unsheathed the knife, thrusting the curved blade into the fire. It turned orange, then red, the skin around her wrist raw and blistering from the heat, although she felt nothing but ice.

It was time.

She stepped toward Beer Breath. The double-blow to the head might have left him stunned, but he still maintained enough wits to recognize what was clutched in her fist. He struggled, but it only tightened the ropes cutting into his arms, turning his hands purple. The gag muffled his endless stream of pleas.

She bent in front of him.

"Shh, shh, shh." She gave him a comforting smile as she reached toward his face.

Ophelia thought his eyes would bug out of his head from sheer terror. He screamed, the veins around his temples, under the crusted blood, bulging. He shook his head from side to side, trying to fend her off, but she slid a hand under the gag without missing a beat.

"Please," was his first word, as she unwound the gag. "Don't hurt me."

Scared. Weak. He wouldn't be angry at the end, the way she preferred her gifts, but he'd have to do.

His face was as hot and red as the blade in her hand.

She stood, her shadow eclipsing him. Next would come the bargaining.

"If you let me go, I'll disappear." Beer Breath's words left him in a rush. "You'll never see me again. I'll never contact my wife."

Almost word for word what the others said. They were all so predictable, even in the end.

"Yes," she agreed.

His expression turned from pleading to surprise.

She leant back over, adjusting the dagger. "You're right. You *will* never tell anyone about this."

"No, no, no, please. Stop!" His voice broke, tears streaking down his cheeks.

"I have one question." Ophelia leaned in close, her breath fluttering over his ear. Although she knew his fear would weaken the gift, she couldn't resist. "Did you stop when your wife begged?"

His screams fuelled the fire within, bringing warmth to her cold bones.

Under the cypress tree again, Ophelia's arms trembled as she filled in the final shovelful of dirt. Sweat broke out between her shoulder blades as she packed the earth.

To the field ... down the left-hand path we go ... her mind sang in circles.

The ground beneath the dead cypress tree never froze when the rest of the world did. Her snow-covered cottage gleamed silver under the swollen moon, but neither the snow nor the moonbeams penetrated the tree's bare branches. Just death and darkness under here.

Hand in hand, we will never be alone.

Less than two weeks until the solstice. One more full moon and the ritual would be complete. All the work, the spent energy, the unrelenting hunger, would be worth it when she and the Queen transcended worlds and became one. Ophelia would never know what pain and starvation were again.

The shovel slipped from her fingers, landing on the freshly packed dirt. She wanted nothing more than to collapse beside it.

She took two stumbling steps, tripping over her feet. The tree caught her fall. Leaning against it for support, she placed her palms on its trunk. She closed her eyes, plucking out a strand of thought, reaching out to the Queen.

Nothing happened. She'd become too weak.

No.

She hadn't come this far. She pushed harder, the bark spiny beneath her flesh.

My Queen ... her thread of thought burrowed through the tree toward its core, touching the membrane of the next world over. She inhaled sharply as a thread from the other side snaked up, entwining with hers.

The tree thrummed under her outstretched hands. The Queen emerged, her consciousness climbing down Ophelia's thread. Concentrating on the ground behind her, Ophelia guided the Queen to where the gift lay buried. The Queen paused, tentative, like an animal sniffing out food. Ophelia held her breath as the Queen examined it, contemplating the offer.

The next gift will be greater, Ophelia said, when the Queen had been silent for too long. *This one was too scared in the end. I won't let you down again.*

A pause. Then, understanding.

The Queen lashed out, devouring the gift, as ravenous as Ophelia herself. A glow pulsed from the tree's centre, the same colour as the moonbeams that never reached it. Ophelia cried out as the Queen's energy surged into her with the intensity of a dam breaking. Out of instinct, she tried to step back, but her palms were glued to the tree.

The Queen sucked the gift dry, scuttling back to her own thread. She released Ophelia. Their thoughts unravelled, their realms separated by the membrane once more.

Ophelia fell to her knees, every rock, every bump, digging into her flesh through her skirt.

"I—I thank you," she stammered, the power almost too much to bear. She drew in a breath, the approaching snowstorm thick on the back of her tongue.

"The Drove thanks you, our Mother of Most." Her voice swelled as the energy melted the ice in her veins. "I am not worthy of your gifts."

She raised her hands to the cypress tree.

"I render every part of myself to you."

The bond running between them strengthened.

"My Queen."

Chapter 8

Redux

A COLD DRAFT blew from the vent above. The skin under Atra's too-thin sweatpants prickled. The asylum was doing a damned good job of matching the inside temperature to the bitter outside.

Dread dispersed under the airflow, drifting across the padded walls.

Growing. Again.

How was she ever supposed to destroy it?

Dread churned overhead, her personal storm cloud. Lex told her it wanted to go to the rift.

Why?

Atra lifted her head off the floor as it swirled closer.

"What are you?" Her words came out gravelly after not speaking for days.

No answer. Of course.

She rested her head back on the padded floor. She was only aware of the passage of time from the food shoved through a slot in the door twice a day. Breakfast, powdered eggs. Dinner, powdered potatoes. They didn't serve you a third meal when you were in isolation.

Lying here, pretending to be a Good Little Psych Patient, was the only way she'd leave this room faster. The way she reacted to Creepsley made them think she was a Bad Little Psych Patient. They didn't like it when you made a scene.

You would think she would've learned that the first time she was committed.

No, she got to make that mistake twice.

Only the last time she'd screamed for longer. Screamed until her voice broke, and even then she couldn't accept no one was coming back for her. Her stepmother had succeeded. Drove Dad away, then finished taking out the trash with her.

But she didn't tie anchors to those memories to have them come floating from the depths now. She shouldn't be focusing on the past; she should be focusing on how to get out of this mess.

Maybe this was how Vanishing Plains had always been.

But there were too many gaps in that theory to hold. It didn't explain the fire, the rift, the escape. It didn't explain Creepsley in the car crash. It didn't explain Lex. And it sure as shit didn't explain why Atra was suddenly the new patient when she had years of memories here.

There *was* another explanation she kept pushing away, but it kept pushing back. That she was dead, dead, dead. Crushed flat in that car crash and this was some fever-death dream.

Stop it.

She didn't escape Vanishing Plains to die in a car crash hours later.

And who was that woman in the beige camper van who'd picked her up on the streets of Telos? Evie, she claimed her name was. In collusion with Creepsley?

No. Atra remembered her sprawled out in the back of the van with a broken neck.

A rattle from behind snapped her out of her thoughts. Another meal already? Atra almost didn't roll over to accept it, but the powdered food was so offensive it distracted her from this hellish predicament.

No tray at the door. Instead sat a cat, black fur with bright-orange tips. He was close enough that she could read the name on his swaying collar.

"Hello, Oriens."

The cat stood, shaking himself off.

"Do *you* know why there are two separate people chasing down a psych patient?" she asked him, not expecting an answer.

Oriens skulked toward her. Atra extended a hand to pet him, but he snaked past. Rolling back over, she followed his path.

The padded wall had disappeared, replaced by a bay window that opened out to a dark snow-blanketed forest. Oriens perched himself on the bench in front of the window.

Atra's heart galloped.

The purple rift was zigzagging across the sky behind the cat.

She pushed herself off the floor, keeping her eyes glued to the rift. Dread floated toward the window, mirroring her movements.

Atra couldn't deny the pull the rift had on Dread. On her.

Insane.

Dead.

But there was a third option she hadn't explored: that all of this was really happening.

"Find Magnus. Find the planes." Those were Lex's last words.

But Atra didn't want to do either. She didn't care about the Queen, or saving the world, no matter how insistent the kid was. She just wanted out, back to her old reality.

At least, that's what she told herself as her gaze remained glued to the rift.

And where was Lex?

Last Atra knew, the kid had been leaning against the bookshelf. Nothing there now but a gaping hole between the crowded volumes.

What happened to the book that crossed over with her? She remembered its worn leather under her fingertips, the twinkling, lopsided figure eight on its spine. She tried to recall when she'd last held it but came up blank.

It was lost.

Lost, like her.

The door to the padded room swung open.

In the split second she turned to face Creepsley, the wall behind her had turned back to white.

"Are you ready to behave, Miss Heart?"

Atra nodded, not trusting herself to speak. Anything to get out of this room.

Creepsley didn't move from the doorway, forcing her to walk past him. She clenched her teeth, grazing the sleeve of his lab coat as she stepped out into the hall.

The door boomed shut. Her spine crawled as Creepsley's warm, damp fingers wrapped around her arm like a slug.

He steered her down the hall. Through the sleeping quarters they went, every door open in a perfect line, the neatly made beds behind them all dressed in blood-red sheets.

Wrong.

Like her name.

Like Dread.

Her former shadow, in its new misty form, floated in the fringes of her vision, confirming so.

"You will be sharing sleeping quarters with Beryl." Creepsley's sulphuric breath fell on her, as he spoke. "I trust you won't have a problem dealing with her Nightsickness?"

Nightsickness. Not Sundowners. Wrong, again.

At least, Beryl remained her roommate.

"No problem," Atra responded softly. She would go along with what the creep said. At least until she had more answers.

"And I will not tolerate disrespect or unruliness. There will be no more flights of fancy, no more talk about imaginary stepbrothers."

Atra pressed her lips together, fighting against her instincts to call out the fake doctor on his bullshit. He was egging her on, itching to issue a strike two and throw her back in the padded room.

They arrived at the common area. Creepsley shoved her inside. She resisted the urge to wipe off her arm where he'd touched her, his slime lingering.

No blood-red tabletops in here. The common area remained the same.

Only now it was filled with people she'd never seen.

Atra crossed her arms over herself as she weaved through the tables, searching for an empty spot. She almost wished for the padded room back, just her and Dread.

Behind her, Creepsley blocked the exit, wearing a smirk. No escape.

Finally, she recognized someone.

"Beryl." The name escaped her as she made a beeline for Beryl. Beryl didn't see her, though, head turned away.

"Beryl!" she called again, closing in on the table. Beryl didn't turn at the sound of her name.

Harmonica Mouth plopped herself down beside Beryl, putting an arm around her bony shoulders.

Atra's cheekbone throbbed where Harmonica Mouth had walloped her with the broomstick. The bruise had turned an ugly yellow.

"Keep moving, Ater." Harmonica Mouth didn't miss a beat.

Atra faltered.

"Beryl?" She hated how small her voice sounded.

Beryl kept her face averted, wiry white eyebrows knitting together.

"I said, keep moving," Harmonica Mouth repeated, through clenched teeth.

Atra wanted to shove Harmonica Mouth off the chair—she was nothing but a pest, a mosquito you squish with your finger—but Creepsley's stare still bore into her from the doorway.

Atra swallowed a remark and walked away.

Every table was full, every hard plastic chair occupied by a hard, plastic stranger. No one looked up as she passed. No one noticed her.

Invisible, like Dread.

At the back of the room stood a bookshelf she'd been well acquainted with in her old reality. Maybe Lex's book had ended up there.

She rushed up to it, its thirteen volumes now unfamiliar, changed like the rest of this place. No sign of the book with the lopsided figure eight on its spine, though.

Of course, it wouldn't be that easy.

"Check."

At the table to the right of the bookshelf, someone was crouched in a chair too small for their hulking body. Finally, another face Atra recognized.

Pepe had been institutionalized here before Atra was born. But that was in the other asylum, where she wasn't the new patient.

Fuck, this was confusing.

Pepe loomed over the table, focused on the chessboard in front of him. He moved a white knight, then shook his head, reached across, and captured it with a black bishop.

"Wrong move," he muttered to himself.

Atra hesitated. What if he ignored her too?

She strode over before she lost her nerve.

"Mind if I sit?"

Silence. Nothing from him too. She was about to walk away when—

"Your mind can go anywhere it likes."

Atra took that as a yes. She slid into the weighted chair, studying Pepe's face. Was that recognition behind his eyes?

"Have we met before?" she asked.

"Not in this place."

She couldn't stop staring at his head. This wasn't the same

Pepe she knew. Her Pepe had a big dent in his big bald head. Tumour removal that resulted in a brain injury. This Pepe's skull was smooth. No tumour. No brain injury.

Then why was he still here?

He gestured to the board in front of him. "Want to play?"

"Looks like you're already in the middle of a game," Atra said.

Pepe picked up a white pawn grimy with fingerprints and wiggled it in the air.

"No time like the present to join."

"Umm ... sure." This was the first time any patient, apart from Harmonica Mouth, had acknowledged her. He might not be the Pepe from her version of the Plains, but he was better than nothing.

"Don't mind Rei." Pepe shifted a rook along. "She's still adjusting. Grandiose delusions and all."

This Pepe unnerved her. The one Atra knew could barely string two sentences together and had the impulse control of a toddler. Hell, he would've eaten these chess pieces before he'd finished arranging them on the board.

"Who's adjusting?"

Pepe grinned, stretching the corners of his mouth as wide as they would go. Atra looked over her shoulder at Harmonica Mouth—sorry *Rei*—who stared daggers back at her.

"Gotcha."

She pushed her bishop across the board, taking a pawn. Pepe immediately captured it with the rook. Shit.

She set the discarded pawn on the table. Its fallen comrades, from before she joined in the game, should've been on the table too. But the pawn sat alone.

"There are pieces missing."

Maybe Pepe did eat them. Maybe this version wasn't so different after all.

"Nah, they aren't missing; they're hanging out on another plane."

"Another pla—?" She broke off as Nurse Silvia strode past. She and Pepe pretended to be deeply invested in their game until she was out of earshot.

"Your turn." Pepe dropped the subject.

A shiny, new piece now stood in the middle of the board.

"Hey," Atra blurted. "Was this always here?"

"Because you see something different doesn't mean it isn't real. It's how you look at it that makes it real to you."

His comment jarred something in her memory from the episode in the house. What did Lex tell her?

"The lie is quicker than the mind," Atra muttered.

"Exactly." Pepe leaned over and pulled a cold breakfast sausage from his sock. "You get me."

He took a bite and offered it to her.

"No, I'm good."

The new piece gracing the board was a queen.

Lex's voice filled Atra's head. *"The Queen will use you to end the world."*

It all kept funnelling back to that, didn't it?

Atra grazed the top of the queen's crown with a finger. The lettering on her medical bracelet flashed at her. Maybe it meant *Vanishing Planes* in the most literal sense. Lex said the house was a thin spot. Where it was easier to climb the altered planes.

Maybe Atra had accidentally climbed into one and gotten herself trapped.

"Pepe, when you said the missing chess pieces were on another plane, did you mean an altered plane?"

Pepe laughed through a mouthful of chewed sausage. "Of course! The altered planes are *everywhere*." He tapped his nose and winked, as if they were sharing an inside joke. Too bad Atra was on the outside. "Imagine reliving an experience you didn't know you had."

Reliving an experience.

"Well, I'm doing that, aren't I? The new patient, all over." She advanced a pawn, giving the queen on the board a wide berth. "The question is, if I *am* trapped in an altered plane, how do I climb back out?"

"You've got a lot of questions. It's not like I wrote the book on them!"

Atra's eyes flitted to the flimsy bookshelf beside him. Pepe was using a figure of speech, but there *was* a book. One that existed on both sides.

Where did it end up?

"Have you seen a book, though? Brown leather, with—"

His head jerked back and forth. "No."

All traces of his cheery demeanour were gone. These weren't the mannerisms of the Pepe she knew.

That's because the Pepe she knew had died in the blaze that had consumed this common room. Even if the asylum's front doors were wide open, it wouldn't be her reality beyond them she'd be running into.

"Not out. Forward." Lex had already given her the answer. Atra just didn't want to hear it.

"What about Lex? Do you know who Lex is?"

"No." But he wasn't agitated this time. He really didn't know.

"What about Magnus?"

Pepe swiped one of her pieces off the board, lips pressed in a thin line.

"What about Magnus." When Atra spoke, it wasn't a question this time.

Pepe bowed his head. "Your turn."

"And for my turn, I'm asking if you know about Magnus."

"Magnus went away." Barely louder than a whisper.

"Where?"

He fidgeted in his chair, muttering, "No, no, no," over and over again.

"Where did he go?" Atra pressed. "Do you know who he is?"

The front chair legs left the floor as his fidgeting turned to rocking. His head snapped up, eyes glistening.

"No, I don't want to talk about HIM!!!"

The room fell into a hush behind her. Pepe inhaled, about to let out a scream.

"Please. Don't. Creepsley will take me away again." Atra's words came out in a rush, panic clambering up her rib cage. "You're the only one in here who isn't ignoring me."

Pepe closed his mouth, nostrils still flared.

She threw a glance over her shoulder. Creepsley stepped forward from his spot in the doorway, uncrossing his arms. Ready to pounce.

"Pepe, you're the only one in here who can help …" Atra trailed off, as she turned back around.

The chair across from her was empty.

"Pepe?"

She scanned the room for him; it would be impossible to miss his lumbering frame. Creepsley still blocked the door. Rei still stared daggers. Beryl still had her head turned away.

But no Pepe.

Reaching over the table, she felt the back of his chair. Cold. He'd vanished.

Back into another plane?

The queen on the chessboard stared at her.

"Find Magnus. Find the planes." A warning from Lex?

You're grasping at straws. Seth, always the voice of reason, at the back of her mind.

"Shut up, Seth. You don't exist here."

No big bro here to rescue her from her nightmare this time around.

She had a book to find. And a person to find. The question was, which one would she find first?

Chapter 9

The Messenger

TOM TUMBLED down the college's hallway in a hungover haze. The light reflecting off the glass trophy cases blinded him, their insides filled with idols of false victories.

Wait till you're done with your courses and the college has no use for you. It'll spit you out like a wad of over-chewed gum, those trophies were saying.

Exactly as Tom's parents had done to him.

"Once you're eighteen, you're on your own, Tommy Boy." His mother's favourite threat throughout his childhood. His father would grunt in agreement from his recliner as he downed his obligatory evening six-pack. A part of Tom never believed it.

Yet here he was. A college student. Not even twenty and buried in crippling debt. Playing poker had been easier than finding a part-time job. And that was working out well, until someone had put one too many whiskies in him and he woke up with empty pockets. Had he lost the money on his own, or did he get robbed?

Either way, he was fucked.

Tom recited The List of everyone he owed money to. It'd grown so long he'd never reach the end of it. He imagined calling his parents, who still lived in the ass-end of nowhere.

"We love you, Tommy Boy." He could hear his mother, her voice razored away by years of sucking back cigarettes. "But you know the rules." *Click.*

Something tugged on his esophagus. Last night's bad decisions were threatening to rise.

Hastily, he turned the corner, hoping he'd make it to the bathroom in time. He ran smack dab into someone. Whoever it was dashed off before Tom could fully take in what had happened.

He picked himself off the floor, his nausea knocked aside for the time being. In front of him, the college job board. Its multi-coloured flyers filled with phone numbers from desperate employers stared him down. He almost laughed at the cruel irony.

If you weren't such a lazy piece of shit, Tom, you could've worked for one of us.

And then he saw it. What he believed to be the deus ex to his machina, the solution to all his problems, in one tiny flyer.

Becopra Corporation.

WANTED: Subjects to participate in sleep study. 2–3 nights. NO experience necessary. ALL ages welcome.

His eyes widened at the amount of money they offered.

He reached for the tear-off tab with the phone number. If he could go back in time and slap his hand away, he would. Sleep study his ass.

He didn't know it, but those were simpler times. Before Polaris, the Cynosura Experiments, Glasser turning him into a human lab rat.

Before Atra. Before the Polaris accident.

Before the new name, new wife, new life.

Before the fender bender that had brought him full circle, right back into Glasser's clutches—

Tom snapped awake from the half-lucid dream, clammy with sweat. A hideous straw lamp illuminated the room, but the dark crack between the curtains told him it was still night.

This was not his bedroom. He was sprawled on a prickly comforter instead of Naomi's 1,000 thread-count cotton sheets. *Those* ridiculous sheets she could afford, yet if he tried buying smokes more than three times a week …

"Tom."

His neck was so stiff from the car crash he couldn't turn it. Instead, he was forced to roll his whole body over, the movements agonizing.

Glasser sat on the bed beside him.

"I see no expense was spared for our weekend getaway," Tom muttered. His memories after agreeing to come here were distorted by sleep deprivation and stress.

He took in the cheap motel room. The carpet was an enigma —where did the stains end and the pattern begin?—and the bulky TV in the corner was so ancient it still housed a VCR player.

He could've easily laid down and closed his eyes again, but his urge for nicotine was greater than his urge for sleep. He fumbled in his jeans pocket for his pack, squashed from sleeping on it.

"The motel has a strict nonsmoking policy." Glasser's eyes ticked to the sprinkler system on the ceiling.

"Like I give a shit."

Tom's words came out muffled from the cigarette dangling between his lips. He flicked his lighter, igniting the end of it.

He inhaled deeply. That first inhale always took his troubles away. If only life could be that one inhale.

"Proof." He exhaled, crashing back to reality. "You have proof Atra is alive. I want to see it, or I walk. It's not like I'm handcuffed to this bed."

"I gave you my word. I won't break my promise, Tom."

Tom clenched his jaw at the way Glasser used his name in that slightly pandering tone.

Glasser got off the bed and walked over to a shoddy table behind the door. Its foul, turquoise laminate top held a four-cup coffee maker.

Tom's cigarette plume formed a smoggy barrier between them. The events of the past two days threatened to surface, but he suppressed them as he took another long drag.

Inhale.

And exhale.

Nothing else mattered in those moments.

Glasser pulled a manila envelope out of a briefcase and tossed it onto Tom's bed. A stack of photos fell out, fanning across the scratchy comforter. They appeared to be stills from grainy security footage, all featuring the same girl, the sequence progressing from teenager to young adult. She wore the same white T-shirt and grey sweatpants regardless of her age.

Atra.

For all Tom knew, these could be fake. Glasser could have found anyone who slightly resembled her. He hadn't looked at a picture of his daughter in years. Those were left behind when he became Thomas Henderson. Only one photo of her remained in his possession, tucked away in the lining of his wallet. He'd nearly thrown it away after he fled, but couldn't bring himself to do it.

It *was* her, though. The girl in the photos had the same wild black hair and slumped posture as him.

"Where is she?" he asked, after going through the stack. He carelessly ashed his smoke onto the bedspread.

These weren't photos of her in school or at work. These looked more like she was in a hospital. But could he really be surprised if she was sick?

"In a home for the mentally disturbed."

Tom's stomach sank. A nuthouse.

"How'd she get there?" His smoke burned down to his fingers. Nothing left to inhale.

"Your ex-wife had her admitted when she was thirteen. Or rather, your first wife, since you never got divorced."

Tom scowled.

"But *why*?"

"We both knew the risks when it came to Atra."

Tom traced the outline of her face in the last photo. What went wrong in her mind? She was fine for seven years, dammit!

That was a lie.

He remembered when she'd started talking about keeping the shadows out, gripped by a hysterical fear no child should know.

He was caught off guard when a yawn wracked his body.

"Coffee?" Glasser offered.

Tom nodded, mashing his smoke on the bedside table.

Glasser already had brewed the coffee. The same cheap stuff they drank in their Polaris days. Tom instantly recognized the silver packaging sitting beside the coffee maker.

All those late nights gathered around the portal, trying to find a way to enter the Otherside.

Glasser poured the coffee into styrofoam cups.

"I'll need those photos back, please. In the envelope, if you would be so kind," he murmured the words, slightly out of breath, as if the simple task of making a coffee drained him.

Tom complied, fingers stiff as he fumbled to arrange the photos in a stack. He turned them around, unable to look at Atra anymore, knowing this was her fate. Maybe she would've been better off staying trapped in that bunker.

He wound the string around the envelope button as Glasser pushed a cup of coffee under his nose.

"Still take it black?"

Tom nodded, exchanging the envelope for the cup. He noticed Glasser wince as he returned the envelope to the briefcase. Glasser's hand flitted up, as if about to rub his chest, but he caught himself at the last moment and stopped. The lamplight illuminated the cavernous hollows of his cheeks, his sagging skin giving away that he'd dropped weight too quickly.

Not looking so well, Quillon.

Glasser glanced at Tom, as if feeling his stare. Tom diverted his attention to the cup, the oily film from the beans swirling on the surface.

"Who else survived?"

Glasser raised his eyebrows.

Tom forced the words out. "At Polaris. You survived. I survived." He inhaled sharply, unable to say his daughter's name. "Who else? Deadmarsh? Maris?"

"No one."

A lie?

Tom plucked at the bedspread. Questions about Atra bubbled, but he popped them before they could form.

Not his fault. He didn't know she was alive.

Liar. You saw her chest moving.

That was Tom Hart. He was Tom Henderson now.

Sure, compartmentalize. That'll make everything okay.

Just inhale.

Now do everyone a favour and never exhale.

"What's the plan?" he asked, to distract himself from the churning thoughts. "Close the rift only we can see, save the world?"

Then deal with charges of fraud and attempted murder.

He could do it again—change his name, slip between the cracks.

"We stay in this five-star resort for a few days," Glasser replied. "Then east to Telos."

Tom's old stomping grounds. "That's where the rift is, isn't it?"

Glasser shuffled to the motel's door, sliding open the chain lock. The spasm of pain flitting across his face would have gone undetected if Tom wasn't looking for it.

"See for yourself."

He swung open the door. A chilly blast of air entered the room. Tom stood, styrofoam cup in one hand, pack of smokes in the other.

He saw it before he got to the doorway. Over the second-floor balcony, the purple light blossomed on the horizon, brighter than last night. But that wasn't what he focused on. A single car was parked in the icy lot below. Its keys were resting on the table, next to the coffee maker.

"You can run." Glasser took note of where Tom's gaze was directed. "I'm not going to stop you."

Tom had a flash of grabbing the keys, shoving Glasser aside. Running down the metal steps and driving away.

Run, Tom. Run.

He squeezed the styrofoam cup, forcing the coffee nearly to the rim, his eyelids still heavy. Having to drink it to wake himself up seemed like too much effort.

"Do you think Becopra would've started their experiments if they knew the outcome?" he asked.

"They knew the risks associated with tapping into the altered planes."

"Then why aren't they fixing the problem?"

"We *are* Becopra."

Tom's mouth twisted into a sardonic smirk. Of course, he'd end up as the last one of two.

"Why not go now? If that thing"—Tom gestured to the horizon—"is growing, what are we waiting for?"

"A few days. We leave in a few days."

"Not good enough."

"We're waiting for the solstice."

"Why?"

"It's when the worlds are the closest."

"And how do you know it's gonna stay shut this time?"

"I've had years to assess what we did wrong. So many variables we were unaware of had to align that didn't before."

"So, you don't know."

"Drink your coffee, Tom."

Tom raised the cup to his mouth, then paused. Poking out from under the cuff of his rolled-up and crinkled business shirt was his old keloid scar. There was a reason he preferred long-sleeved shirts, even in the summer. That damned scar was his single physical reminder of the experiments Glasser had put him through. Every time he saw it, he thought of the pearlescent substance he'd been injected with. Under the buried memories, he still remembered the squelching sensation of that thick liquid entering his body.

Glasser had lied when he said it wouldn't hurt.

For weeks, Tom thought he was dying. He'd convinced himself his arm would combust from the inside out.

Becopra had him holed up in that bunker with nothing but a cot in a room the size of a broom closet. At first, he remembered the whitecoats coming in like clockwork to check his vitals, hook him to the EEG, watch his brain waves. He demanded to see Glasser, to know what was happening, but Glasser never showed himself.

Hours blurred into days, his body racked with feverish chills. Maybe this time, when he passed out, it would be the last, if only to end the agony.

Then it happened. The walls around his cot no longer aligned, defying logic, defying gravity, the angles warping toward the spot under where he slept. That's when Glasser finally made his appearance. Out of all the test subjects, Glasser announced, Tom had been the only one to succeed.

"Succeed at what?" Tom asked, barely able to speak through his nausea.

The goal was to tap into an altered plane. But Tom exceeded

expectations. He'd actually opened a doorway to one. One where death reigned and nothing living could enter.

The rift beyond the motel room pulsed in the sky, as if responding to the memory. Tom almost didn't notice Glasser brush past him, silent as a mouse.

Glasser's shoulders shook and his lips pulled down, a far cry from his usual composed self. He stumbled into the bedside table, entered the bathroom and slammed the door shut behind him.

Whatever transpired in there was quickly muffled by the faucet turning on. And frankly, Tom didn't want to know.

Tom closed the door to the outside world, taking one last wistful glance at the car in the lot. If Glasser had never shown him those pictures, he'd be in that car, keys in the ignition, ready to peel off into wherever the night would take him.

Were those pictures of Atra? He remained unconvinced. He turned to the table, where Glasser's briefcase sat. Should he open it?

Setting down his coffee cup, he threw a glance over his shoulder, expecting the bathroom door to open. Out of nervous habit, he reached into his pocket for his smokes. His fingers wrapped around something hard and plastic instead.

His cell phone.

He took it out, turning the screen on. It lit up with the familiar wallpaper of Naomi. One night, after too much wine, she'd replaced the default image with one of herself. She pretended to be joking around, but Tom knew she wasn't.

There was no signal. He wandered around the room, phone held high, hoping to get a bar. He didn't know why he was so determined to find reception; who would he call? The woman staring at him from the screen with a not-quite-content smile on her face?

Sorry for wasting ten years of your life, babe.

He never gave her the love and security she so desperately

craved. He was never the husband she wanted him to be. She was never his idea of wallpaper material.

Tom stopped searching for a bar and put his phone away. Naomi oversaw his cell phone bill. She probably cut him off after she left.

A dark shape darted out of the corner of his eye. He twisted around, tripping over his feet and crashing into the side of the bed, phone tumbling out of his hands.

A black cat stood beside the coffee maker. Jumping down from … where? The cat stared at Tom with bottle-green eyes and then leapt down, knocking Tom's coffee cup to the floor, before disappearing under the bed.

Shit cat.

Tom crouched, peering under the bed. Nothing there but the styrofoam cup.

Where had that cat come from? There was no ledge or window above the table. In all probability, the thing snuck in while the door was open. But that didn't explain where he'd vanished to.

A rough, hacking noise filled the room. At first, Tom thought it was the cat coughing up a hairball, then realized it came from behind the bathroom door.

How sick was Glasser? The man sounded like he was going to eject a lung.

Tom rose, about to step outside for a smoke and let Glasser suffer in peace, when the bathroom door opened.

They locked eyes, each caught off guard by the other's candid stare.

"What's going on in here, Tom?" Glasser was the first to break the silence.

"Nothing. What's going on in there?"

"Nothing."

Chapter 10

Eye

December 11
Four days before the Vanishing Plains Fire

OPHELIA WRAPPED HER HANDS around the mug on the table in front of her. Her fingertips whispered over the tiny ridges in the ceramic, reverberating through her ears. Wisps of steam floated off the surface of the chamomile. She could smell the exact temperature of the water.

The energy of the café buzzed through her. If she closed her eyes, she could sense the mood of each individual in the shop. The barista—bitter that her boss was taking a cut of her tips—was serving a customer worried he would be late for work. The man waiting in line behind sighed, the muscles in his chest contracting as his impatience gave way to anger.

So many people angry.

If Ophelia lingered on the emotion too long, it fed the uncontrollable rage that grew as the cypress tree took more from her.

She reached out beyond the walls of the café, scanning the

people walking past, driving down the street. More of the same emotions out here. One block, two ... how far could she go? Ah—there was Evie, her beige camper van stuck in traffic. She radiated anxiety, late for their meetup.

If Ophelia concentrated harder, she could wind her way through the streets, to the farmland on the outskirts of Telos. She found where her house stood, taking the path through the fields and behind it to the cypress tree.

The tree that gave her this power. The tree that sucked the very life from her if she didn't feed it.

Pushing the dying branches aside, she worked through the bark to the glowing centre of the tree. The membrane separating her world from the Otherside. Where the Queen lay in wait.

A foul odour snapped her back to the café. It wafted through the room like rotting garbage on a summer day.

The undeniable stench of a man.

She could smell his intent before he slipped into the booth across from her.

Not the visitor she was expecting.

"Ophelia Lampard?"

She pressed her lips together. Even without her enhanced senses, she would've known he was with law enforcement. It was the way he carried himself above everyone else, chest puffed out like a rooster.

Did she completely cover her tracks after Beer Breath's attack last night?

She'd destroyed the security footage of the alley behind the resource centre. She'd scrubbed her house of DNA evidence.

As long as no one looked at the base of the cypress tree too closely, she'd be fine. It was easier to hide the bodies before the snow fell.

The man in the booth cut right to the chase. "I worked security detail for Lyall Lampard."

Now there was a name she hadn't heard in almost three decades.

As hard as Ophelia tried to maintain her composure, she couldn't control the sharp inhale at her ex-husband's name.

Sorry—ex-husband wasn't the correct term. That's what you call it when you divorce the son of a bitch. She was a widow.

She wondered if she'd seen this security guard before—possibly while her piece-of-shit ex gave his campaign speeches she was forced to attend with their son. Sitting there, with a baby in her lap and a smile plastered on her face. No one had known how much pain that expression caused, the fresh bruises on her cheekbone and temple meticulously covered up.

The perfect family. That's all it was to Lyall. Image. The public never knew what their precious mayor was like behind closed doors.

The man in the booth noticed Ophelia's reaction, his piggy eyes gleaming.

"I'm sorry, what was your name again?" She failed to keep the petulance out of her voice.

"Chuck. Chuck O'Flennek."

He said it too quickly. Too stiffly.

A fake name if she ever heard one.

She ran the tip of her index finger across her thumbnail. Time to trim them again. The cypress tree didn't affect only her senses; her hair and nails were growing at an accelerated rate.

"There's been a breakthrough in the cold case of your husband's disappearance," Chuck went on.

A stone dropped in Ophelia's gut as she struggled to keep her expression placid. How was she still being haunted by something that happened almost three decades ago? Why couldn't the case have died when her husband did?

"Don't you have anything to say?" White spittle collected in the corners of Chuck's cracked lips. "I thought you'd be happy to hear your husband's murderer might finally be found."

Ophelia knew what she should say in response—that she'd suffered enough knowing her husband's murderer had gotten away with it, leaving her a single, grieving mother—but she couldn't force the words out. She could still feel his hands around her throat, the bruises she constantly wore, her shattered elbow that never healed properly. It was bad enough she still had to carry the asshole's last name.

"He was a great man," Mr. Chuck *O'Flennek* continued to goad her. "He never deserved what happened—"

"They never found a body," she said, but he continued talking over her.

"—being murdered in cold—"

"They never found a body," she repeated, louder this time. Too loud, judging by the way the surrounding tables fell into a hush.

The ruddy splotches on Chuck's cheeks spread, turning his nose red.

Ophelia shouldn't have said anything. Self-restraint was becoming difficult. The anger twisted its way through her veins like the roots of the cypress tree. Her grip on the mug tightened. The microscopic fractures in the ceramic whispered to her that they were on the verge of shattering. She pulled her hands away, balling them into fists. Her too-long nails bit into her palms.

Chuck's mouth twitched.

"Lyall's shirt was recovered in the forest close to where you used to live." He produced an envelope from the inner pocket of his jacket. Ophelia found it hard to believe the shirt hadn't disintegrated, exposed to the elements for decades. "On it, a hair. Belonging to one Evelien Charles."

Evie.

Evie had better not walk through that door right now.

"Records indicate you and Ms. Charles were not acquainted then. You two started your witchy cult after packing your bags and moving to Telos. So how did her hair end up on Lyall's jacket all those years ago?"

Ophelia's fingernails punctured her skin, palms warming with blood.

Fucking Evie. How could she be so careless?

And how did Chuck know about The Drove? And how was he privy to details about her ex's disappearance if he was a lowly security guard?

"Can I see some identification, Mr. *O'Flennek*?"

She could hear the gears in his walnut-sized brain turning.

Got you.

She leaned back in her seat. A vigilante security guard with a grudge; that's all he was.

"C'mon, Ophelia." The way he murmured her name made her insides squelch. "You're not doing yourself any favours. Anyone can see a pattern. Twenty-eight years ago, Lyall goes missing, suspected dead. Eleven years ago, after you start up your second family, husband number two goes missing, never heard from again. Seven years ago, your son dies under mysterious—"

"Enough. We're finished here."

Ophelia could hear the rumblings of a grunt of anger threatening to escape Chuck's throat.

"Keep this." He pushed the envelope closer. "There are copies."

He leaned over the table, close enough for her to see the dead skin clinging to his copper hair. The scent of his unwashed scalp churned her stomach.

"Women like you disgust me." He heaved himself out of the booth, belly hitting the table, causing her tea to slosh over the envelope.

The door chimed as he exited the café.

Through the window, she watched him don a pair of sunglasses too tiny for his face, then climb into his truck. He sped off without a backward glance.

Chuck may be a nobody, but this envelope meant *someone* out there was investigating her ex's disappearance. Could they pin anything on her?

"The solstice is ten days away," she muttered. "I'll be with the Queen before that happens."

But was she telling herself, or merely reassuring herself?

Moments later, Evie arrived in her rattling old van, bald tires taking the place of where Chuck's jacked-up ones had been. Ophelia froze. What if Chuck was still slinking about?

Call Evie? Tell her to abort?

Instead, Ophelia reached out, as she did earlier, searching for Chuck's truck. He passed through a set of lights, leaving the city centre of Telos. Satisfaction oozed from his oily pores, a smirk plastered on his face.

Not coming back. Although Ophelia was draining the gift, she couldn't stop. She could follow him to wherever he worked, wherever he lived, prevent whatever mess he was trying to cause—

A purse slapped down on the table. Her connection to Chuck severed as Evie plunked herself into the seat.

"Sorry, I'm late. The pharmacy's swamped and I couldn't get away," Evie said breathlessly. "What's that?" She motioned to Chuck's envelope.

"Nothing." Ophelia stuffed the envelope into her bag.

But Evie wasn't paying attention as she shrugged off her coat. Her buggy eyes looked like they would pop out of their sockets with excitement.

Ophelia wished they would.

"I got it." Evie couldn't hold in her news any longer. "A visitor's badge for Vanishing Plains."

She produced a laminated rectangle, waving it around. Ophelia forced herself to concentrate on it.

"Did they give you any trouble?"

"No. It was easy enough. I told them I was a family friend. Not a lie ... exactly." Evie smirked as she put the badge back in her purse.

She tucked a lock of her short, blond hair behind her ear. Ophelia stared at it. The cause of all these problems.

"Good."

Evie cleared her throat. "Are you going to tell me why you need me to get her out? The girl at Vanishing Plains?" Her voice wavered. Things did not go well the last time this topic was broached.

"Why won't you tell me?" Evie had screamed at Ophelia, pink in the face. *"What are you—"* she'd gasped at the revelation. *"You're planning to sacrifice her, aren't you? I have a right to know. If I'm doing this I have a right to know!"*

"Don't act so innocent," Ophelia had shot back. *"Remember what you were doing before the Queen."*

"The Queen will divulge why the girl is needed if and when she sees fit." A politician's answer. Ophelia had learned a thing or two from her ex after all.

"Fine." Evie wasn't satisfied with the response, but Ophelia knew she wouldn't make a scene here. "I'm just worried. What about that ... man?"

Ophelia's eye twitched before she could stop it. Evie saw Chuck?

"The doctor. Glassman, or whatever his name was."

Relief washed over Ophelia. She'd almost forgotten about him.

"You're the pharmacist. Did you do what I told you?"

"Yes."

"Then he shouldn't be a problem anymore." Like Chuck should hopefully not be a problem soon.

"Hey." Evie reached her hand out, gently placing it over Ophelia's. "Are you okay?"

"I'm fine." Ophelia jerked her hand away. "Will you be bringing another gift?"

"Yes." Evie's hand twitched, as if she didn't know what to do with it. She squirmed in her seat, clearly uncomfortable with the task. "It might take me two or three days to ... gather everything."

Ophelia winced inwardly. Too long. Nothing she could do about it. With Chuck watching, she'd had to leave the harvesting to Evie. Ophelia had no choice but to trust her.

The Drove wasn't what it used to be. They used to be women, survivors, coming together. A group. Strength in numbers.

Now, The Drove was Ophelia and the Queen. They never had plans to bring Evie along. The Queen made that decision long ago.

The night of the solstice was for Ophelia and the Queen. Evie would be long gone. Like Chuck. Like Dr. Glasser, who had come nosing around. Evie was only useful until she delivered the girl. As the moon overhead turned blood red, the gateway within the cypress tree would open. The Queen would reach out, accepting the final gift, Atra Hart. The girl's shadow was the linchpin that connected life and death. It would allow Ophelia and the Queen to move freely between the worlds, united as one.

Ophelia suppressed a shudder, tasting the power. She drained the last of her tea from the mug. Her stomach contracted, wanting to retch it back up.

Not the sustenance she needed.

Picking up her bag, she stood.

"I have to go. Don't you have a busy pharmacy to run?"

Evie's face fell. Clearly, she'd been expecting more praise for the visitor's badge.

Ophelia exited the café with more grace than Chuck had. She hesitated at the door, contemplating throwing away the envelope. The hair on her arms bristled, feeling Evie's sad, confused gaze. No wonder the Queen wasn't taking her.

Ophelia dug into her bag. The envelope went into the trash, buried alongside the spent coffee cups. She wouldn't be weak like Evie.

Chapter 11

Molly

GLASSER'S SNORING cut through the silence of the hotel room. Tom didn't mind being kept awake by it. In fact, he welcomed it.

Was Glasser really asleep? Hard to fake that phlegmy snore that put a pneumonia patient to shame.

Tom sat up, fumbling for his phone under the pillow. He tapped on the flashlight feature, shielding the glow with his hand so it wouldn't wake old Quillon. The light illuminated the two sets of shoes by the door. Tom's shiny new pair, and Glasser's. The heels of Glasser's otherwise pristine leather shoes were squashed down; his feet were too swollen to fit into them anymore.

The man was sick, there was no doubt about it. Although Glasser had cleared away all evidence in the bathroom after one of his coughing fits—no used tissues, no blister packs of popped pills in the trash—Tom had still managed to find something. An empty pill bottle, between the plastic bag and the bottom of the trashcan. Glasser had ripped most of the label off, but the top corner showed a *PH. CHARLES, EVELIEN* had recently filled a prescription for him.

Glasser constantly rubbing his chest, the wincing, the breathlessness ...

This was for the old ticker, Tom bet.

The car keys sat on the laminate table. Tom lingered on them for too long. Glasser kept them in plain sight for the sole purpose of taunting him.

Run, Tom. Run.

He nearly had. The first night, while Glasser was out cold, he'd grabbed those keys, shoved his feet into his new shoes, and booked it to the car. He sat inside, knuckles tight against the wheel. But he couldn't peel his hands off the freezing leather to start the damned thing.

Those photos of Atra—growing up while the asylum around her stayed the same—haunted him.

His fault.

All his fault.

You let her shadows in. Coward.

He opened his mouth. The scream billowed around his head in a cloud of white breath.

That first night in the motel had been his only sleepless night. He'd passed out soundly for the next three of them. Uncharacteristically soundly. His guilty thoughts did not churn their familiar storm. And at this point, they should've been a hurricane.

Every evening, Glasser brewed that no-name, silver-packaged coffee.

Every evening, he poured a styrofoam cup full.

Every evening, "Drink your coffee, Tom."

"Finish your coffee, Tom."

"Go to sleep, Tom."

This had been their song and dance for three nights now as the solstice inched closer.

But on that first night, he hadn't drunk his coffee because the imaginary cat had spilled it. And he hadn't fallen asleep.

Was it so farfetched to think Glasser was drugging him?

And if he was, what was he doing while Tom drooled unceremoniously in his doped-up slumber?

Tom only had tonight to figure it out; Glasser had announced this morning they'd be heading for Telos at the crack of dawn tomorrow.

Tom lifted the briefcase, careful not to bang it against the table. He sat at the foot of the bed, placing the briefcase on the mattress beside him. He clicked open the fastenings, gritting his teeth at the noise, but Glasser's snores droned on.

A business card fell out of the top pocket. Someone had scribbled a phone number on the back in pencil, with the name *Creeley* underneath. Tom stuffed it away, disinterested. He shifted aside the manila envelope of photos—*Coward,* they whispered—revealing a laptop underneath.

Aha!

He removed it with the same delicacy as if dismantling an atomic bomb.

All Glasser did was sit on that fucking laptop, typing away. *Clickclickclickclickclick*, as Tom turned up the volume on the TV trying to drone it out.

He was sick of watching television. The endless game shows, save for the occasional news report. All he needed was a microwave dinner and some cheap beer and the transformation into his father would be complete.

The local weatherman wouldn't shut up about the impending lunar eclipse. The Cold Blood Moon. Tom had the weatherman's spiel memorized: "*The last one to occur on a winter solstice happened 205 years ago, folks. A once-in-a-lifetime astrological event, and we will have clear skies tomorrow to see it!*"

Whenever Tom couldn't stand the *clickclickclickclickclicking* and the game shows anymore, he stepped out for a cigarette-fuelled walk around the motel. Even that did little to smooth his frazzled nerves, because the rift was now visible in the daytime. Watching it was like trying to pin down an aurora as it shimmered over the foothills. What would the weatherman say if he could see the rift? An eclipse, the solstice, *and* an interdimensional tear in the sky? He'd shit himself.

At the end of every walk, after Tom put his smoke out in the empty pop can on the balcony, he took out his wallet. Peered inside the torn lining. But he couldn't bring himself to take out the picture within. The only one he had left of his daughter, buried all these years like the memories. He couldn't bring himself to remember what her face looked like.

He turned off his phone's flashlight and opened the laptop, squinting from the screen's white light.

Quillon Glasser, the login window said.

Password? the blinking cursor mocked.

Of course, there would be a passcode. Did Tom really think it would be unlocked? He went to work, typing as softly as he could, guessing letters, numbers, symbols. Phrases Glasser used. Phrases Glasser would never use. Every time, the login window shuddered, *incorrect password, try again.*

He waited a few moments for the system to reload. He didn't come this far to get locked out.

Between his clicking at the keyboard all day, Glasser had peered between the closed curtains every half hour like clockwork. Every time Tom opened the door to step out for a smoke, Glasser would crane his neck toward the outside world.

"Expecting someone?" Tom finally asked as he lit a cigarette.

"No." But Glasser couldn't hide the agitation in his voice.

He was up to something. Sick and up to something. It wasn't as simple as him just needing to close the rift. It was never that simple with Glasser.

The cursor on the laptop blinked. *Password. Gimme the password.*

Atra Hart, Tom nearly typed, then decided at the last second to enter his name instead. A pause, and then—

Are you fucking kidding me?

Glasser's desktop was clear, sparse, tidy. Not giving anything away. Tom searched through the files, aimless and at random, not sure what he was hoping to find. A folder called *Tail of the Dog* piqued his interest. He clicked it open, to find another folder. And within that, another, and another.

Where are you leading me? he thought as he ignored the random documents scattered within each folder, impatient to get to the end.

He was about to abandon his search through the nest of folders when he finally came to the last one. Inside, a single document, titled "M."

He held his breath as he double-clicked it. *This* was going to contain the answers to Glasser's web of mysteries and lies. Tom could feel it.

The document opened, revealing a page of scanned typewriter notes. The first entry was dated thirty-five years ago. Long before Tom's involvement in Polaris and the Cynosura Experiments.

> <u>*05 Mar*</u>—*Patient M (female, age 4) shows the most promise out of all of them. My best guess is it has to do with her brain disorder. She's a fascinating case; something is eating away at her brain but we can't determine what. No foreign bodies or bacteria are present. It shows similarities to Huntington's, but advancing at a more aggressive rate.*
>
> *During her EEG, her brainwaves seemed to go ... somewhere. They're atypical, but not from the neurodegeneration. I want to order further tests, but that's the hospital's decision, not mine. They don't notice anything abnormal in her results because they're not looking for it. Of course, they're not looking for it.*
>
> *They don't know what I'm doing.*

Tom paused. This had nothing to do with Becopra or the rift. This was Glasser's life before Polaris, his personal medical diary or some shit. Disappointment curdled in his stomach—he wasn't going to get any answers after all—but he continued reading.

13 Mar—They want to move me off Patient M's case. Start working with a patient who will make it out of the terminal ward. The only thing that stopped them was me saying I could cure her.

They don't need the full truth. I might be able to stall it. We're going to track the progression of her disease. Hopefully, I can extrapolate the data I need from her tests. But cure? No.

Everyone assumes we pediatricians try to save every life, that every child matters. That's a lie. I've seen and participated in it enough times to know. M has no parents, no family, nothing out there. She's a burden to the system. If anyone understands, it's me.

Tom re-read the entry. He was wrong to assume this had nothing to do with Becopra. This kid, Patient M, was *she* Glasser's original Cynosura Experiment?

29 Mar—M recognizes me when I come around. Her eyes are unsettling—a striking colour of thunder. They look right through me, like she knows what I'm really here for. They say the eyes are the window to the soul, but where is her soul going?

She says she likes me better than the other doctors. I stay with her, talk to her. I suppose it's true, if only to make sure every last drop of those drugs goes into her IV.

Still too early to know if I've slowed the degeneration.

09 Apr—Are her brainwaves going to the altered planes? Is this the proof I've been searching for? Could they theoretically exist? The minds of children are still forming. They're capable of perceiving things adults don't.

My efforts are doing nothing to slow the degeneration. The bad days outweigh the good. I can't deny she's leaving us. The sun behind the thunder is fading.

One evening after dinner, M tried to give me a mangy stuffed animal, a black cat she'd named Ori. I refused, telling her that Ori would be happier tucked in bed with her than in my cold lab. She doesn't have much in the way of comfort.

<u>*30 Apr*</u>*—I'm writing this very late. Or it is early? Can't remember the last time I slept. I got to the lab late after my shift. Patient M has been having trouble falling asleep as the disease takes her. She doesn't recognize where she is, who is around her. Except me; she always recognizes me.*

So many children have died; it comes with the territory of my work. But why does the death of this particular child trouble me? It's more than the brainwaves. I've grown accustomed to putting her to bed at night, reading a story to her and Ori, no matter what state she's in.

And here I am in this lab every free moment, my life consumed by finding a way to keep her alive enough to suit my needs. What am I doing, prolonging her suffering? The hours I've spent in here, trying to slow the degeneration, combing over her scan results, all for my own gain. I could have been finding a cure for her.

I don't know what I'm trying to say. I need sleep.

Me. Why does she recognize me?

<u>*17 May*</u>*—Molly had a terrible day. It comes in waves, but this wave never receded. She can't eat. The muscles she needs to swallow have atrophied. Intubation is the next step. I can't remember the last time she left the bed. Her wheelchair, parked in the corner of her room, gathers dust. Our strolls down the ward to the window overlooking the city are over.*

She had to be sedated. After she was out, I still tucked

Ori under the covers with her. I wanted to pretend she was only asleep. What is happening to me? All my life, I've appreciated my adoptive parents, but I never reciprocated the love they gave. Numbers speak to me, not emotions. They're not quantifiable. I'm not sure I enjoy feeling this vulnerable, this ... human.

A nurse spoke with me tonight. I thought she was going to comment on my attachment—for lack of a better word—to Molly. Instead, she thanked me for spending time with Molly. That it's good for her to have company.

So she's not alone in the end.

The end. Her end. Does it have to be an end? I can't help but notice the parallels between our childhoods. Both orphans. Both in the hospital. But, unlike her, someone rescued me. My parents decided to give a sickly child a chance. They adopted me, gave me the life I have. The reason I'm in this lab now.

Molly doesn't have that. Or does she? She has me. Is this what my parents felt when they saw me in my own hospital bed?

I've failed so far at slowing her degeneration, but maybe I could stop it entirely. I don't want her eyes to close for the last time in that cold hospital room. I want them to sparkle with life. I want them so full of sun the thunder is gone.

<u>18 May</u>—Curing her is plausible, on paper. Hypothesizing and knowing are different things. But if I stop the degeneration, there are two things I must take into consideration:

- Can I reverse it? No four-year-old should know this quality of life. There's no point in her continuing if this is going to be it.

- The experiment ends. I may never have a chance at the altered planes again.

Look at the order of that list. A month ago, I wouldn't

have let anything come between me and the planes. Back when she was a number. When did she cease being that and start being ... well, Molly?

I know I've already made my decision. The long hours in the lab will go on, but my reason for being here will change. These entries will cease. My efforts will now be focused on a cure. No time for anything else. I may be given another chance at the altered planes. To know if this is one world of many.

With Molly's life at stake, this has turned out to be a different kind of experiment. One I wasn't prepared for. One that proved I may be human after all.

Tom scrolled farther, but the document didn't move. For a second, he thought the program had frozen.

But no—he'd reached the end.

That's it?

He felt like he'd read through an entire novel to find the last chapter ripped out. Did Glasser cure her? Did he stop his research into the planes for her, or did his obsession win in the end?

Tom's mind hummed, desperate for more. Only the sound wasn't coming from inside his head. It was the shitty heater pumping air, bringing him back to reality. Had the fan always been that loud? He exited out of the document, unsure if he should cut his losses before Glasser caught him, or keep digging.

He paused, squinting beyond the laptop, but with the glow of the screen, he might as well have been staring into the abyss.

The room was too quiet. Glasser's snores had ceased.

Chapter 12

Go Here, in the Dark

Dread buzzed around Atra's head, clouding her vision as she walked down the hall. It was no longer a wisp of smoke. More like a swarm of flies, the way she kept swatting at it.

She'd scoured the common area for Lex's book as best she could without drawing unwanted attention from Creepsley but came up short. As for finding Magnus?

Next to impossible, given all the patients acted like she didn't exist.

And the one patient who did notice her had vanished. How dare Pepe speak in riddles, dangling the answers in front of her, and then leave her hanging. It reminded her of a certain creepy kid in a certain creepy house.

Atra had decided to cut her losses in the common area and go back to her sleeping quarters, the last place she remembered having the book. Doubtful it was still there, but worth a shot.

Fuck this place. Fuck this whole situation. She was ready to bust the walls down; if none of it was real, why was she afraid of any of it?!

The light at the end of the hall went out.

She imagined Rei standing on the cusp of the darkness,

Creepsley looming beside her. If Atra looked hard enough, she could make out the pearly whites of Rei's harmonica smile.

Above her head, the fluorescent light flickered.

Her nerve broke. She sprinted for her bedroom before she was left in total darkness.

Whatever solace she sought from her room disappeared the moment she stepped foot in it.

"What the fuck?"

Her bed wasn't there. Or rather, it was; it had just been flipped sideways and pushed against the wall. An impressive feat, considering the legs had been bolted to the ground. Beryl's bed had suffered the same fate. The linoleum around the bolts stuck up, shredded. The shared night table had been thrown across the room, its splintered remains strewn around the closed bathroom door.

Ta-ka tik-et, ta-ka ...

She strained her ears. What was that? A faucet dripping, or machinery ...

... tik-et, ta-ka tik-et ...

Something alive.

"*... ta-ka tik-et, ta-ka tik-et ...*"

The sound was human. And it came from behind the closed bathroom door.

Atra stepped over the remnants of the night table, biting her lip as she reached for the handle.

The door creaked open.

Dark in here.

Something glittered around the sink and floor. Broken shards of a mirror.

Above the sink, a section of plywood was exposed where the mirror used to be. Smeared on it, in red paint, the same lopsided infinity loop as the one on the book.

"*Ta-ka tik-et, ta-ka tik-et ...*"

Beryl had squished herself into the area between the toilet and the wall, her bony shoulders hunched over. An odd noise came from her throat, like a pig grunting. Her arthritic fingers clutched a mirror shard. Rivulets of blood ran down her hand and wrapped around her wrist.

Atra swallowed a lump. That wasn't paint on the wall.

"Beryl—" Her breath hitched. Streaks of red crisscrossed Beryl's shirt, standing out against the white fabric.

Too much blood.

"*Ta-ka tik* ..." Beryl trailed off, noticing Atra. Her chestnut eyes swam with tears. "It hurts so bad." She didn't mean the gashes in her hand.

She'd never had a sundowning episode this bad before.

If Atra could get her cleaned up, examine the cuts ... she could wrap them in toilet paper, wash the blood off the walls, flush the evidence down the drain. Because if the nurses found Beryl like this, they would take her away. And Atra needed Beryl now more than ever, alone in this awful—

She gave her head a shake. This wasn't her Beryl. This wasn't her asylum.

"Beryl," Atra repeated her name, careful not to make any sudden movements. "Put the mirror down."

"You don't understand." Beryl's lips pulled away from her teeth, resembling a dehydrated corpse.

She trembled. Her fingers wrapped around the mirror seeped new blood.

Atra dropped to one knee, inching closer. "I understand."

"No, you don't. You don't know what they're doing to us in here."

Beryl raised the mirror shard. Atra charged her, intending to knock it out of her hand, but the old bat was faster.

Atra was sent tumbling as something warm spread across her chest, shirt clinging to her skin. She scrambled back to her feet, lunging again.

"Leave me alone!" Beryl's voice took on an inhuman, guttural tone.

The next thing Atra knew, the shard had sliced her across the palm and punctured her arm. She cried out as Beryl shoved her off a second time.

A crack of pain shot through her skull. Darkness crept in. Dread, Dread was coming, taking over ...

No, it wasn't Dread. Atra struggled to remain conscious, but her eyelids wanted to shut.

Her cheek pressed into the linoleum, the smell of rubber shoes and cleaning solvent thick in her nostrils.

Somewhere, she was aware of raised voices, of squeaking shoes, as people ran into the room. The screams—whose screams? Hers? Beryl's?—had alerted the nurses that something Bad Was Happening.

Atra tried picking herself up but the floor had changed, turning soft, squishy.

The familiar scents of dust and old hit her. The darkness cleared. So much that the shadows also left.

Back in the house. On ... a couch? The paisley pattern swam in and out of focus. Atra rolled over, disoriented, and crashed to the floor. She braced herself, waiting for her bleeding gashes to cry out, but the pain never came.

Her wounds were gone, like the shadows in here.

The stillness of the house weighed down, eerie after her battle with Feral Beryl. The archway dividing the rooms revealed the kitchen in disarray. The table lay in two, snapped down the middle, its chairs flipped over and the fronts torn off the cupboards.

Red-orange light spilled from the coals of the fireplace. A set of wrought-iron fireplace tools rested against the hearth. She needed something to defend herself from whatever had destroyed the kitchen. She grabbed the top of the fire poker, wiggling it out of its slot. Although she tried to be quiet, nothing could stop the scrape of metal on metal—

An ember popped at the same time someone grabbed her arm. The poker clanged to the ground as she backed into the couch. It was Beryl; she had followed her over, ready to finish her off.

But it was only Lex.

"We have to hide," the kid murmured, the whites of her eyes shining in the dim light.

They weren't playing a game anymore.

Atra grabbed the poker off the ground.

Lex crept out of the room, keeping close to the wood-panelled walls. Atra didn't need to be told to follow.

A tug at her shirt, as Lex turned her down a short hall. At the end of it, a frosted-glass door stood ajar.

They entered a cramped bathroom. Atra tensed as she pulled her foot through the doorway, expecting something to snatch her ankle and drag her back into the hall.

Lex pointed to the area under the pedestal sink. Atra crouched there, the back of her neck pressing against a rusted pipe.

There were no windows in here, but she could sense the rift pulsing against the side of the house. The urge to smash through the wall and bask under the rift's radiance nearly overcame her.

Lex closed the door before joining Atra under the sink.

"What are we hiding from?"

Lex shook her head. "You haven't found the planes yet."

"I was just in one. Vanishing Planes."

"No. You are at the *gateway* of the planes."

"No. I'm at a dead end," Atra retorted. She hadn't come back here to be reprimanded for not doing something she didn't even understand. "I tried doing what you said. There is no Magnus where I am. And I lost your book."

"The book isn't lost. It just hasn't been found."

"Stop speaking in riddles and tell me what you really want from me."

"I'm already breaking the rules by being here."

"Oh, cut the crap." Atra had reached her breaking point. "Why is Dread so important?"

"You have to find that truth out for yourself. Keep going forward. Keep climbing the planes, all the way to the top. To the Tentorum Plane. Unbury the memories."

"Imagine, reliving an experience you didn't know you had." Those had been Pepe's words to her during their chess game.

"The lie is quicker than the mind," Atra said.

Lex nodded. "You need to be one with yourself before you face the Queen."

"But Dread isn't part of me. I need to get rid of it."

"Dread is a part of you as much as my arm is a part of me. Get rid of Dread and you amputate a part of yourself. Stop running from it."

Atra bristled, biting back a remark.

She *didn't* run. That was her father's job.

"And you're exactly like him," her stepmother's voice rang out, so vivid the woman could've been towering over Atra right now. *"A coward like your waste-of-skin father."*

Atra blinked back tears at the onslaught of buried memories. Yes, Tom had run. But Atra also knew how awful her stepmother was. That woman probably drove him away—

A sudden flash of being in the camper van with Evie, after being picked up on the streets of Telos, derailed her thoughts.

"The Drove is going to take good care of you, Atra," Evie's words crashed into her with the intensity of a thunderbolt.

The drove ... a drove of bees ... and what kept the heart of a beehive beating?

"Was Evie taking me to the Queen?" she asked Lex.

C'mon, Attie, even you know that's more than a reach, Seth said.

But Seth was fading.

And the tug of the rift was growing.

Lex didn't answer. "Depending on where Dread goes, it can balance the worlds or end them," she offered instead.

"So, if this *is* real and I do nothing, I'll destroy everything," Atra whispered. The freedom she yearned for all these years would be gone because there'd be nothing left. "But if this *is* a hallucination …"

Maybe Dread could end the asylum she'd created in her head.

"You're right; I have to stop running. I have to learn how to control Dread."

"Yes. Meet me in the Tentorum Plane." Lex's words came out constricted, invisible hands choking the words back. "Uncover the lie. That's where you can face the truth of why Dread is in your mind. It's the only way to defeat the Queen." She licked her dry lips. "Time is running out. For both of us. I can only help you until my brother comes back."

"Lex—"

"You have until the Cold Blood Moon."

Lex stared at the empty wall, forehead bathed in sweat. Atra wanted to comfort her, but she was afraid if she touched her, Lex would disappear.

"Your soul beats for two worlds." Lex choked the words out, between jagged breaths. "You have to decide which one you belong to."

She vanished. Atra's arm—which she didn't realize was wrapped around Lex's shoulders—fell to her side, now supported by nothing.

The floorboards in the hallway creaked. Her eyes slid to the door.

A *stomp!* then a slide, as uneven footsteps approached.

She gripped the poker, her palms as cold and clammy as the rusted pipe behind her.

A silhouette on the other side of the frosted glass appeared. A dripping, from somewhere within the walls, echoed through the room. The figure in the hall craned its neck, trying to get a better view into the bathroom.

The tattered hem of a lab coat swished behind them.

Creepsley. He'd followed Atra into the house, even though he should've been dead from the crash.

Then again, so should she.

The door handle turned, hinges groaning.

Atra pressed herself against the wall.

Everything changed.

In the asylum again.

Ouuuucchhhh!

A searing pain spread through her palm and up her wrist, cutting through her panic. The poker clattered to the ground, rolling under a bed.

She turned, her sweaty feet slipping out from under her. But Creepsley hadn't followed her back over here.

Here she recognized as the asylum's shoddy hospital wing.

The bandage around her palm bloomed crimson. So, her wounds from Beryl didn't cross over to the house, but the fire poker had crossed back over here.

Like the book.

She wanted to grab the poker but was overcome with a swell of terror at the idea of reaching under the bed. Like something was going to reach back for her.

Stop running. Just do it.

She moved forward, but the gash under her collarbone protested the movement. Tears leaked from the corners of her eyes.

Dread swirled around, pulsing in time to the pain, feeding off it. She brought her uninjured hand to her chest, fingers brushing over the gash. She jerked away as if she'd touched a hot grate. The stitches across her flesh surprised her.

Beryl did some damage.

More stitches twisted up her arm, the skin bright red and puckering underneath.

All sutured up, like a corpse after an autopsy.

She resisted the urge to dig her fingers in and scratch the stitches open.

Into the ground you go.

Laughter bubbled at the back of her throat.

Now you're dead, it's time for Dread.

Footsteps approached. Her spine went as rigid as the fire poker. Creepsley.

She tried standing, but her stupid, useless arm wouldn't push her off the ground.

"You shouldn't be out of bed," Silvia said from the doorway.

Atra never thought she'd be relieved to hear that woman's voice.

"And you shouldn't be awake. All this noise—" Silvia let out a sharp gasp. "Your hand!"

She crossed the room, looming over Atra. Worried, or annoyed?

"Can you stand?"

She didn't wait for an answer, grabbing Atra around the waist.

"Ater, get up," she snapped, in a no-nonsense tone.

Atra obliged, grimacing as the stitches under her collarbone threatened to pop open. She grabbed Silvia's pastel-yellow cardigan for support, leaving an ugly, bloody smear on it.

Together, they walked over to the bed. Atra eased herself onto it.

Silvia noticed the bloody handprint on her cardigan, sighed, then removed it and threw it over the end of the bed.

"Don't move."

She walked off, presumably to get supplies.

Atra stared at the cardigan. The front pocket gaped open, something small and rectangular poking out. Silvia's keycard.

One of the magical keycards that unlocked any door to this place.

Before she could think about it, she snapped it up. Her heart raced as she tucked it under her pillow. She didn't have time to check if it was properly hidden as Silvia re-emerged with an armful of bandages. It took everything Atra had not to peek at the cardigan to make sure she hadn't disturbed it.

It was just a hunch, but she'd bet anything that Lex's book was in Creepsley's office.

A deep headache throbbed at the back of her skull. That's right, she'd smacked it in the bathroom when—

"What happened to Beryl?"

Silvia ignored her as she closed the curtains around the bed, shutting out the rest of the world. She sat on the mattress, motioning for Atra to hold her hand out.

"Where is she?" Atra persisted.

Silvia's lips pursed together as she unwound the bloody bandages.

Why wouldn't Silvia respond? Was Beryl in isolation, or—

Atra didn't want to consider the rest of the thought.

Silvia pressed a fresh pad onto the wound. Atra winced.

"Please." A sob threatened to escape her throat. "Can you tell me what happened to Beryl?"

"Enough." Silvia wrapped a bandage around Atra's palm, the motions gentle in contrast to her harsh voice. "There wasn't enough evidence to prove you didn't mean to harm yourself. But if Dr. Creeley hears you making a fuss, it'll be strike two."

Atra clenched her teeth together. Creepsley knew she didn't do this to herself; this was his way of lording his power over her.

"Understand?" Silvia's eyes met Atra's own.

Atra nodded. How very un-Silvia to issue a warning.

Once Silvia finished bandaging Atra's hand, she stood, parting the curtains around the bed.

Atra's mind spun with everything that had happened with Lex: the planes, the Queen, confronting Dread.

"Am I dead?" She spoke so softly she half-hoped Silvia wouldn't hear.

But Silvia did, pausing with her hand up to the curtain.

"I died in that car crash." Atra didn't want to be telling Silvia any of this, but she couldn't stop the words from flowing out. This asylum had to be hell, from Creepsley and Rei taking over, to Dread flourishing in its new form. "None of this is real."

Silvia half-turned, her profile silhouetted in the darkness.

"The lie is quicker than the mind," she offered, before departing.

Her footsteps faded away before Atra had a chance to process her words.

Was she dead? Now that she'd said it aloud, she wasn't convinced. She scanned the empty hospital wing. So familiar, and yet so alien.

She traced the rounded plastic corner of the keycard hidden beneath the pillow. Creepsley had blocked her every step of the way since she'd crash-landed in this fucked-up asylum. Maybe he was trying to prevent her from entering the planes. But was breaking into his office really the best idea she had?

The fluffy black tail of a cat flicked in the doorway before disappearing. Oriens.

She sat upright. Was the cat trying to reassure her she was on the right path?

Find the book. Find Magnus. Find the Tentorum Plane.

Dread floated across the bed, obscuring the doorway like mist on a dark lake.

"Find out what Dread really is," Atra whispered, getting up.

Chapter 13

Castle of Glass

Glasser sat up. Tom could only make out his silhouette, backlit by the glow of the laptop.

Caught red-handed.

Wordlessly, Glasser reached out and plucked the computer off Tom's lap. His eyes danced over the screen, the light illuminating his puffy face.

A streak of pity ran through Tom. He'd gone searching for answers that didn't exist, and instead, had invaded a deeply personal part of Glasser. Once again, he was the asshole.

His fingers itched for his cigarettes.

"Who's Molly?" Tom couldn't help himself. If he was going to be an asshole, he might as well go for the gold.

Glasser placed the laptop on the bed, his expression indecipherable. Tom waited for him to answer, or at least turn the light on. He did neither.

The fan pumped air overhead, punctuating the silence.

"She's the past. Or what should have remained in the past."

Glasser closed the laptop, entombing them in darkness.

"What happened to her?"

Tom wished he could gather the courage to lean over and turn on the bedside lamp. The pitch dark shielding Glasser's expression was more than disquieting.

So much time passed that Tom didn't think he was going to get an answer.

"She died." Glasser coughed lightly. "I thought I put her away after leaving the field of paediatric medicine. Once I started my work at Becopra, there was no more sneaking around. No more bending the rules as a medical doctor for my outlandish hobby to find the altered planes, because finding the altered planes *had become* my job.

"And I was good at it. I didn't just find the planes; I found evidence of an afterlife. Both humanity's greatest enigma and fear, and I had the answer."

The way Glasser spoke so candidly, after years of sneaking around in the shadows, wasn't sitting right with Tom at all.

"After I found the Otherside, my thoughts didn't turn to Molly. At first," Glasser continued. "But then the spark ignited. Could I pull her out of the afterlife? Could I bring her back to our world? Once sparked, the fire was impossible to extinguish."

He broke off in a coughing fit. He'd shared more about himself in the past thirty seconds than he had in the decades Tom had known him. Why?

Maybe because Glasser was about to kill him. One swift blow to Tom's head, wrapping up the last loose thread that knew he had a shred of humanity left in him.

"But we learned nothing can survive crossing the membranes between worlds." Tom's voice shook.

His skin crawled as he imagined Glasser silently getting off the bed, laptop in hand, ready to bludgeon him with it.

Turn on the light, chickenshit.

But his hands were cemented to the bed.

"Our last Cynosura Experiment may have failed, but I was not done with the Otherside," Glasser said.

The bedside lamp came on. Tom squinted, shielding his eyes.

Glasser towered over him, arm raised.

Here it comes.

Tom stiffened in anticipation of the death blow.

Glasser brought up his other arm and ... unbuttoned the sleeve of his shirt.

Tom exhaled. The tension left his shoulders.

Of course, Glasser slept in a business shirt. Not even wrinkled with sleep.

"I became the next Cynosura Experiment." Glasser pushed up his sleeve. Ugly grey tendrils twisted across his arm. "I thought I could go to the Otherside to find her. The girl that started the experiment, I now became the experiment for."

Keloid scars. That's what marred Glasser's flesh. He must've injected himself with the same shit he'd shot into his human lab rats.

"Didn't go to plan, did it?" Tom grabbed his smokes off the bedside table. "I'm guessing if it did, you wouldn't be here."

"No." Glasser rolled his sleeve down as Tom lit a smoke. "It would seem I do not have much shadow DNA to activate. Instead, my experiments have caused my soul to break down. My only hope is to get to the Otherside."

He paused, a crease forming between his brows. It was unlike him to be at a loss for words. "If I stay on this side, I will fade from existence. That I am certain of. Perhaps my soul will fare better on the Otherside. Maybe there will still be something left of me."

For a blink-or-miss-it moment, fear flashed across Glasser's eyes.

"The rift." Tom cut straight to the point they were beating around. "You don't need me to close it. You need me to open it wider."

"Yes."

"Was it you who cracked it open in the first place?"

"No." Again, Glasser paused with that foggy expression, as if his mind was elsewhere.

"And I'm just supposed to believe that? Is anything you said earlier true?" The smoke between Tom's fingers shook as he was overcome with the urge to smash something. Preferably the bedside lamp, over Glasser's head.

"The worlds being on the verge of collapse is still very much a threat." Glasser's placid tone hit turbulent waters. "I told you the truth, Tom. Just not all of it. I may be using the rift to my advantage, but I did not open it. Our original objective still stands: seal the portal for good, but only after I am through."

Beads of sweat popped up along his hairline. Was the old ticker about to detonate right here in this room? With Glasser dead, this bullshit would be over.

Except the accident didn't kill him. Glasser's own brutal medical experiments didn't kill him.

Would he die? Or would he vanish—*poof!*—fade into nothing? Not cross over to the Otherside?

How ironic for the man who found life after death to suffer a fate worse than it.

What if Atra had been a lie? Glasser could've doctored the photos—

Tom stiffened. "Why haven't you brought her into this?"

"Who?" Judging by the spasm that crossed Glasser's face, he damn well knew.

"Wouldn't you like to know if your precious Cynosura Experiments worked? Why go mutilating yourself when you could use Atra?"

"Tom, I—" Glasser rubbed his glistening brow with a shaking hand. Oh ho! Was Mr. Calm, Cool, and Collected *flustered?* "Atra is not part of this equation."

But of course she was! How could Tom be so blind?

Glasser, on edge all day. Waiting for something. Or someone. Atra?

"Can't you tell the truth?" Tom smacked the briefcase off the bed. It ricocheted off Glasser's bed. "For once in your life, can you not twist everything into a lie?"

"I am ... telling the truth." The way Glasser's words came out in laboured breaths reminded Tom of a robot short-circuiting. "I'm trying to protect her, dammit! Protect her from this!"

"The fuck you are!"

"Why'd you leave her?" Glasser's eyes, murky until now, shot daggers. "If Atra meant so much, why'd you leave her on the floor of that bunker when she was still breathing?"

There it was; the blade plunging into his gut. The tiny detail Tom had been running from all these years. It sounded worse coming from someone else than he could've ever imagined.

He opened his mouth but only managed a deflated squeak. Shocking wetness pooled in the corners of his eyes.

Tears.

Genuine tears.

"Why'd you leave her, Tom?" *You coward.* Glasser's expression challenged him.

Run, Tom. Run.

"Because I was terrified of her! I was terrified of what we'd created!"

Glasser clutched his chest, keeling over. He raised his other hand, about to push himself off the bed, but crashed to the floor instead. His head hit the corner of the night table and then he went still.

"Hey." Tom kicked Glasser's leg. Nothing. "Hey!" Louder this time.

Was Glasser breathing?

The car keys on the table by the door called him.

Now, Tom. Now.

But he had to know if Glasser was dead.

Tom bent over, holding his breath as he listened for Glasser's own.

Silence.

Then—

Something between a gurgle and a groan. Visions of a body bubbling to the surface of a lake filled Tom's mind as he backed off.

Glasser's arms shot forward, fingers contorting into claws. Another awful gurgle as his back arched inward. His limbs jerked, tapping in rhythm to a macabre song only his body could hear.

Convulsions.

What the hell were you supposed to do when someone was having a seizure? Flip them on their side? Their stomach?

Fuck if Tom knew.

He bent back over, gripping Glasser's midsection. His hands passed right through the crisp business shirt like it were made of air. What the hell?

He grabbed again, Glasser's body now solid underneath him. He turned Glasser onto his side before his hands once again passed through nothing. Tumbling forward, he caught himself on the bed. With a trembling hand, he touched Glasser. His fingers passed right through the good doctor's torso.

Tom let out a yelp as he jerked back, tripping into the bed.

The shaking stopped. But the gurgling didn't.

"*Nnn ... nnn ...*" Like Glasser's tongue was stuck to the roof of his mouth with plaster. "*Nnn ... crrr ...*"

Tom didn't want to but he found himself leaning down, turning his ear to hear better.

"*Crr ...*" Glasser struggled to get out. "*Crr ... Cree-ley.* Why isn't Creeley here yet?"

Part Three

While the World Lies Dreaming

Chapter 14

Creep

Atra crept down the hall, leaving the hospital wing behind. The plastic keycard dug into her fingers, as if it would disappear if she loosened her grip. She needed to find Creepsley's office, and quickly. It wouldn't be long before Silvia noticed her keycard was missing.

The fire poker banged against the outside of Atra's leg, smacking her knee as she held it close to her body. She'd grabbed it from under her bed after Silvia left the hospital room. Getting caught with it while skulking the halls at night would be Very Bad, but she couldn't leave it under the bed. Like the book she was on her way to retrieve, the poker was special. It existed in both realities.

Not that she knew whether she was headed in the right direction. She didn't know where Creepsley's office was. She'd have to sneak around and hope she found it before—

She paused. Were those footsteps? She peered through Dread, but the hall was too dark to see anything.

Patpatpatpat—

Like a rodent scurrying around.

She doubled back, ducking around a corner and pressing herself against the wall.

Patpatpat—

The footsteps approached as the distinctive shape of Rei's lopped-off hair approached. Atra wasn't far off in thinking it was a rat.

Rei scampered past, oblivious to Atra, off on her own mission.

Atra's eyes narrowed. What was Harmonica Mouth up to?

She waited until the hall was silent again before continuing. Her skin crawled; she was too exposed in the empty halls now that they weren't all hers. What if she didn't hear the next person in time?

Dread closed in, threatening to suffocate her. She waved her hand through the air, but it did nothing to clear her view.

Back when Dread was shadow instead of smoke, her greatest fear was that it would consume her. That one day she'd wake up and her world would be black.

That day was coming.

Beyond the common area was a hallway that hadn't existed before. She knew Creepsley's office would be down there before she found it.

Throughout the years, Vanishing Plains had had its share of patients who believed they could think their ideas into existence. The intensity of their delusions frightened her.

But was that Atra now, standing in front of the door marked *DR. CREELEY*, clutching Silvia's conveniently obtained keycard?

The gashes across her chest and arms pulsed. She rubbed her sunken eyes, wishing she could lay down and sleep for a week.

It was exhausting, using your thoughts to control everything.

Stop.

Just stop it.

She swiped the keycard, holding her breath. Would it work?

Click.

The darkness from the hall followed her inside. The office

reeked of Creepsley's sulphur breath, like he was waiting in the shadows.

She flicked on the light.

Empty.

Behind Creepsley's desk sat a filing cabinet, a stack of papers balanced precariously atop it. And beneath the papers was a strip of brown leather, with something twinkling on it like an eye.

The book.

She tiptoed over to the filing cabinet. She'd be in and out and back to the hospital wing before anyone was the wiser.

She picked up the book, running her fingers over its smooth surface, needing to convince herself it was real. Having the book and the poker together, objects that spanned both realities, made Atra feel powerful. Like they would show her the way out of here.

Like how those crazies feel powerful in their unreal realities.

Atra shook the thought off. Time to get out of here.

But the drawer labelled *PATIENT FILES* on the cabinet piqued her interest.

Silvia had insinuated that there was no Beryl in this asylum and that Atra had sliced herself open with the broken mirror. But if she found Beryl's folder, Atra could prove they were all lying.

She pulled it open. A neat row of files stared at her. She thumbed through them as fast as her shaking fingers would allow.

"No Beryl, no Beryl, no blind-as-a-bat, Feral Beryl."

Beryl existed. Atra didn't trash the bedroom and rip up the beds herself. She didn't break the mirror and stab herself with it.

Right?

Beryl's file *had* to be in this cabinet.

Creepsley could have removed the file. One patient disappears, one file goes out. Putting the "Vanishing" in Vanishing Planes.

She stopped at a familiar name, but not the one she was searching for.

Atra Hart.

Her real name, not the fake one on her wristband. Fucking Creepsley, gaslighting her.

What did that big, fat file have to say?

She scanned her patient history—involuntarily admitted after assaulting her stepmother (a lie)—and dug into the juicy heart of it.

A stack of glossy photos, paper-clipped together, was at the front of the file. The first one featured a kid, four or five, standing in front of a concrete wall. The over-exposed lighting washed out their features, but she recognized the haunted eyes as hers. The watermark in the bottom corner read: *Cynosura Experiment: ATrA/Polaris Division 502.*

"I don't remember this." That didn't say much, since most of her childhood was as murky as the veil of Dread now surrounding her.

She flipped to the next photo. Same kid, a few months older. Same wall, only this time with a smudge on it, like someone had smeared a finger across the lens.

Next photo.

The smudge grew larger, streaks of black darkening the edges of it.

Next.

The smudge devoured the wall, swatches of black and red all over. Atra stared at it.

A face stared back.

She slammed the folder shut before she could meet its eyes.

Dread, attaching itself to her years before its official appearance. Always a part of her.

Who took these photos? Did *they* know what Dread was?

A *click!* and a swing.

The door.

She was flat on the floor before she thought about it.

In three steps, Creepsley would be at his desk to discover her crouched there.

Strike two.

Over the adrenaline surge hammering her heart into her ears, she realized Creepsley wasn't coming over.

"Get in before someone sees."

Still by the door. Muttering. Whispering.

Atra pressed herself back with the heels of her feet, sliding into the farthest corner under the desk. She held the poker up to avoid banging it against the floor. The other hand—the one with the gash—gripped both the file and the book. She let out a silent hiss, grimacing as the cut across her palm stretched.

Fuckity, fuck, fuck.

The worst place to hide. She tried balling herself up as small as possible, but it was a futile attempt with this stupid piece of metal down the side of her leg.

"Don't rush me. Rude." The vocal equivalent of a spider sneaking across your flesh. Rei.

"You stupid girl, get in before you start flapping your gums."

It was hard to tell who sounded more agitated.

"I'm not stupid. You know what's stupid"—the door clicked shut—"Your. Stupid. Plan."

Atra could visualize Rei jabbing her pointy finger into Creepsley's chest.

"They still have free will. We're losing control," Rei went on.

An abrupt *slap!* clapped through the office. Atra assumed Creepsley had struck Rei.

"It's *you* who can't control them," Creepsley said as Rei sobbed over-dramatically. "I had to take care of Beryl because you couldn't."

The image of Beryl, bloody on the bathroom floor. *"You don't know what they're doing to us in here,"* she'd moaned.

"Pull yourself together," Creepsley commanded. "There are still souls to collect." The door opened. "Get back to your sleeping quarters before that wretch Silvia finds you out of bed."

The door closed, but only one set of footsteps went out.

Why wasn't Creepsley leaving?

The filing cabinet.

Fuck.

Was its wide-open drawer visible from the door?

In answer to Atra's question, Creepsley's footsteps approached the desk at a mockingly leisurely pace.

The hem of his frayed lab coat swept into view. His polished shoes almost brushed her bare toes as they stopped in front of the filing cabinet. She could see him up to his chest, his head cut off by the top of the desk.

In a slow, exaggerated movement, he pushed the drawer shut with his index finger.

Atra's arms trembled, the poker slipping out of her grasp. She caught it before it hit the floor. The hasty movement caused the papers in the folder to rustle.

Creepsley paused, his finger still touching the drawer.

She sensed his smirk radiating victory. His lab coat swayed in front of her face as he bent over the desk.

Chapter 15

Diary of a Madman

A BOOMING KNOCK VIBRATED the door. A scream threatened to rip out of Atra like the roar of an oncoming tidal wave. She managed to suppress it, a sharp gasp leaving her instead.

Creepsley paused.

His finger tapped the cabinet. If he moved an inch lower, she'd be in his line of sight.

Another series of knocks.

The finger, still tapping, still contemplating.

Go to the door. Go away, Atra screamed in her thoughts.

"Dr. Creeley!"

For the second time in less than an hour, Atra was relieved to hear Silvia's voice.

"What?" Creepsley called, still not moving.

"We have a problem."

Creepsley exhaled, standing up straight, then walked to the door.

"What?" he hissed, swinging it open.

"A patient is missing."

Another long pause.

"Who?"

Two patients were out and about. Atra and Rei.

Which one was Silvia talking about?

And which one was Creepsley concerned about?

"We've started a sweep." Silvia dodged the question. "The exit doors are guarded."

Atra noticed how Silvia's voice wavered when bringing up the doors. She didn't want Creepsley to know about the missing keycard.

"Should I sound the alarm?" Silvia suggested, when Creepsley said nothing.

"Don't be foolish," Creepsley said, through what sounded like clenched teeth. "Get out of my way. It seems you need someone competent out there."

Their voices dimmed as the door shut.

Leaving Atra alone again.

Her mouth hung agape. In her mind, Creepsley had already caught her, dragged her out from under the desk, and issued his second strike.

MOVE. NOW.

For a moment, Atra didn't think her limbs would obey, and then she was out the door. Where to go? Silvia had thwarted her plans of slipping in and out of the hospital wing unnoticed.

Speaking of which, she'd left the keycard on the floor of Creepsley's office, and the door had self-locked behind her after she left. No way to get back into the wing, even if she wanted to.

She'd forgotten her file, too.

Oops.

At least she had the book.

Dread obscured her vision. Atra kept close to the wall, grazing it with her hand as she blindly navigated the hall.

Her fingers touched something warm and spongy. A set of fingers grabbed her back.

She shrieked as a hand covered her mouth.

A pair of eyes stared down at her in the darkness. But they were far, far too high to belong to either Creepsley or Silvia.

Pepe. Dread parted enough for her to make out his massive frame blocking the narrow corridor behind him.

She relaxed as he removed his hand from her mouth.

Where have you been? she wanted to ask, but the urgency in his face kept her silent.

He motioned in the direction of the corridor behind him, as the sound of shoes squeaking down the hall grew louder.

She nodded. He moved aside to give her enough room to slip past. Hurrying along, Atra cast a final glance over her shoulder. Pepe stepped out of the corridor and into the main hall.

"GET HIM!" Creepsley bellowed.

Commotion, footsteps, yelling. When Pepe was caught, would he suffer the same fate as Beryl? Cease to exist?

Atra skidded to a stop, nearly doubling back. But Pepe had sacrificed himself so she could escape.

Why?

Because he knew about the altered planes.

Run, Atra. Run.

So, she did.

The other end of the corridor opened out to … the hallway in front of her sleeping quarters?

This wasn't right. Like the asylum had turned into a dollhouse some kid was snapping apart and reassembling at random.

She halted, her wounds pulsing in time to her heart. Surely this would be the first place Creepsley would look for her.

As soon as she entered her room, the odour of bleach blasted her nostrils. She rubbed her eyes in an attempt to rid them of the burning sensation.

The room had been put back together. There was no evidence of where the bolts had ripped up the floor. The beds sat in their respective places, crisp sheets pulled taut, a new bedside table between them.

Atra clicked the door shut. Her entire body thrummed; a bird caught in a cat's mouth waiting for the jaws to clamp down.

The skin below her knee burned from where the fire poker smashed against it while she ran. Her hands trembled as she shoved it under her mattress. She didn't know why, but her instincts told her to do so.

Just another crazy idea.

She backed into the bathroom, where the bleach smell was coming from. The walls and floors in here were scrubbed clean, some patches whiter than others where the worst of the blood had spilled. They hadn't bothered replacing the mirror, but the plywood backing had been scoured of the symbol.

Atra opened the book. The gash across her palm oozed fresh blood, smearing the pages red. Proof that even if the asylum wasn't real, it could still hurt her.

Property of Becopra/Polaris Division 502

Same name as the watermark on the photo of her and Dread.

Magnus Deadmarsh

"Found you," she whispered.

Maybe she'd also find the planes and get the hell out of here before Creepsley caught her.

Atra's arms shook, barely able to hold the book. Exhaling deeply, she leaned against the sink to steady herself. She tried to focus, but her eyeballs were threatening to vibrate out of their sockets.

The first two pages of the book were a mass of ink splotches and scribbled-out words. Then—

They don't understand what they opened. The altered planes are not what they seem. There are shadows beneath Polaris.

Her breath caught as she turned the page.

The lopsided figure-eight symbol, same as the one on the book's spine, took up the entire sheet of paper.

The Solstices and the Solar Analemma was scribbled across the top.

The name of the symbol, Atra gathered.

The Tentorum Plane is the most accessible on the solstice. That's why the shadows have come to play now.

The Cold Blood Moon. Lex warned her time was running out.

Fuck. Atra didn't know the date.

Think.

The last full moon ... she remembered staring at it from behind her reinforced bedroom window. She couldn't sleep, partly because Beryl was sundowning, and partly because Seth was visiting the next day. Her late birthday present.

Her birthday was November 22. Which meant ...

Time was indeed running out.

A blood-curdling cry echoed through the asylum.

Had Creepsley caught Pepe? And if she was next, would she scream the same way?

She shut the bathroom door. It could give her the seconds she needed if Creepsley burst in.

Take me to the planes. Please.

But the bleached walls did not dematerialize.

Back to the book. More ink splotches dotted this page.

Good shadows. Bad shadows. Everywhere. I can't unsee them. An ancient evil, one that has always been here, has awoken now that the worlds are too close. Glasser and Hart—

Hart? As in her? No. Magnus must've meant good ol' Tom, the original disgrace to the family name.

—won't see reason. They're too wrapped up in their Cynosura Experiment. They're blinded to what's really on the other side of their portal.

WHAT ARE THE ORIENS? I am at the gateway of the planes.

"So am I," Atra muttered. "Now, are you going to tell me how to get into them?"

Existence is planes, stacked atop one another. At the apex lies the Tentorum Plane, where all knowledge resides. A place to let go of the lie. A place to relive memories you didn't know you had.

Hadn't Pepe said something similar during their chess game? Pepe, who was currently being dragged away by Creepsley and Co., never to be seen again. Pepe, who seemed to know what Magnus meant. She wished he was here.

The Tentorum Plane, so close. Like a 3-D stereogram, stare at the dots on the picture long enough and a hidden pattern emerges. Only now you're unfocusing your mind. That's what these realities are; altered states, hidden behind one another.

Just because I see something, it doesn't mean that's what I'm really seeing. I can look at it in any way to be whatever I want it to be. It's my own perception. It's how I look at it that makes it real.

For me.

The lie is quicker than the mind.

The barriers are thinner in the dark. The cat is already

in both places but can see farther into the dark plane this way. He misses home.

If the lie is quicker than the mind, then the mind is heightened. I can do it. Access the Tentorum Plane. Face the evil there. If my plan fails, maybe someone will hear my echo in the planes and correct it.

June 21

The date was circled three times, the pressure of the pen denting the paper.

The portal must be open for the solstice. For the planes.

It will be the beginning. Or the end. It depends which side I'm on.

I have decided to head home. It's time.

Voices from the hallway dragged Atra out of the pages. She snapped the book shut, pressing herself into the corner behind the door.

She waited for the voices to grow, for the footsteps to approach, for the bedroom door to swing open.

It never happened.

The whispers weren't coming from the hall.

She faced the plywood backing of the mirror. More garblings, like someone talking from under a babbling brook. But definite voices. She leaned in closer.

"... a soul."

Her jaw tensed. The voice was clear. Like someone was standing on the other side of the wall.

"Another Cynosura Experiment?"

Homesickness twisted in her gut. Her dad.

Was she doing it? Unfocusing her mind, tapping into the planes? She was just thinking about her father, this could be her manifesting her own realit—

"Glasser, are you talking about a living being?"

It was him. Tom. Atra didn't think she'd remember his voice after all these years.

"D—Dad?" she asked, holding her palm against the plywood.

She hated the swell of excitement that grew in her. Was he right there, beyond the wall?

"We can do it," the other voice said, a smooth juxtaposition to her dad's abrasive tone. Who were they? "Create an aperture to the Otherside."

Her brows knitted together. No—she wasn't talking to her dad. She was overhearing a conversation that had already happened.

"What makes you think it'll work?" Dad asked. "Maybe we should pull the plug. Shut the portal down for good."

Portal? Like in the book?

She pressed her ear against the plywood, holding her breath.

"Think of the possibilities," the other voice said. "We can know what happens after death. Find an answer to it. One last experiment."

Dad replied, but his voice was muffled.

Atra cupped a hand over her ear. She needed him to keep talking. She needed to hear a familiar voice. She hadn't realized how desperate she was not to feel alone anymore.

"Are you listening to another dimension?"

A new voice behind her.

She gasped, spinning around. She didn't hear the door open. Beryl.

"What happened to you?" she blurted.

"Yes, I'm fine." Beryl's words came out stilted.

Not an answer.

"Beryl, are—" The words stuck in Atra's throat. "Are you okay?"

"Yes, I'm fine."

Repeated, like a machine on a loop.

"I didn't think I'd see you again."

Something was wrong. Although Beryl's face was composed, the tendons in her neck bulged, under pressure.

"Are you listening to another dimension?" Beryl asked again.

The tension in the air swirled between them.

Beryl approached. It happened too fast and too slow at once. She reached out with hands that should've been covered in deep gashes from the mirror. Instead, the skin was smooth, intact. She plucked the book out of Atra's limp grasp and turned around.

"Hey," Atra called out, as the reality of what happened sunk in.

Beryl didn't flinch.

"Hey!" she repeated, as Beryl left the bedroom with *her* book.

Atra followed. By the time she got to the door, Beryl was halfway down the hall. How did that old bat move so fast?

Atra ran, determined to catch up before Beryl disappeared around the corner. "Give me my book back!"

She closed the gap, grabbing Beryl's T-shirt. Beryl plowed forward with unnatural strength, the fabric yanking out of Atra's hands.

"What's wrong with you?"

Atra grabbed both her shoulders, forcing Beryl to turn around. It was a harder feat than she'd imagined for someone who was skin and bones.

Beryl's face remained unnaturally placid. The expression unnerved Atra so much she lost her grip.

Beryl pulled away. Her gaze unfocused, her cataract eye off-centre as she began walking backward.

Atra lunged for the book.

Beryl jerked her hand away, moving the book out of reach, in that horrible fast-yet-slow motion.

Dread whirled around, in front, behind. It filled Atra's mouth, funnelling into her lungs. It seeped into her eyes, swirled down her ears.

She could hear it. Not words, but an impression.

Hurt her, Dread was saying. *It's not really her.*

She lunged for the book, more aggressively this time.

She's not real. She can't feel a thing.

Beryl deflected her. She jabbed her free hand into the stitches lacing up Atra's chest, nails burrowing in.

The resulting scream that erupted from Atra didn't sound human.

She jerked back, shoving Beryl away. Beryl stumbled, but her grip on the book remained tight.

Dread surged, so dark it almost obscured Atra's world entirely.

That's not hurting her, Dread taunted. *Hurt her.*

Atra's hand balled into a fist. It flew through the air, clocking Beryl in the face.

Hitting her was not as satisfying as Atra anticipated. In fact, it did nothing but make her knuckles throb.

How could she ever hurt Beryl? Beryl was her best friend.

But Dread was pleased. If Dread was pleased, then she was pleased. It felt what she felt.

And Dread wanted more.

Suddenly she was on the floor, pinning Beryl to the ground.

Dread pulled the strings, moving her arms like she was nothing but a marionette. Atra knew it was manipulating her, feeding off her anger, but she couldn't stop …

Tears dripped from her eyes, clearing her vision enough to see the face beneath her had changed. Not Beryl, but Rei, with a big bloody nose, or was that blood from Atra's hand?

Yells, screams. Rei, telling her to stop?

A pair of hands grabbed her under the arms, lifting her up. She writhed like a wild animal caught in a trap. Another hand grabbed her face, trying to force her into submission.

Crunch! went Atra's teeth as they chomped down on the finger digging into the side of her mouth.

"Bitch bit me!" Silvia wailed.

Stars shot through Atra's vision as someone hit her across the face. They faded to reveal Creepsley standing there. His glasses had become two bottomless pools, devoid of life.

"Strike two, Miss Heart," there was a certain triumph to Creepsley's words, like he'd been dying to say them since her arrival. "Silvia, restrain her and take her to my office."

The hands gripped her tighter.

"And be so kind as to set up the ECT machine. I'll be along in a moment."

Atra tried to dig her heels into the linoleum but it was futile. Creepsley's ghoulish grin bobbed in the darkness like some macabre moon as she was dragged away.

Chapter 16

Nearly Witches

December 14
One day before the Vanishing Plains Fire

Ophelia stepped out of her back door, numb to the night's chill. The pinpoints of light from the distant neighbourhood were brighter than she remembered.

She'd come to hate the night. During the day, she could distract herself from the hunger that gnawed away at the last of her humanity. Nothing could distract her in the dark while the world lay dreaming.

No need to sleep.

No need to eat.

She entered her greenhouse. What had she come in here for?

It wasn't just her body becoming a burden; her mind was too. The synapses fired off into nothing.

In front of Ophelia bloomed a sunset of foxgloves. Their tiny, bell-shaped buds grew in the dead of winter. Her flower garden surrounded her, thriving and vibrant when it should've been withered and brown.

And yet she felt nothing.

Where was Evie with the new gift?

For months, they'd alternated turns. Find someone like the man who tried to corner her behind the resource centre. An abuser. Scum of the earth. Something you'd scrape off the bottom of your shoe. Harvest them for the gift. The angrier they were in the end, the longer the gift lasted.

Plant it beneath the cypress tree. Bask under the cypress tree's glow as the Queen sucked it dry. Reap the reward when the Queen transferred the energy.

What was taking Evie so long? Two or three days. That's what she'd promised. Ophelia could've done the deed in less than one. But that security guard with a grudge left her perturbed.

The Queen had warned her months ago when they opened the gateway in the cypress tree: If there are no gifts, you become the gift.

The past three days had slowed to a crawl. Burying the last gift under the cypress tree seemed a lifetime ago.

The translucent walls of Ophelia's greenhouse became tinged with grey as dawn approached.

How long had she been standing here?

A noise. Coming from ... where? She cast an uncertain glance around the greenhouse. With her senses on overdrive, a clap of thunder or a whisper on the wind sounded the same.

She had to move. She had to get out of here before the ground swallowed her.

Out of the greenhouse and back to her home. Through the narrow kitchen and into the living room. Everything seemed in order. The heavy curtains were shut, her bag on the couch undisturbed. The knickknacks sat on the mantel in a neat row. She lingered for too long on the urn in the centre.

What would her life be like if her son hadn't died at seventeen? If she hadn't remarried after Lyall? If she hadn't started chasing the Queen's dream?

A footstep crunched on the icy snow outside.

She grabbed the silver dagger off the mantel.

The cloying stench of Chuck O'Flennek permeated the room from outside. She imagined him poking around, his puffy eyes trying to peer through her curtains.

Unsheathing the dagger, she clutched it behind her back. She zeroed in on the front door. She'd forgotten to lock it.

Stupid, stupid, stupid.

The door handle turned slowly.

The *audacity* of that man!

She crossed the room with a split second to decide whether to lock the door or swing it wide open.

She chose the latter.

Chuck *O'Flennek* jumped at her abrupt appearance, his boot slipping on the icy step.

For a moment she thought he'd fall on his ass.

No such luck.

"Get off my property," she seethed.

"Not your property, is it?" He straightened himself out. "You're renting this piece-of-shit place."

"*Get off my property*," she repeated, through clenched teeth.

"Have a chance to look through the envelope I left you?" He craned his neck, attempting to get a view inside. She blocked his line of sight.

"What do you want?"

"Thought I'd drop by and see if you would consent to a search of your premises before I get a warrant."

Bullshit. It was six in the morning.

Ophelia gripped the dagger, contemplating. He'd make the perfect gift for the cypress tree. Enough to tide her and the Queen over until the solstice.

The Queen's claws sunk into her neck. A warning not to act rashly.

"*Get off my property*," she said, for a third time. "A pathetic security guard with a grudge can't get a search warrant."

He closed in on her, face red as a beet. He puffed out his chest. As if that was going to intimidate her.

"No. But a pathetic detective with a grudge can."

He held a shiny badge up to her face.

Fuck. Guess *Chuck O'Flennek* wasn't a fake name after all.

Images of plunging the dagger into his chest flooded her mind. She couldn't do that, though. If he went missing while investigating a cold case related to her …

Chuck was, unfortunately, untouchable.

And his smirk said he knew it.

"I'll be back with a warrant."

Bits of his spittle landed on her cheeks. She didn't want him to see her wipe them off.

Chuck turned, not able to stomp away aggressively, she noticed with a modicum of satisfaction, lest he slip on the ice again. She could see the bulge of his gun holster, hidden under his jacket.

SCREEEETCH!

The sound of his truck keys scraping along the side of her car sent shooting pain through the fillings in her teeth.

Coward. That all you've got?

She stepped back into a house that no longer felt safe, tainted by Chuck's lingering presence. Her body shuddered, becoming one raw, exposed nerve.

Why was Lyall coming back to haunt her twenty-eight years later?

She slammed the door shut. It splintered, jamming into the frame. If she hadn't pulled back at the last moment, the door would be lying on the crusted ice of the front stoop.

Resheathing the dagger, she placed it on the mantel beside her son's urn. From the outside, the dagger appeared to be nothing more than a simple letter opener. The same went for the black candles around her bathtub, the crystals hanging in the windows, the jars of poisonous herbs hidden among her dried spices.

She'd cleared her closet of its skeletons and had hidden them in plain sight. If an investigation was launched against her, they would open her closet to find it empty.

At least, she hoped so.

Because Chuck O'Flennek was just getting started.

Back at work. Her office in the resource centre didn't feel any more comfortable than her house had.

Heavy. So heavy in her chair.

Why hadn't Evie returned her text?

The lavender walls surrounding Ophelia dulled to grey. Or was she just perceiving them that way? She held her hands out in front of her.

Also grey.

Her veins protruded, seeming to sit over her skin rather than under. They throbbed in time to her leaden heart.

So many hours spent at this resource centre, counselling women, helping women, recruiting women ...

What would come of this place when she and the Queen joined together? Would it—along with the rest of the city—be reduced to rubble? Did Ophelia care? It was hard to care about such things when she was on the cusp of becoming immortal.

She scanned her phone messages, knowing she hadn't missed anything.

How could she have been so naive to think Chuck was a security guard? Because she was in denial. Pushing him aside like a dusty cobweb could very well be her undoing.

The solstice was mere days away, but Chuck could throw a wrench in her plans before then. And sitting in a jail cell as the 21st of December passed was not an option. That crooked cop had her in a deadlock. He'd left her entirely dependent on Evie for the gifts; Ophelia couldn't afford any more blood on her hands.

She checked her phone again. Nothing. If Evie wasn't going to respond, then Ophelia would go to her.

She closed her eyes, intending to reach out through the office walls to the outside world. Evie shouldn't be hard to find. Ophelia knew her habits, her daily routine. Probably manning the counter at her pharmacy, no doubt.

Her nerves electrified when she discovered Evie was standing right outside her office door.

What was she doing here? Evie knew it was too risky to meet at the resource centre.

Ophelia barely had time to gather herself as the door opened.

The emotions radiating off Evie—terror, mixed with adrenaline and determination—crashed over Ophelia. Patches of red stood out on Evie's cheeks, yet the hollows under her eyes were more prominent than ever. She hadn't been sleeping.

Chuck paid you a visit, too, was Ophelia's first thought.

But something else churned in Evie's emotions.

"Hello, Ophelia."

"Hello, Evelien."

Without being invited, Evie strode in. She stood awkwardly in the middle of the room, as if trying very hard to be assertive.

Ophelia smelled her intent. There would be no more gifts from her. She knew this before Evie spoke.

"You've been poisoned. This isn't what we're supposed to stand for."

Ophelia cocked an eyebrow. Her assumptions in the café had been correct; Evie was pulling away. The crack in the foundation had been left to grow too large. The crack Ophelia had foolishly hinged her plan upon.

"You've sullied the name of The Drove," Evie continued, her voice wavering. "You've destroyed our years of hard work and dedication." She sounded like she had rehearsed this. Many times.

"We were supposed to be a band of women helping women. Not women murdering men."

A flutter ran through Ophelia. The word had never been spoken aloud before. What if someone overheard?

"I won't play into your sick game anymore. You either stop this madness and turn yourself in or I—" Evie faltered. "Or I will."

Ophelia weighed her options. Evie's hands weren't clean, either. She was in this just as deep.

"You're not going to do anything. If you take this to the authorities, you're admitting your guilt too. And as noble as this cause of yours is, I don't think you're willing to serve time for it."

Ophelia leaned in closer. Evie's skin looked even worse up close—coarse and dry. No, she hadn't been sleeping well at all, had she?

"I could take your head and twist it 'round like a spin top before you even knew I had moved." Ophelia's voice was a stream trickling down bedrock. "Feed you to the cypress tree. You could be its final gift before the solstice. The only reason you're still alive is because we need that psych patient. You *will* go to that asylum tomorrow and retrieve her. You don't have the spine to turn me in, but we both know I won't hesitate to kill you if you fail me."

Evie struggled to maintain her composure. Ophelia wondered what other outcome she'd imagined for this. Did Evie really think she'd roll over and play dead?

"Get out." Ophelia didn't give her the chance to respond. "Don't show your face again unless you have the girl, or I *will* make you the next gift."

The drive back home, parking her car, dumping her bag on the couch, a blur.

Fucking Evie.

Useless.

Worthless.

But Ophelia still had time to get this under control. Evie was good and scared when she'd left, but Evie had already been good and scared before her grand "confrontation." There was still a chance she wouldn't go through with retrieving Atra. But Ophelia had a contingency plan.

She went to her kitchen. Opened the cupboard above her stove, lined with cookbooks she never used. Grabbed the fattest volume. Flipped open the cover.

The inside was hollowed out, containing a vial for almost every member of The Drove, past and present. She grabbed the one with Evie's name on it and held it up to the light. Within, a single, blond hair. Like the blond hair that found its way onto her ex's shirt.

The hunger no longer clawed her insides. It shredded.

Ophelia set the vial on her dinky, made-for-one dining table. Then she dug into another cupboard, reaching to the far back for a mason jar. She clutched the jar and went outside. Entered the greenhouse, shovelled a handful of dirt into the mason jar. Then back to the kitchen. Slammed the mason jar down beside the vial. To the bathroom. A black candle. A book of matches. A scrap of paper and a pencil off the coffee table on her way back.

Almost in the kitchen, then turned back. Plucked the dagger off the mantel that sat beside her son's urn.

She seated herself at the table, scooting in close. With a shaking hand, she wrote *Evelien Charles* on the paper. Popping open the vial, she tipped the hair into the mason jar. She poked the pad of her thumb with the dagger and squeezed a drop of blood into the jar alongside the hair.

Wiping her sweaty brow, she pushed away the strands of her own hair that had fallen out of their twist. Her hands trembled harder, struggling to grasp the paper with her too-long fingernails. The high hum of anticipation rang through her head.

Evie was going to regret ever trying to turn against her.

Ophelia's tongue lolled like a mad dog baking in the sun.

She opened the matchbook. Struck a match. Held it under the paper, flame wavering.

The echo responds to the call.

The phrase rang through her head.

Those words had been hammered into her when she'd first joined The Drove. Whatever you put out into the world, harm or good, eventually came back full circle. The phrase was meant to placate abuse victims, to give them peace of mind that their abusers would get what was coming to them.

She always thought it was a bullshit phrase.

Yet it nagged at her now.

"No, it won't come full circle."

The Queen's arrival would interrupt that.

The flame licked the corner of the paper. It smoked, the edge turning black. She dropped it into the jar as it curled from the heat. The hair sizzled, its burning stench filling the kitchen.

"You will see the error of your ways."

She fastened the lid on the jar and set it on the table. She stared at it, chest heaving as the paper turned to ash.

Evie would be retrieving Atra whether she wanted to or not.

Chapter 17

As Ugly as I Seem

Awake.

In her room, with the blood-red sheets.

Right, but wrong.

Something told Atra she hadn't fallen asleep here.

Scritch, scritch.

Swimming in the ether between dream and sleep, the sounds came from nowhere and everywhere.

Scritch, scritch.

Scritch, scritch.

No—they came from under the bed.

Like a tree branch squeaking against a windowpane in the dead of night. Atra imagined a fingernail, long and twisted like the tree branch, scratching the underside of the bed, piercing through the mattress, skewering her.

She gasped, breaking the surface of consciousness.

Her eyes flew open. For real this time.

The light blared in. Her lids clamped back shut. How did she end up here?

The answer ground to a halt, the gears in her brain clogged with cotton.

She tried cracking her eyes open again. Still too bright. She brought a hand up to shield them, but her wrist snapped against something. Something leather, with a buckle. She twisted both arms.

They had her strapped down. She wasn't going anywhere. The cotton clogging her head caught fire, a pressure building behind her sinuses.

The blanket on top suffocated her. Her skin prickled, hot as a hare, but she couldn't throw the blanket off.

The room glowed like sunset on a summer day. But it was the dead of winter. Close to the Cold Blood Moon. Close to the Queen's arrival.

How'd she end up here? Memories of the fight trickled into her groggy brain.

The book was supposed to get her out of here, but Beryl had stolen it. Only it wasn't Beryl, it was Rei. She didn't know where Beryl was and she didn't know what was wrong with her mind and what had they done to her?

Movement in the strange glow. Lex, sitting beside her. Grown-up Lex. She didn't seem afraid anymore. She wore turquoise nurse's scrubs, because it wasn't Lex, it was Silvia. How could Atra ever have thought it was Lex?

Just because I see something, it doesn't mean that's what I'm really seeing. I can look at it in any way to be whatever I want it to be. It's how I look at it that makes it real. For me.

Silvia—Lex?—noted she was awake.

Atra wanted to ask what happened to her but the words stuck to the back of her throat.

The wood-panelled walls in here reminded her of the house. Like how Lex was Silvia. Or Silvia was Lex. Were her two realities bleeding together?

Silvia clasped her hands in her lap, her index finger swathed in a heavy bandage. Atra recalled chomping on someone's finger, the coppery taste of drawing blood.

"I'm sorry." The words took a terrifyingly long time to travel from her brain to her mouth.

Silvia looked at the bandage. "You didn't really do it."

That didn't make Atra feel like any less of an asshole.

"The lie is quicker than the mind." Atra wasn't sure if she thought it or spoke it.

Her body ached in the sort of way it did when you were sick and spent too long in bed. What was the date? How close was it to—

"The Cold Blood Moon approaches," Silvia finished her thought.

"I have to find the Tentorum Plane."

It was her only shot at conquering Dread, but Atra was *so tired*.

"You're close." Silvia's face changed to Lex's again. "But so is the Queen."

Who was she? Atra wanted to ask, but her thoughts drifted apart.

Her lids closed again. It was too bright in here because Dread wasn't swirling around.

Where had it gone?

She stood in a hallway. In the asylum or in the house? Atra couldn't be sure. Was it dark because Dread had returned or because it was night?

It didn't matter; her world was perpetual night now.

Sorry, Lex. I failed. I couldn't control Dread.

Her head pounded. The skin stretched too tight around her temples, burning like a thousand fire-ant bites. Her fingers ran over the rough scabs along her hairline.

What did they do to me?

She stood in front of the door to her sleeping quarters. When did she get here?

It didn't matter.

Steel double doors with heavy handles blocked off the hallway past her bedroom. They looked like they led to a morgue.

She may be drowning in the deep end, but she knew with certainty those hadn't been there before.

She shook it off and entered her room.

Rei sat cross-legged on Beryl's bed, nose swollen and eyes blackened from Atra's attack.

"Hey, roomie. I've been waiting for you." Balloons surrounded Rei, blood red, matching the bedspreads. On each balloon glimmered a pearlescent analemma, identical to the one on the spine of Lex's book. "Did the electroshock therapy treat you well?"

"What did you do to Beryl?"

"Beryl went *bye-bye*," Rei emphasized the last two words, with her signature grin.

"Why are you here?"

Atra didn't mean *here* in this room. She meant why was Rei here in this asylum. Where had she come from? What were she and Creepsley doing in this place?

Rei scooped up a handful of little papers off the bed that resembled confetti. Her mouth split open unnaturally, the corners almost reaching her ears.

"You are dead and I am dead ..." she started in a horrible sing-song voice.

She threw a handful of confetti. It danced in the light as it rained back down on the bed. Black cats. They were shaped like black cats. They were shaped like Oriens.

"... and Seth is dead and Dread is dead ..."

Atra jerked away. Why was Rei talking about her brother? And *how did she know about Dread*?

"... and we are all DEAD!"

The confetti continued to fall, a surprise party just for Atra.

You're nuts. Surprise!

Atra needed to lie down. Although she'd rather do so far away from Rei, she couldn't manage anything but the two steps to her bed.

Nausea bubbled in the back of her throat, almost like she'd been hit by the flu. But that wasn't it. This was from whatever they did to her, in the room where she'd been strapped to the bed.

She curled up on her side. Her skin prickled, body alternating between hot and cold currents. Shivering or trembling?

"Going to sleep, buddy?" Rei's voice came from the other end of a tunnel with a train barrelling between them. "The fun has just begun."

"Leave me alone."

Atra felt Rei's stare burning into her back. Rei could do whatever she wanted, this was her chance …

And Atra didn't care.

She crushed her head into the flat pillow, brain too heavy.

Everything bled together, trapped in a fever dream.

She tried to bring a hand up to cradle her head, but the distance to cover was impossibly vast.

Had she been sleeping? Her head told her it hurt too much to sleep, but then there were periods when the pain came back stronger. Did she manage to drift off and forget it?

A sound she couldn't place. A spring in Rei's mattress as she shifted on it? A nurse coming in?

No, it came from under the bed. A scratching, made by a creature with one long fingernail and a featureless face. Two horns protruded from her head … or was she wearing a crown? Atra knew in her heart this was the Queen, hunting her, haunting her.

Her eyes opened. At least, she thought they did. Darkness pressed all around.

Dread suffocated her.

She remembered its first appearance.

It began with the shadows, darting in and out of her vision.

Their insidious presence had transformed into shapes and figures without her noticing.

Standing outside her bedroom window, reflecting off the television screen.

Always watching.

Those were the first true memories of her childhood. She had a vague sense of her dad, of Seth, of her stepmother, but they were ... impressions. Feelings. She knew it wasn't normal for your memories to start at nine.

They said lack of memories could indicate a repressed trauma. Wait ... who said that?

Atra sat up in her bed. Her bedside lamp illuminated the ugly flowered wallpaper. Her dad had promised he'd get rid of it, but he never did and now he was gone.

She was nine years old again.

She'd stuffed boxes under the bed and barricaded the closet doors shut so nothing could sneak up on her in the night. The light stayed on, even when she slept.

Because the shadows could be anywhere. They could slip under a crack in the door, sneak in between the sliver of the curtains ...

Her own shadow splayed out long on the wall beside her. The only one she had control over. The only one she didn't fear.

A whisper in her peripherals.

Oh no. A shadow had found its way in.

She turned to face the wall. Her shadow mimicked her. It was herself; that was all.

Just herself, moving to look at her shadow.

It loomed over her, grazing the ceiling. Was it that big due to how the bedside lamp was casting the light?

No. Because a pair of spindly arms were now reaching up, creeping along the ceiling, the fingers too long. They couldn't belong to her, because hers were cemented in her lap ...

A scream rose in her throat, but she swallowed it back and shut her eyes.

One, two, three ...

It was in her head.

Four, five, six ...

When she opened her eyes, the shadow would be gone.

Seven, eight, nine ...

But she couldn't stop picturing the clawed hand peeling itself off the ceiling and sinking its nails into her head.

She peeked through her squinted lids. The shadow was still there. It formed a fist, one long finger wagging at her.

Tsk, tsk, did you think I'd leave?

Atra sat upright in her bed, in the asylum. The metal frame poked at her from under the mattress. She was twenty again, but the terror she'd felt as a nine-year-old remained.

Cold sweat drenched her forehead and ran between her shoulder blades. Her mind had cleared, like a buzzing you notice only after it ceases. How long had she been out? Long enough that her stomach grumbled in hunger. Long enough that she had to use the bathroom.

She stood on unsteady legs. Rei was an unmoving lump in Beryl's bed.

Atra could barely make out shapes as she walked to the bathroom. Dread clung to her eyes, nose, and mouth, like the smoke from the fire. Maybe she did die in it. Rei said they were all dead.

That room was my tomb.

Laughter tickled the back of her throat.

But she didn't make a sound. Because Rei was asleep. And when Rei was asleep, she wasn't dangerous.

Dread's murmuring filled her ears. Atra hummed, trying to block it out as she sat on the toilet.

The voice grew more distinct. No longer a gossamer thread of thought. A female voice.

Rei?

She stopped humming, squinting through Dread, but it was too thick to tell if Rei had awoken.

Out of the corner of her eye, something glinted through the gloom. She turned, looking up from her seat on the toilet. The mirror above the sink had finally been replaced.

"... *Atra* ..."

Her blood ran cold.

The mirror. The voice came from the mirror.

She stood, shaking. As much as she wanted to run back to bed and bury herself under the covers, she had to face the voice.

She went to the mirror.

"Did you think you could get rid of me?" The voice was as ancient and evil as the beginning of time.

It came from the reflection.

It came from her.

But it wasn't her face.

Hollow eye sockets stared back at her. They matched the gaping hole in the bottom of the face where the mouth should be. The skin was grey and green, like a bloated corpse in water.

"Go look under the bed." The unhinged mouth didn't move, but the words were clear.

The thing's features disintegrated like sand on the wind.

"Then see if you can escape me."

Out of reflex, Atra's hand slammed down on the mirror. Anything to destroy that horrible face. Anything to stop that horrible voice.

The mirror shattered, pieces of glass raining around the sink. Did any of them cut her? She didn't care. The voice was gone. And the face—

She didn't want to look, but yes, the face was gone. Nothing but plywood underneath. The plywood and the—

Her breath hitched.

And the analemma. The one Beryl had drawn. The one that had been scrubbed off with bleach.

Her gaze danced around the mirror frame, unable to find the corner. At first, she thought it was a trick of the light. She tried following the edges, but they didn't exist. Everything warped toward the analemma.

She turned, running to her bed and retrieving the fire poker stashed under her mattress. Miraculously, the nurses hadn't found it.

The metal vibrated in her fingers, like it was a conductor and she was the lightning strike.

Atra slammed the pointed end of the poker into the analemma, over and over.

"Stop wasting your time," the foul voice returned. *"Under the bed is where you'll find what you're looking for."*

She smashed the plywood harder in retaliation, trying to drown out the voice, but it wouldn't shut up.

"What are you doing?"

She paused, turning around. Rei stood halfway between the beds and the bathroom, nothing but a shapeless blur through Dread. Atra held the poker up defensively, ready for an attack. But Rei didn't sound hostile.

In fact, she sounded sleepy and annoyed.

"That's what she wants you to believe." So loud, coming from everywhere Dread was, siphoning off Atra's darkest desires.

"Finish Rei before she has the chance to finish you."

But Rei had the chance for hours while Atra laid in bed delusional. Rei could have done anything. Instead, she fell asleep.

Rei took a step forward.

Don't come any closer, Atra wanted to say, not for her sake but for Rei's.

Rei spoke, but Dread's intrusive commands drowned her out.

"Don't forget what she did to Beryl. Do the same to her."

Atra still held the poker over her head, arms locked in place. Dread gave her a push forward. That's all she needed. A push. She wanted to do it. She'd wanted to do it since the day they met, when the bitch attacked her with a broom handle. The poker came down.

This is it. I'm going to kill Rei.

The certainty of it sickened her. This wasn't her; she wasn't some violent, deranged animal. She was Atra Hart. She knew her name.

Instead, she slammed Rei against the door, holding the fire poker against Rei's throat.

Rei's dark eyes were wide and glassy as they darted around Atra's face.

"Do not fuck with me." Atra's voice was low and deep. The voice of Dread. "Not now, Rei."

Rei's throat ticked behind the metal rod pressed against it.

"*Please*," Atra pleaded, not for her safety, but for Rei's.

Rei nodded, jaw clenched. Atra realized she was terrified.

For a moment, Atra considered not letting her go. Push the fire poker deeper, cut off her breathing.

That was Dread talking.

Instead, Atra stepped back. Rei slipped past, scampering out of the room without a word.

A hot wetness had spread across Atra's face. She rubbed away her tears as she rounded on the shattered mirror.

The frame still warped around the splintered analemma.

"*You missed your chance.*" She smashed the poker into the plywood, trying to ignore the voice. "*Follow her. Find her.*"

"SHUT UP!" she roared.

She wrenched the poker back and forth, trying to widen the crack.

The wood splintered, brightness streaming through. She jerked away. The light reminded her of the rift splitting open the sky. Atra threw the poker aside, limbs trembling, heart racing. She pressed herself against the sink, holding her eye up to the gap.

Beyond it sat a familiar paisley-patterned couch bathed in firelight.

The house.

Backing away, she reached down to retrieve the poker to pry the gap open farther, when a puff of air fell across her neck.

Dread?

Or had Rei returned?

The stench of sulphur filled the room. Worse than Rei. Much, much worse.

"Strike three."

Chapter 18

Dead Meat

Tom rounded the bend, putting the motel out of sight. *No* —he wasn't running away. He was getting some air.

Or whatever the hell you call it when you've fucking had enough.

Goddammit, it was cold out here. Naomi always said he swore too much when he was stressed.

She was fucking right.

Oh, Naomi—absence really did make the heart grow fonder. He'd read somewhere how you don't miss a person, you miss the memories surrounding them.

Truth was, he didn't have many good memories of her—at least, none that sprang to mind—but his stagnant existence with her seemed far better than the shit show it was now. He was caught in some convoluted sci-fi drama you would watch on TV after work when fuck else was on.

Glasser convulsing on the floor haunted Tom. The way his spine had buckled. The way his throat had emitted those guttural noises. The way his body had flickered out of reality.

Glasser had come around long enough to vomit on the carpet, heave himself onto the bed, and pass out.

Tom flipped him onto his side, in case he puked again, then immediately considered flipping him onto his back. But he wasn't ready to stoop to that level. Yet.

The low drone of Glasser's snores filled the room.

Tom should've stayed with him, to make sure he kept snoring. But he needed out of that fucking room.

Back outside, he threw a glance over his shoulder. The exposed hand clutching his cigarette went from cold to numb.

Turn around and go back?

Nah.

He was already more than halfway around the block. He puffed on his smoke, a cold hand up to a cold face. His last smoke, too. He doubted Glasser would be buying him anymore. Hell, he doubted Glasser would be the same after the ol' grand mal.

The solstice was tomorrow, but Tom didn't think Glasser would make it till then.

Glasser's only chance at continuing to exist hinged on his assumption he'd survive on the Otherside. Frankly, Tom didn't think he would. Even if Glasser managed to activate a minuscule portion of his shadow DNA, it wasn't enough. Same reason why Tom could open the portal but never step through. You needed something else to survive over there. What did Glasser call it? Ultramatter. Ulma, for short.

From what they'd gathered, the soul—or the closest thing to it—was what crossed over. The body, obviously, did not.

But there had to be a *third* part they were missing. Because the soul had never survived when they sent living matter through. It was almost like it needed a body to go into *over there*. That's where Glasser got his idea of an ulma. A vessel on the Otherside to house the soul once it arrived.

No way in hell Glasser had one of those. They'd tried to splice one into a human but every attempt failed. Even on Tom, the prized lab rat with the exceptional shadow DNA.

It was impossible for a living being to possess an ulma.

Bottom line.

Tom puffed his cigarette to the filter, the taste of bitter plastic lining his mouth. Dammit. He didn't get to enjoy the final drag.

Woe is me.

The cigarette butt fell to the snow-crusted sidewalk. He stuffed his frozen hand into his jacket. Between his chattering teeth, his breath billowed out in white puffs, the only cloud in an otherwise clear night. The rift, growing ever brighter on the horizon, washed out the stars.

Tom turned up the street. The sodium lamps of the motel parking lot stained the icy asphalt yellow. Back to the beginning. Back to where he started.

The rift was behind him. He breathed a sigh of relief. Watching light filter in from another world sent his skin crawling.

His chest racked with shivers, but he didn't want to go back to that stifling room. The car keys, resting beside the coffee maker, taunted him.

He could still get in the car. Get out of this place while he still had time. Why didn't he? Fuck the world. Fuck it if it all ended tomorrow. He didn't have a reason to be alive anyway.

Yet something nagged him that he did.

Atra.

Did Glasser really know where she was?

Tom couldn't abandon her. Not again.

He paused in front of a closed retail shop. His reflection showed himself hunched over like a spineless jellyfish. He shuffled past, unable to stand the sight of himself.

Coward.

His frozen fingers curled around the fake-leather wallet in his pocket. He pulled it out and opened it.

He gripped the photo inside the torn lining before he could chicken out. It didn't want to budge after being jammed in there for years. He was about to give up, in fear it would rip, when it came free.

Clutched in his hand was a shitty-quality school photo.

It was wrinkled and worn with age, but there was Atra, forever seven, smiling at him with her two missing front teeth.

She had a sad smile. One that said, *When are you gonna be back, Dad*? Was her smile always like that, or was he projecting his years of crushing guilt onto it?

His throat threatened to close in on itself. He cleared it, tugging at the collar of his jacket.

Almost like he was having an allergic reaction.

No, you idiot.

His eyes welled, causing the photo to swim in and out of focus.

A loud sob escaped him before he knew what was happening. It shocked him back to sobriety. He blinked rapidly, causing the tears to spill down his face.

What a horrible sensation. Shaking his head, he tried to get himself under control, but the choking refused to abate.

He couldn't stand to look at the photo again but forced himself to. So much of her he didn't remember.

He didn't remember the freckles dotting her skin, just like his, the messy black hair, just like his, or the eyes ...

The eyes were not just like his. They were grey, stormy.

Another wave of emotion crashed through him, but this time it wasn't anguish.

The colour of thunder. Exactly how Glasser had described Molly's eyes.

Tom fumbled, stuffing the picture back into the lining with fingers that refused to stop shaking.

The tightening in his throat returned, although he wasn't about to cry this time.

He was about to vomit.

Swallowing the urge, he shoved the wallet into his jacket. That fucking picture made the outside world shrink to the size of a matchbox, more suffocating than the motel room.

At least the motel room wasn't fucking freezing.

He walked through the parking lot, up the slippery metal steps to the second floor, and to his room. The hot, acrid stench of Glasser's puke wafted out before he stepped inside, worse after being out in the crisp winter air.

Glasser's bed was vacant.

Holding a hand to his nose, Tom went in. He checked the spot between the beds, thinking Glasser might have rolled back onto the floor.

Nada.

Bastard. Did Glasser really have a seizure, or did he fake that too? But Tom had seen him disappear. He'd felt his hands go through nothing where Glasser's body should have been.

He couldn't have imagined that.

Right?

He eyeballed the car keys on the table.

Time to go, Tommy boy.

He reached for them when the laptop on Glasser's bed caught his attention instead. He grabbed it, struck with an idea.

Sitting on the edge of the bed, he clicked the internet icon on the desktop. The browser opened, cursor blinking in the blank window of the search engine.

Where to start?

If Atra *had* been placed in a mental institution, his bet was it was located near Telos, where he lived with his family before he flew the coop.

He typed in his search, not sure what it would accomplish. It wasn't like he'd get a list of psych patients and their exact location. But maybe he could figure out where Atra was. Then he'd get in the car and drive away.

But not run away. No.

Save his daughter.

There was a mental hospital in Telos. *Was* being the operative word, he learned, as he scanned the news articles. It had burned down.

Recently, too. December 15. Less than a week ago.

The same day Glasser flushed him out of hiding.

Tom's eyes narrowed.

Coincidence?

Heavy footfalls thumped up the stairs outside.

Shit. Was that Glasser?

Tom exited the search screen. He shut the laptop and stuffed it under his pillow as the door opened. Glasser had aged fifty years overnight.

Tom opened his mouth to ask Glasser where he'd been, but Glasser's gaze darted to something over Tom's shoulder. In the years they'd known each other, Tom had never seen Glasser frightened.

Until now.

Tom didn't want to know what had him scared shitless.

He turned, neck stiff as a rusty hinge. Something black came into view. His vision crossed, focusing on the muzzle of a handgun pointed at his forehead. The hand holding the gun had an odd, cracked appearance like sun-baked clay.

Veins, some far-off part of Tom's mind registered. *They aren't cracks. They're bulging veins.*

A woman towered over him, her long auburn hair cascading to her hips. She wore sunglasses in the dead of night, the large black frames contrasting against her sunken cheekbones. She reminded Tom of a giant walking fly.

How long had she been standing there with one long-nailed finger on the trigger?

Tom's breath hitched, the choking sensation back. Because behind the sunglasses, behind the veins, he recognized the woman.

Ophelia? he wanted to ask, but his tongue was glued to the roof of his mouth.

The veiny hand lashed out like a cobra striking. The butt of the gun clocked him between the eyes.

Tom's world exploded into a field of white.

Chapter 19

Monster Hospital

"Strike three." Creepsley's voice oozed victory.

His feet crunched on the broken mirror as he lunged for Atra. She hit the floor, rolling to the side.

Creepsley slipped on a shard of glass. An *oof!* escaped him as he collided with the edge of the sink.

Flashbacks of their first meeting streaked through Atra's head. Before the flames. Before the car crash that led to this whole fucked-up asylum.

A narrow escape then.

Would there be a narrow escape now?

She darted out of the bedroom, moving off muscle memory; Dread had reduced her world to a dim blur.

"*Go back, finish him off.*" Dread's sinister whispering was relentless. "*Slide a mirror shard between his ribs.*"

She chomped down on her lip to keep from screaming back.

Where to go?

The new morgue-like double doors beside her room yawned open, ready to swallow her.

She went left, heading for the common area instead.

Was that her bedroom door opening? Impossible to tell over her booming heart and Dread's chatter.

She slammed into the door of the common area and yanked at the handle. The door wouldn't budge. She threw her weight against it, panic gripping her in a vise. It thumped open an inch before slamming back shut. Like something on the other side was trying to keep her out.

"Where'd she go?" Creepsley bellowed.

A high, grating voice—Rei's—answered, but Atra couldn't make out the words.

Keep running, or try to open the door? Only time for one option.

She rammed her shoulder into the door, digging her feet into the ground and pushing with all her might. Resistance and then—

The door banged open. She lost her balance, falling into the room.

Her feet hit the floor. Old chipped hardwood, to be precise. She could see it clearly because there were no shadows here.

She'd entered the house.

The kitchen remained in disarray, the overturned table and chairs blocking off the area in front of her.

Where was Lex?

Atra drew a deep breath, about to call out for her, when a pair of hands wrapped around her waist.

Small hands. Bony hands. Rei's hands.

The split second of surprise was all Rei needed to gain the upper hand. Before Atra could fight, she was yanked back.

She clawed at Rei's hands with her own, trying to break their iron grip, but couldn't get her footing, couldn't gain the advantage. Her wounds ripped open in her struggle as another pair of hands added to Rei's.

Cold, terrible hands.

The strength left her as Rei and Creepsley pulled her back into their asylum. She screamed for Lex.

The darkness of Dread returned. Something stung Atra's thigh. Did they inject her with something again?

She struggled, limbs sluggish. Her eyelids wanted to close, and how easy would that be, to close them and never open them again? Fade to black.

"No!" She shook her head.

Rei and Creepsley dragged her out of the common area, down the hall. Atra dug her heels into the linoleum, but it did nothing to slow them. She flailed, but the despicable duo tightened their grip, pinning her arms to her side.

"Help!" she screamed, into the void. "Lex! Pepe!"

Rei's grin bobbed above her like a sinister crescent moon in the night sky.

"Silvia! Anyone!"

But no one answered. Because no one was left.

Rei and Creepsley dragged Atra through the morgue-like double doors and into the unknown.

Windowless wrought iron doors lined the hall. One after another, so close together.

They dragged her to the far end of the hall. Through another set of doors. Past a gleaming array of machines and instruments.

They forced her onto a bed. No, not a bed; a chair, ankles strapped down, wrists strapped in.

"Bring me the tray," Creepsley commanded Rei.

Atra arched her spine, but a cold hand shoved her back. Creepsley fumbled with something around her head, his glasses askew, sulphur breath panting in her face.

"Why are you doing this?" Atra hated the way her voice broke with fear.

"This is all for you—" The end of the sentence was drowned out by the cart rolling toward him. "You have a special soul, Atra. Dr. Glasser wanted it, but I think I'll keep it for myself."

Creepsley ducked out of view as the rattling of metal

instruments filled Atra's ears. He was grabbing something off the tray. Then, to Rei—

"Hold her head. I don't trust the strap."

More pressure against Atra's forehead. Creepsley returned, his watery black eyes magnified under his lenses. He clutched a pointed stick of metal in one hand and a small hammer in the other.

A whimper escaped Atra's throat as she pressed her head farther into the chair.

Creepsley's stupid glasses still hung crooked as he poised the pointed end of the ice pick over her eye. Rei's head popped up beside his, slobbering through her grin. Was this really going to be the last image Atra remembered seeing?

Surely, she could imagine something else—Seth, Beryl—hell, she'd take her deadbeat dad over these two goons. Could she convince her mind to lie in these last moments?

Just because I see something, it doesn't mean that's what I'm really seeing. It's how I look at it that makes it real.

The ice pick swung toward her in an exaggerated movement.

You are at the gateway of the planes.

She concentrated on the metal tip. Was she slowing it down?

She must be if she could think all of this. The metal should've been digging into her tear duct.

Was Vanishing Planes a lie, or a gateway?

Or both?

She was ready to uncover the lie. She was ready to find out the truth about Dread.

All she had to do was unfocus her mind. Find the hidden plane behind this one. Magnus had put the answer right in the book.

I have decided to head home. It's time.

She was getting out of here.

Atra sat upright.

No Creepsley.

No Rei.

Nothing left to bind her limbs because there was nothing left of the chair.

She stood in her sleeping quarters.

Start over?

She squinted, the fluorescents buzzing overhead.

Where was Dread?

It no longer shrouded her vision. In fact, there was no darkness at all, not even a shadow behind her. But there *were* other shadows, unlike in the house.

Just not one for her.

The bedspreads had been restored to their former white. Oriens the cat sat on top of them. He jumped off, padding toward the bathroom.

Through the bathroom door, the mirror glinted, whole once more. The red analemma dripped down it.

"It's time to move on." Atra's words startled her. "The Cold Blood Moon approaches."

Time for answers.

She walked into the bathroom, toward the analemma—

—and came out in a hospital room. But not one belonging to the asylum. A young woman lay on a bed, surrounded by monitors.

Beep ... beep ...

A tube was shoved up her nose and taped to her face. Didn't look comfortable, but Atra didn't think the ashen-toned body in the bed was asleep.

Unconscious was putting it lightly. More like dipping dangerously into the territory of deceased.

Beep ... beep ...

But not dead yet.

Atra recognized the orange hair. It had lost most of its lustre, like the skin.

"Lex!" It *was* Lex, but older. Closer to Atra's age. She didn't stir at the sound of her name.

A clipboard hung off the foot of the bed.

DEADMARSH, ALEXIS, the chart clipped to it told her.

Atra's veins turned to ice. She read the last name again, as if doing so would magically change what was written.

Magnus was Lex's dad?

She was suddenly afraid to get any closer.

You've come this far. Don't be a coward. Don't be your father.

Atra didn't notice Lex's eyes crack open.

Green, yet dulled, like the rest of her.

Dying.

The eyes broke Atra's paralyzing fear. This was still the same Lex she'd met in the house. Well, not quite the same because this one was all grown up.

Atra wanted to ask about Magnus, the man who wrote the book on the planes. He'd mentioned her own dad; how did they know each other? Why didn't Lex say anything earlier?

But this wasn't the time for those questions. Atra could feel the passage of time pressing in on this place, trying to squeeze her out.

"Is this real?" she asked instead.

"It is if you allow it."

Typical Lex answer.

"Are you real in the house? Or is this you?"

"I am as real in the house as you are in the asylum."

Atra took that as yes, this was the *real* Lex. This is what she meant by time running out for her.

"What happened to you? How'd you end up like this?"

Lex's eyes were still open, but they stared into nothing. Had she died?

Atra stepped closer, leaning over. She was about to wave a hand over Lex's face when—

"It doesn't matter what happened to me. You're here. I was afraid you wouldn't make it. They're about to let me go."

What? Did she mean put down like an animal abandoned at the pound?

Lex must've seen the fear flash across Atra's face.

"Don't worry. It's what I want. I've been in this bed for years."

Comatose. Not dead, but not living, either.

"Yes," Lex replied, as if reading Atra's thoughts. "It's why I could communicate with you. But I'm going to the Otherside. My time with the living is over."

A lump rose in the back of Atra's throat. Lex had been her guiding light in this mess of insanity.

"Do you need help? Don't you want to live?" Atra asked this for selfish reasons. The idea of being alone here gripped her with panic.

"Don't worry." Lex extended a hand. Atra grabbed it, her fingers grazing the rough tape over the cannula. "You're not alone here. I can help you now."

"Because I made it to the altered planes."

"The one you're looking for is that way." Lex released her, pointing to the bathroom door from where Atra had come.

Atra expected the doorway to be glowing, inviting her, but it remained dark.

"The Tentorum Plane." It wasn't a question.

Lex nodded. "The answers are within. Where the truth no longer lies."

Footfalls approached the room.

Lex smiled.

"My brother."

Coming to say goodbye, Atra finished in her head.

"You can stay if you want," Lex said.

Atra knew it was an empty offer. She shook her head; this was a family affair.

The footsteps grew closer. She left the bedside, running for the bathroom doorway. She didn't want Lex's brother to see her.

Right before the doorway, she paused. She hadn't said goodbye to Lex nor thanked her for ... what? For being there?

She turned, unsure of what to say, but sensed movement in the hallway.

"Hey, Lex." The brother had arrived.

Atra felt a tug. It was the same way Seth used to greet her. *"Hey, Attie."*

You are dead and Seth is dead and we are all dead!

Rei's voice, as she sat on Beryl's bed, ripped her out of the moment. Atra pushed the words aside. She wasn't dead and neither was her brother.

She stepped through the doorway. Her foot plunged through where the floor should be, stomach bottoming out. She grabbed at the doorframe, but her fingers slipped off the smooth painted metal.

She was falling before she could scream.

Chapter 20

The End of the Dream

Atra hit the ground hard. Darkness pressed all around. She pushed herself up, cool tile under her fingers. Where was she?

The blackness swirling reminded her of Dread. Was it? Couldn't be sure.

A woman's voice cut through the misty dark, coming from far away. Atra couldn't make out the words.

The darkness dispersed, revealing vinyl-wrapped cabinets and chipped countertops. She stood in the kitchen of her old house. An archway led to the living room.

And in the archway—

Oh no.

"The police are on their way."

Still, after all these years, she recognized the voice. Her stepmother towered over her like a gigantic spider.

"I didn't do anything!" Atra heard herself reply, felt the words vibrating her throat, but she didn't think to say them.

Because this was a memory.

One she never wanted to relive.

She tried to run. But her feet were cemented to the ground, stuck in the exact position as the first time this happened.

"They'll lock you up for violence against your own stepmother." That awful woman clutched a yellow-handled screwdriver, a grin of malice twisting her face.

"I've never hurt you!" The words flowed from Atra on their own accord. She didn't want to watch this—not again, not her last memory of being in this kitchen, in this house.

"The police will never know that."

Her stepmother raised the screwdriver, positioning it over her leg. Her intense dark eyes never left Atra's. No fear of pain hidden behind them.

Atra had screamed but her stepmother hadn't. The metal shank had dug deeply into the muscle as she pushed it back and forth. The awful satisfaction in her expression that said, *I won,* as the yellow handle stained red with blood.

The room blurred as Atra ran back into the dark cloud—or had the world blurred from her tears? She hastily wiped at them. What *was* this place?

She ran in the direction she came, hoping to emerge in the hospital room.

Thwack!

An immense crack of pain radiated up her shin. She cried out, doubling over from the unexpected agony. She fumbled, still blind, hands grazing a plank of wood.

The mist drifted apart. What horrors would it unveil this time?

A bed.

Her bed.

Not the one from the asylum, but the one she'd burrowed into at night as a kid, hiding from her stepmother, from Dread, from the world.

Something cut through the silence.

A *scritch-scritch* scratching.

She pictured a faceless creature under the bed, never seeing but always running those long fingernails across the planks beneath the mattress.

It was a bed—just a bed!—but the terror that seized her was worse than watching her stepmother stab herself in the leg again.

She fled back into the black mist—

Run, Atra. Run

—not caring where she ended up. The Tentorum Plane was madness. The place she'd been searching for had reduced her to the very thing she'd been staving off her entire life.

A light pierced the darkness.

A doorway.

To Lex's hospital room?

No. The frame wasn't the smooth painted metal of a medical facility.

Atra recognized that damn doorframe, like she'd recognized the kitchen cupboards and the bed. All from her childhood house.

Why was her mind turning this place over, churning memories that best lay buried?

The downstairs bathroom was as she remembered. Seth crouched on the floor in front of the scummy shower curtain, his back to her. A pair of scissors lay on the bathmat behind him, the blades glinting.

Atra's breath caught in her throat. She knew exactly what this memory was. Only she wasn't experiencing this one, because Seth was leaning over to hug a younger version of herself. He was thirteen here and she was nine.

An eye mask lay on the floor behind the kid-version of herself. Atra's face grew hot. She'd forgotten about that mask.

When she was nine, she'd strapped it over her eyes to keep Dread out, but it didn't work. Dread's presence still crushed her over the darkness of the mask. When it became too much, she grabbed the scissors and headed to the bathroom.

She'd leaned over the mirror, scissors trembling in her hand. Out of the corner of her eye, Dread mocked her with its exaggerated movements. But she wouldn't be seeing out of the corner of her eye much longer.

The mask didn't work.

Maybe the scissors would.

Atra brushed her fingers over the faint scar under her eye.

Seth knew she couldn't be left alone. He'd barged into the bathroom at the last second, talking her off the ledge, prying the scissors out of her hands. She struggled while Dread bounced off the walls as if laughing at her.

Then she'd spilled her guts, unable to hold in the crushing secret any longer. She was crazy, she was crazy, nothing could save her …

And he'd hugged her, as he did now, at the end of the memory. Always there for her, always saving her.

"I won't let anything hurt you." He held her tight. "We'll get through this together."

In her small child's voice, between sobs: "Don't tell Mom. Promise me you won't tell her."

Seth had kept his promise, but it didn't matter. Her stepmother had found out. Dread got too big to hide.

Atra stepped closer. She hadn't seen her brother in so long, even before the fire that plunged her world into madness.

But he wasn't there. The two kids were only an illusion. The tiled floor turned back to carpet, the sink now a bed. *That* bed.

Her gaze never left the dark crack as she backed away. She should've hit the wall, but never did. No matter how far she retreated, the bed remained in the corner, never fading.

She tore herself away from it to find herself in the kitchen again. She expected her stepmother to enter the archway, caught in a nightmare loop, but this wasn't the same kitchen from when she was thirteen. Instead of the sparse countertops, this one had dirty dishes stacked by the sink, homework scattered on the table, a cereal box tipped over on the island.

This was before Dad jumped ship.

Bang! Bang! Bang!

Atra flinched.

Bang! Bang! Bang!

A cupboard door slamming shut.

Bang! Bang! Bang!

But none of the cupboards above the counter moved. Where was the noise coming from?

A shuffling from behind the kitchen island. Atra's ears rang in the silence, and then another explosion.

1! 2! 3! 4! 5! 6! 7! 8!

"Atra, what are you doing?" Dad's voice.

The cupboard banged once more—*9!*—as Dad emerged from the living room. He rubbed at his five o'clock shadow, the skin underneath red and crinkled, like it had been crushed into a pillow. Napping, no doubt, after another all-nighter at his mysterious job he never talked about.

Atra stepped toward him, wanting him to acknowledge her.

No, not wanting. *Yearning.* The feeling caught her more off guard than his presence did. *He'd* left *her*, dammit, yet here she was, still seeking his approval, like when she was a kid. Wanting him to see her.

"I have to keep the shadows out!" she heard herself, hidden on the other side of the island, say. Her voice was so small; she couldn't have been more than five.

Dad ducked behind the counter, both of them out of sight. But not before Atra caught the terror that flashed across his face.

"What are you talking about, kiddo?"

But he *knew*. That was the worst part.

The cupboard banged open and shut—*1! 2! 3!*—then stopped abruptly.

Dad must've grabbed her arm, because she heard herself shriek, "I have to do it nine times! To keep the shadows out. To keep the world safe!"

Atra didn't remember this.

"We can create it."

A third voice, not hers or her dad's, reverberated from everywhere.

"Then what?" Dad's voice replied, but it didn't come from behind the island.

A flash, like a negative image of a photograph, of two figures in shadow. They stood in a concrete room. The word "bunker" sprang to mind.

Was one of the figures her dad?

"From ... your shadow ..." The other voice crackled.

The kitchen, the voices, disappeared as the bedroom once again took its place. Atra turned to run, but a bed occupied that corner of the room too.

No escape. It was time to face whatever she'd seen all those years ago and suppressed. This place wouldn't stop calling her back.

She clenched her jaw, warding off the fear gnawing at her stomach. The walls grew taller, looming over her—or was she getting shorter? She held her hands out—they were too small, not the hands she was used to. She was nine again, the bed stretching out in front of her, comically oversized.

She crouched in front of the gap, holding her breath, waiting for a pair of long-nailed fingers to dart out and grab her ankles.

But it didn't happen. Because there was nothing here at all.

Her breath rushed out, a nervous laugh trying to escape with it.

Empty.

Wait ...

Her vision adjusted to the darkness. A lump, in the far bottom corner.

It stirred.

She tried jerking away but was locked into place by an invisible hand.

The lump drew closer. Was it crawling?

She strained against the hand, but it pressed her harder, closer to the ground, closer to the crack, closer to the *thing* drawing near.

No escape. No escape.

Because she remembered now, she *remembered*.

The thing beneath the bed was wearing her face.

Atra's mouth opened, a scream tearing through her, but she couldn't feel it, couldn't hear it, because she remembered, yes, the thing hiding all along was her.

Dread appeared after this because she'd awoken it. By looking under here and finding herself.

She was Dread.

I am Dread and Dread is dead.

The thing pulled itself forward. Its face twisted into a grin—her own face, but not quite right, not quite her—as the glinting whites of its eyes locked onto her own.

The darkness closed in, but this time the shadow was Dread, coming to bind them, her and the doppelgänger beneath the bed—one and the same—together forever.

Her shadow-self lunged for her. If it caught her, it would never let go, but she still couldn't move—

The darkness parted.

She no longer kneeled on the carpet. Instead, her palms were splayed out on cold concrete. From the bunker that had flashed before. She was inside it.

She stood, not sure if her legs would support her. Lex was right. She couldn't destroy Dread, because she *was* Dread.

But what was this place? Her feet shuffled against the concrete, skin prickling with goosebumps. She hugged herself, the damp cold chilling her to the bone.

Polaris.

That was the answer, whatever it meant.

This was no memory of hers. It belonged to one of the two figures standing in the corner, speaking in low murmurs.

"Imagine, reliving an experience you didn't know you had," Pepe had told her so long ago, while they played chess.

One of the figures was her dad. He hunched over a lab bench, his sloppy clothes a stark juxtaposition to the other man in his plum-coloured suit.

"We can create it," the polished man said. "An aperture to the Otherside, created from your shadow DNA. The last Cynosura Experiment."

Atra's footsteps echoed off the walls as she approached, but the two men didn't react.

A deep crease formed between Dad's brows. She'd never seen his face so young.

"Then what? You're talking about creating a human being. This isn't some lab animal you can leave in a cage, Glasser. Is one of us expected to take care of it?"

"Yes," the other person—Glasser—said. "It will be worth it. We'll do something no one has done before. Send a living being to the Otherside." The gleam in his eyes reminded Atra of those delusional patients lost in their own beliefs. "Imagine it. A being who can fully exist on both sides. If we manage it, maybe we can understand how to do it to ourselves. Forever conquer death.

"We'll create a vessel containing all three components—body, soul, and ulma. The shadow. The component humans lack. The third part that can traverse planes and dimensions. *Cross over* to the Otherside. A test subject that is both alive *and* dead."

Dad seemed troubled, but the gleam in Glasser's eyes had sparked something in his own. "Okay. But we get a whisper something is going sideways and we pull the plug. We don't get attached."

"Our own artificial transcendental aperture." Glasser grinned.

Dad nodded, the spark catching light. He spoke his next word softly.

"Atra."

Part Four

Cold Blood Moon

Chapter 21

Queen of the Night

December 14
Eve of the Vanishing Plains Fire

Something burrowed into Ophelia's eyeball. She leaned in closer to her bathroom mirror, pulling up her eyelid, but saw nothing. The sensation had started an hour ago as she drove to Charles Family Pharmacy to pay Evie a visit.

To make sure the jar spell worked.

"Oh, Evie," she had muttered, parking across the street. "How am I going to fix your mess now?"

The block was quiet. Ophelia glanced at the time on the dashboard.

5:02 p.m.

The pharmacy's storefront windows spilled light onto the empty sidewalk, despite the *CLOSED* sign in the window. But Ophelia could sense Evie still inside.

The deadbolt lock on the door might as well have been a twig, snapping in two as Ophelia barged into the store.

A burning wave rippled through her eyes as they adjusted to the overhead lights. She rubbed at them, trying to clear her vision.

The same calm eeriness out on the street lingered in here. Her boots clacked across the worn linoleum as she walked to the back counter in search of Evie. This place smelled old, washed up. Like its owner.

No one back here. Ophelia stopped. Listened. Felt.

Fear. Confusion.

Was Evie hiding?

Ophelia went around the back counter toward the staff room. She followed the trail of emotions to the closed bathroom door. Evie sniffled behind it. Crying? Not quite, but almost.

This door gave less resistance than the one out front. Evie cried out in a mixture of pain and surprise as Ophelia grabbed her, slamming her against the wall.

"Hello, Evelien." Ophelia's jaw clenched as her hands dug into the fabric of Evie's winter coat. "Thought I'd check in. Make sure we're still on track."

"Ophelia, please," Evie choked out. "Think about what you're doing."

Ophelia's eyes danced over Evie's terrified face, then up to the hood covering her head.

"Ophelia, the Queen is something evil you're letting in—"

She cut Evie off with a hard slap to the face. Evie's eyelids fluttered in surprise, tongue darting out to examine the split at the corner of her lip.

"The Queen didn't pick you. Understand?" Ophelia's voice dripped poison.

Evie nodded.

"I own you." Ophelia let go of the coat.

She yanked back the hood, revealing what had left Evie so disturbed. Patches of Evie's skin were visible under her thinning crown of hair.

The jar spell had worked.

"You made a mistake trying to defy me. Your hair is just the beginning if you don't go to that asylum tomorrow morning and extract Atra." Her voice hitched, saying the girl's name aloud. "Deliver her to me. Don't be late."

Evie nodded, her newly-revealed scalp shining in the light.

Ophelia smacked her cheek almost playfully. The skin under her fingers was too warm, too spongy.

Too human.

"We're in this together, Evelien. Never forget that."

Ophelia was ripped out of the memory by a searing sensation in her eyes. The mirror revealed burst blood vessels blooming, smattering the whites like drops of red ink. Between the inflamed veins, something worked its way to the surface. Not burrowing in as she first thought, but rather crawling out. It reminded her of a worm.

No—not a worm. More like the end of a rat's lashing tail.

Her eyelids quivered under her pinched fingers, desperate to close, to blink away the foreign object. Instead, Ophelia brought her free hand up, lightly touching the tip of whatever was jutting from her eyeball.

Hard. Bristly. She managed to pinch it between the long nails of her thumb and index finger, giving it a tug.

She pulled.

And pulled.

And pulled.

Her vision blurred, tears springing forth, begging her to stop.

Finally, the searing pain abated. She blinked rapidly, wiping the tears away to see what she'd removed.

A single hair.

Not hers. Hers was dark red and too heavy to be confined in its usual twist because it had grown so long now. This hair was blond, short. Exactly like the hair Chuck found on that jacket.

Exactly like the burned remains of the hair in that mason jar.

Exactly like the hair falling out of Evie's head.

The echo responds to the call.

What she put out into the world would eventually come back full circle.

She examined her eye, now swelling out of its socket. Behind the inflamed sclera, more hairs. Swirling, circling, making their way to the surface. An entire head of them.

Ophelia ran into the greenhouse with the mason jar. Unscrewed the lid. Dumped the dirt back into the hole. But it wasn't enough, because she couldn't take the hair back.

She rubbed furiously at her eyes. Nothing stopped the burning. The hairs would continue to swirl within until every last one fell out of Evie's head. Ophelia would end up gouging out her eyeballs before that happened.

I take it back, please; there has to be a way …

She smoothed the dirt into the hole, contaminated with the single hair now reduced beyond ash. Going to the door, she grabbed a set of pruning shears off a hook.

Which herb, which plant, which flower would help her out of this predicament?

She knelt in front of her greenery. The shears slipped out of her grip.

Concentrate, Ophelia.

But she couldn't, not with these damn hairs swimming in her eyeballs.

She bit back a scream of agony, heart beating like a hammer.

Wait. That wasn't her heart. The noise came from beyond the greenhouse walls.

Footsteps. Running.

She recognized the lumbering footfalls.

Chuck *O'Flennek*, Detective Extraordinaire.

Fuck. Did he get a search warrant already?

Don't panic. There was nothing for him to find, as long as he didn't go digging around the cypress tree. Technically, it was on the neighbouring farmland, but Chuck wasn't a technical kind of guy ...

Forget the search warrant. Why wasn't he driving? What was he doing, travelling out to the sticks on foot?

Ophelia cocked her head. Something had changed. His foul stench was different from the one lurking outside her front door this morning.

She looked at the mound of dirt, the empty jar beside it. She hadn't just been thinking about Evie when she'd burned the hair. She'd been thinking about Chuck too. He was entwined in this mess with them. All that anger she'd directed at the jar—

Chuck wasn't here with a search warrant. She sensed the intent on him.

He was here to kill her.

She couldn't fight him, not in this state. Time to get out of here. Now.

She hightailed it back into her house. Was there time to grab her car keys and drive away before—

The front door banged open.

Chuck stood there, hunched over. His eyes blazed as sweat poured down his face in rivulets. He was being driven by primal emotions.

Exactly like her.

The echo responding to the call.

He exhaled loudly, nostrils flaring. He charged like a mad bull, letting out an incoherent yell.

Ophelia flew through her kitchen, watching as the back door drew closer.

She greyed out as the top half of her body shattered the window. Her world was nothing but hot pain as the glass shredded her neck and back into ribbons.

Chuck barrelled through the kitchen, fixated on her. She

curled into a ball, ignoring the screaming of her torn skin, rolling between his legs as he approached. The air above her *whooshed!* as Chuck's hands clapped together where her head had been. He lost his balance, falling over.

He let out another yell, this one confused. Ophelia scrambled to her feet, bolting back inside the living room. Her car keys sat on the glass-top coffee table. She had to grab them, had to get out of the house, had to get into the car …

Shit, why hadn't she taken a knife from the kitchen to defend herself? Why didn't she bring those fucking gardening shears inside with—

A sweaty hand clamped around her ankle. She went down, face-first. A suffocating numbness spread across her face as her nose smashed into the carpet.

Broken? Who cared.

She twisted around. Chuck's grip on her leg tightened as he climbed forward, pinning her to the ground. She beat her fists against his chest but she might as well have been beating a slab of concrete.

Why was she so fucking weak? For a split second, it was twenty-eight years ago, and it wasn't Chuck trying to kill her. It was her ex-husband. It was Lyall.

She shook off the notion, snaking her hand up to Chuck's face. She gripped the back of his head as she plunged her thumbnail into his eye. It gave way like a popped grape.

Chuck's neck snapped back as he howled in pain, forgetting about her as he clasped a palm over his eye socket. She shuffled out from underneath him, clambering to her feet.

The car keys.

She almost grabbed them but stopped. It didn't matter if she drove away; he'd follow, he wouldn't stop. Like Lyall. She could run but she couldn't hide.

A horrible sensation ripped through her, of being in two places at once: here, and the night her ex nearly killed her.

She was weak then. So weak.

But now she had The Drove. And her Queen. And her strength.

She was not that helpless woman anymore.

Instead of grabbing the car keys, she grabbed the sides of the coffee table. With a primal cry that put Chuck's to shame, she lifted the table above her head.

Chuck stood, crimson pouring between the gaps of his fingers over his face.

She brought the coffee table down on his sweaty head. The glass top shattered as he collapsed under it. Tossing it aside, she seized a broken shard and plunged it into the front of his soft neck.

Ophelia stood, catching sight of herself in the mirror above the mantel. She drew a breath through her chattering teeth, eyes wide, bright, standing out against the red splattered over her face and body. She didn't know which blood was hers and which was Chuck's as he gurgled at her feet.

Dead.

Gone.

Like her piece-of-shit ex.

She had won. Again.

But her work wasn't done. The body had to go. And the Queen had to be fed.

Perhaps the echo had turned in her favour, Ophelia mused as she rolled Chuck up in the living room rug, beginning the slow and exhausting process of dragging him out of the house and to the cypress tree.

The adrenaline surge had worn off, leaving her spent. The gashes across her back pulsed fresh blood. She needed medical attention, but that wasn't an option.

She dropped the body next to the tree, marching back to get a shovel from the greenhouse. Keep going, keep marching. If she stopped, she'd never start again.

She speared the shovel into the earth. The ground offered no resistance. The circle of snow had melted almost to her house, the cypress tree at the epicentre.

She dug the grave, the hole never getting any deeper, any wider. Her arms trembled, her back on fire. She was reliving the night she'd killed Lyall, digging his grave all over again.

She'd killed him in self-defence too. At least, that's what she'd told herself. After a shattered elbow and broken cheekbone, it was damned well time she defended herself.

She could've maimed him, grabbed her son and run, but the years of suffering through his abuse overcame her.

She'd vomited after the deed was done, standing in her kitchen over a puddle of his blood and her puke, her infant son screaming from his crib down the hall.

She didn't know what to do. She should have called the cops, but he was their mayor; they wouldn't believe her. But maybe they would have. Maybe if she'd called, her life would have taken a less gruesome path. There would be no Queen, no Atra, no digging another hole for yet another body.

Instead, she'd called Evie, who'd handed her a pamphlet for The Drove months earlier. Ophelia had buried it inside a cookbook where Lyall would never find it.

The line rang and rang and rang. All the while her son screamed from his crib, and she couldn't comfort him, not like this ...

"Hello?"

Just as she was about to hang up.

She'd broken into tears. Told Evie she didn't know what to do.

Evie came with two others. They helped bury the body in the back garden. Scrubbed the house. Cleaned her up.

When she asked why they buried the body so close, Evie said it was so she remembered what she had done.

It meant she was one of them. Her blood was on their hands.

Lyall might be gone, but she was The Drove's now. And then she became The Drove. And then she had become the Queen's.

Would she ever just be herself?

No, the answer was certain. The grave beneath the cypress tree was becoming wide enough, deep enough, as the sky lightened on the prairie's horizon.

She and the Queen would become one, forever trapped as two. And where was Evie?

Ophelia couldn't afford to deplete the energy she didn't have, but she reached out. She had to make sure Evie was doing her job.

Evie was sitting inside her van. She'd tied a blue bandana around her balding head. A great sob escaped her as she leaned over the GPS mounted to the console.

Vanishing Plains Psychiatric Hospital, she programmed into it.

Sitting upright, she gripped the steering wheel, jaw set. A great bubble of snot popped out of her nostril.

Her van rattled down the freeway toward Vanishing Plains.

Still on the right path.

Good girl, Evie, Ophelia thought, as if she were training a stupid dog.

Grabbing the corner of the rug, she tugged it toward the hole, then stopped. Unrolled it. Took the gun out of Chuck's holster. Might come in handy.

She hesitated. The gifts were only as good as the men were angry in the end. And Chuck was angry, all right, but he'd also been under the effect of her jar spell. Would that contaminate the gift, taint her connection to the Queen?

Too late to second-guess anything. If she didn't feed the Queen, she'd die.

Into the grave the body went, every inch of her on fire.

"Here, take it!" she screamed, at the Queen as the body thudded to the ground. "Have your precious gift!"

The trunk of the skeletal cypress tree burst into light. She shielded her eyes, the after-image scarring her retinas. The blinding whiteness bolted up the tree like a lightning strike, branching across the sky.

There was her answer about the jar spell.

Her connection with the Queen surged so intensely she thought she'd faint, every sense thrust into overdrive.

A tremendous cracking echo rattled her bones. She shrank away, protecting her head with her hands, thinking the tree had split in two, overwhelmed by the deluge of energy.

But it wasn't the tree. It was the sky. Lowering her hand, she watched as an unnatural purple rift shimmered above like a mirage, polluting the dawn.

What had she done?

Back in the house. Scrubbing, cleaning, bleaching. No one to help her this time. She had to move fast. Evie would be delivering Atra at any moment.

Though she couldn't see it, Ophelia could feel the rift in the sky through her roof. The unnatural break between worlds, an extension of the cypress tree.

After she finished cleaning and burning her clothes, she stepped into the shower, letting the final remnants of her crime wash down the drain. Every water droplet pelted her as if it were sand. The water too hot, too cold, no in-between. The unnatural gift from Chuck granted her more strength than her body could handle.

The lacerations across her back and neck stitched themselves together, the smooth flesh unscarred. The only things that didn't heal were her eyes. She was still pulling hairs out of them.

After she put on fresh clothes, she combed the house, making sure every drop of blood, every fingerprint, every shard of glass had been wiped away.

The busted window in the kitchen might draw suspicion. She grabbed a trash bag from under the sink to tape it over when a voice spoke from behind her.

"Mom?"

The fire in her veins crystallized. Her heart churned in her ears as she fought to stay conscious.

She didn't hear the door open, nor the footsteps approach. She didn't *sense* anyone behind her, in any way, shape, or form. But the voice. She'd recognize the voice to her grave.

"Mom? Are you okay?"

Breathe, she told herself.

Stand.

Turn and face him.

An internal battle raged inside her, torn between sheer terror and running to throw her arms around him.

Her son stood in the archway of the living room, just as Chuck had, fully grown into a young man. But that was impossible, because he'd passed away at seventeen. His ashes sat on the mantel behind him.

Finally, she managed to stammer out his name, the word like a knife puncturing her lung.

"Seth?"

He stepped closer. It took everything in her not to shrink away.

"How ... what are you doing here?"

Crazy. The cypress tree had made her crazy. This wasn't happening. Seth was dead.

"Sorry for coming unannounced, but there's something you need to know." His voice cracked, choked up and thick. "There was a fire this morning. At Vanishing Plains. When I was on my way to visit."

Seth wiped a tear from the corner of his eye.

"Mom—what if Atra didn't make it out? What if my sister is dead?"

Chapter 22

A Place for My Head

The concrete bunker gave way under Atra's feet as the Tentorum Plane dissolved. Her stomach lurched as she fell. Looking down, she saw herself still in Vanishing Planes, strapped to that chair. Rei and Creepsley hovered over her, ready to lobotomize her.

Her world tipped upside down, then ...

She crash-landed back into the asylum. Back into the chair.

Her eyes focused on the ice pick poised between them. She moved her head aside, unable to execute the motion. The leather strap pinned her forehead in place.

The lie is quicker than the mind.

Creepsley brought the ice pick down.

She *could* move her head, though. Because there was no strap. There was no chair. There was no asylum.

It had burned to the ground. Its ghost now trapped her, haunting her memory.

Creepsley hammered the ice pick into the leather cushion instead of into Atra's eye socket. She tried to push him out of the way, but her limbs were fastened into place.

No—they weren't. Like her head wasn't.

She raised her leg, kicking at Creepsley, using every ounce of her pent-up aggression at him, at Rei, at her stepmother for throwing her in this place, at her father for creating her in the first place.

She caught Creepsley square in the stomach, causing him to fall over with an *oof!*

Movement, out of the corner of her eye. Harmonica Mouth.

Atra lunged for the metal tray beside her. Rei beat her to it, snapping up a scalpel.

Atra's hand clamped around Rei's wrist. Rei's face contorted as she struggled to bring the scalpel down. Their eyes locked.

One of them wasn't getting out of here alive and they both knew it.

"You're not real," Atra said, through clenched teeth.

Confused realization crossed Rei's features.

It was all Atra needed to bend the scalpel toward Rei's face and bury it in her forehead.

The blade glided effortlessly through Rei as if she were made of smoke. Her eyes drooped as the skin around the scalpel turned grey. The mouth that housed her horrible grin melted away, and the scalpel clattered to the floor as Rei dissipated into nothing.

Because like the chair, like the straps, Rei was never here.

Atra hopped off the chair. She still had Creepsley to deal with.

Bending over, she picked the scalpel off the floor, a wave of calm washing over her.

This place wasn't real. Nothing here could hurt her if she didn't let it.

The lie is quicker than the mind.

Finally, she understood what Lex meant.

Creepsley got back to his feet, crouching low in the doorway with his arms out. He didn't notice the scalpel in her hand.

She burrowed the scalpel into his thigh. But unlike when she stabbed Rei, she met resistance. A warm stickiness coated Atra's hand as Creepsley shrieked.

She let go of the scalpel, but it remained upright, wedged between the muscles in Creepsley's thigh. The sight was too similar to the screwdriver that had burrowed into her stepmother's leg.

Atra's world tipped sideways as a blast of pain radiated through her skull. Creepsley's blow sent her crashing into the rolling cart. The back of her head clicked against the floor.

She pushed herself onto her elbows, only to collapse again as the world dimmed.

Don't you dare pass out. Not after all this.

Gritting her teeth, she lifted herself up. She sensed Creepsley behind her, getting over his own shock, closing in.

She grabbed the sides of the aluminum rolling cart, tossing it at Creepsley. It grazed the side of his hip as he jumped out of the way. His foot landed in the puddle of his own blood and he slipped, temple smashing against the doorframe.

Atra darted past him before he had a chance to recover.

Her ringing headache intensified. A pressure built behind her eyes with every step she took down the hall.

Why didn't Creepsley disappear like Rei? He could still harm her. He could kill her if he wanted.

And Atra had a feeling he did.

She glanced over her shoulder at the empty hallway. Maybe she should go back and kill him first.

Nausea bubbled in her stomach from the familiar stench of the asylum but it was ... *different.* A recreation, almost ... but not quite. The place looked fake, sounded fake, felt fake. A copy. The Tentorum Plane had changed her perception. They didn't call them the altered planes for nothing.

She burst through the morgue-like doors at the end of the hall, stopping dead in her tracks when she got to her sleeping quarters. Standing between the two beds was Beryl.

"You're alive," Atra stammered.

"No more alive than I've been before," Beryl responded cryptically.

"That seems like something Lex would say."

Although Beryl didn't know about Lex, she replied, "It does, doesn't it?"

"I thought Creepsley took you away, and—" Atra broke off. "That wasn't real, was it?" She didn't know if she was talking to herself or to Beryl. "None of it was. I was the only one here."

"Trapped in your own head." Beryl tapped her own. "The mind's way of coping. But now that you know the truth, you don't need this place."

"Lex said this was the gateway to the planes."

Time to get to the mirror over the bathroom sink. Time to get out of this asylum for good.

"Come with me," Atra said. "Please, come with me and be saved—"

But Beryl shook her head.

If the asylum was an illusion, that meant Beryl was too.

There *had* been a fire, and Beryl *had* probably perished in it, but that *wasn't Atra's fault*.

She wasn't speaking to Beryl. She was speaking to herself. Everything in here, every person she'd come across, was a part of her, distorted and extrapolated.

The loud bang of the morgue doors shocked Atra out of her revelation.

She was wrong. One thing in here wasn't part of her.

"Creepsley."

"I'll hold him off." Beryl strode past her.

That was it. No goodbye as Atra sprinted for the bathroom. As soon as she stepped through the doorway her stomach bottomed out like she'd missed a step.

The warping around the mirror frame had spread, the walls and floors rippling against angles that shouldn't exist. Over the sink, the crack in the plywood twisted in on itself.

Her escape.

She reached for the fire poker still lying on the floor, only the floor was now halfway up the wall. She grabbed a fistful of air instead, the room spinning.

Closing her eyes, she fumbled around until her fingers grazed the metal. She gripped it, bracing herself against the wall as she tried to orient herself.

She attempted to stab the poker through the fracture in the plywood but instead stumbled into the edge of the sink.

The lie is quicker than the mind.

Atra didn't have to aim where her eyes told her to, because everything they told her was a lie.

The poker wedged itself into the crack. Atra pushed down with all her might, the plywood squeaking under the strain.

The crack split open. She stumbled forward, holding her hands out to brace against the sink.

It was no longer there.

In fact, the entire wall was gone, peeled away to reveal the house underneath.

Footsteps squeaked on the linoleum behind her.

Beryl could only hold Creepsley off for so long.

The house's shadowless living room, bathed in the warm light of the fireplace, called to her.

She leapt toward it. For a moment—no longer than a split second but it felt like an eternity—she was weightless, part of both realities. The air surged behind her. Turning to look over her shoulder, she saw Creepsley charging forward, reaching for her. She raised the poker, whacking his arm aside. The metal made a satisfying *thunk!* as it smacked into his wrist bone.

She tumbled into the house, landing hard on the floor. The gap in the wall closed, trapping Creepsley behind it, as she left Vanishing Planes for good.

Chapter 23

When Things Are Said

Atra slipped on the hardwood floor as she tumbled out of the other side of the mirror. Staggering to her feet, she knocked over the stand holding the fireplace tools. She still clutched its missing fire poker in her hand.

She pounded her fist against the wall beside the crackling fireplace.

Solid.

But something wasn't right. Her hand should've been bandaged. Instead, it was unmarred. Brushing her uninjured hand over her collarbone, she grazed smooth skin instead of puckering stitches. She stomped a foot on the floor.

Real.

Atra ran for the kitchen before remembering the walls had swallowed its door out of here.

No matter. She'd smash through, just as she'd smashed her way out of the asylum. Raising the poker, she slammed it against the wood where the door should've been. Instead of denting, the walls rippled out, deflecting the blows.

She may be done with the house, but the house wasn't done with her.

Those familiar claws of panic threatened to close around her throat. She wouldn't let them this time.

"Lex!" she called out, turning away from the unyielding wall. "Where are you?"

If the house wasn't done with her, that must mean Lex wasn't either. At least, she hoped so.

"Lex!" Atra's voice faltered, as she doubled back to the living room. The claws worked their way around her neck. What if Lex *was* gone? How would she get out of here?

But another set of thoughts crept in too.

You're fake.

You're a medical experiment.

"We're not playing games anymore!" she screamed, trying to shove the thoughts out, not ready to process what she'd learned in the Tentorum Plane.

The thoughts shoved right back.

You're not human.

You shouldn't exist.

Something brushed against her ankle. She gasped.

It was that fucking cat, weaving himself between her legs. He trotted through the living room, black tail with its orange tip bolt upright.

Atra followed. Oriens turned a corner, taking them to a part of the house she hadn't visited yet. Thick carpet cushioned her footsteps as she entered an infinitely long hall. Photographs covered the walls, rows upon rows, stretching up to the high-vaulted ceiling.

She trailed Oriens down the hall at not quite a run.

"Lex!"

The people in the photographs stared as she passed them. Endless faces, so many lives intertwined, forgotten.

"I want some answers!"

The hall ended abruptly.

The house had listened. An open door stood in front of her, the room beyond it dark, filled with wavering candlelight.

Inside, a long dining table with a candelabra in the centre. Oriens leapt up, slinking across the mahogany top and stopping in front of the person seated at the other end.

Lex, all grown up, like in the hospital bed.

"You're not dead?" Atra wasn't sure if it was a question or a statement.

"Not yet." Lex's voice cracked.

She appeared worse off than before. Her skin had a green hue to it, the lines in her face exaggerated by the shadows of the candlelight.

The shadows! When had they returned? Atra did a sweep for Dread, curious what form it would possess, but it was too dark in here to tell.

Speaking of Dread ...

"I found the planes." Atra's voice shook. "You said I'd get answers there. The truth. But I still don't know what's going on. Your dad—Magnus—how is he connected to this? How does he know my dad? How do you know me?"

Lex let out a sigh, gesturing Atra over.

"I don't have much time. It will be faster this way."

She extended her hands. They were green, like her face. Atra hesitated. She didn't want to touch them.

"You wanted answers."

Atra nodded, placing the poker on the table and lightly brushing her fingertips against Lex's palms. They were clammy, the texture of something left underwater too long. She shuddered as Lex enveloped her fingers with her own.

A corpse, I'm being touched by a corpse.

It took everything Atra had not to pull away.

"*Close your eyes.*"

But Lex didn't speak. The voice came from inside Atra's head. This time, Atra did jerk away, but Lex's grip tightened. Their hands locked as a shock coursed through her. She knew before it happened that they were going to the altered planes, and please no, she didn't want to go back, never again, but she couldn't twist out of Lex's hands because neither of them had hands anymore.

"*We have to go back to the beginning,*" Lex told her, through a mouth that didn't exist.

To the Tentorum Plane again, but this time it was different. Atra could still feel herself standing in the musty house as she and Lex moved along. How were they moving? Not having a body in this plane meant having no perspective.

They passed through a hatch door, going underground, deeper than she thought possible.

Atra wanted to say she'd never been here before, but something told her otherwise.

Imagine reliving memories you didn't know you had.

Concrete walls closed in on all sides, reminding her how far away the surface was.

"*Becopra.*" Was it she or Lex that thought it?

Somewhere in this place was a room with a lab bench, where her dad and a scientist decided to create her.

"*This is Polaris. This is where my dad worked, isn't it?*" Atra asked.

"*Yes. This is where the first weak spot formed. Because of him.*"

Tom lying on a cot, screaming as someone administered a shot into his arm, flashed across Atra's eyes. It didn't make sense, and yet it did.

Lex came to a halt as they entered a room. Did they pass through a doorway or float through the walls?

"*They were searching for other planes of existence when they found the Otherside.*"

In the centre of the room was a pulsing light, suspended by nothing. Atra knew this was the same light she'd witnessed flood through the rift. The light of another world.

The Otherside lay beyond, tantalizingly within reach.

"*They should have left it alone,*" Lex finished.

The portal mesmerized Atra. It pulsed brighter, the area surrounding it warping in the same way as the mirror frame in the asylum had.

"*The portal was a two-way looking glass.*" Lex's voice—thoughts?—snapped Atra back to the matter at hand. "*Becopra wasn't the only one trying to get into another world.*"

An image of a silhouette stalking a dark corridor, wearing a crown that resembled horns, came to Atra's mind.

"*The Queen.*"

"*Yes. Becopra woke her. My father—Magnus—learned the truth about her because he worked for Polaris, too.*"

"*But no one listened to him,*" Atra deduced, "*because they were too busy with me.*"

"*Yes. Magnus tried to face the Queen himself. He thought if he found the Tentorum Plane, he could overpower her there. He had to do it on the solstice. When the worlds are closest. But Becopra closed the portal early, and my father failed.*"

The light drawing Atra in flared. Before she had a chance to shrink away, it flooded the room, enveloping them.

"*Closing the portal ended in catastrophe,*" Lex said.

Atra could feel it, beyond the light; death everywhere.

"*Lex?*" Because she saw something else in the light as well. "*Was I there?*"

No answer.

They floated through the light, weightless, untethered. Leaving Polaris. Another presence attached to her. Magnus. Atra was following the path his soul had taken to the Tentorum Plane.

She couldn't handle the influx of emotions that weren't hers. She yanked her hands out of Lex's grip. No more; she didn't want to experience anymore.

She swallowed back her nausea, holding a shaking hand up to her clammy forehead.

Lex slumped over in her chair, supported only by the armrest. Atra grabbed her shoulders and sat her upright.

"Lex?" Atra gave her a shake.

Lex's eyelids fluttered, her eyes not coming back into focus. The light behind them had nearly faded.

"You understand, don't you?" Her voice scraped against sandpaper as she struggled to draw a breath.

Atra nodded, blinking back tears. Because during her last moments in the Tentorum Plane, she knew what Magnus knew. She felt what he felt, the magnitude of terror, the clawing desperation.

"His soul passed through the Tentorum Plane as it left his body," Lex said. "Only for a moment, but enough to leave an impression. Enough for another soul to find the planes and become aware of the Queen."

"That other soul was you," Atra whispered.

"I've been in a coma for years. My mind is between life and death. I heard the echo my father left in the planes. I learned about the Queen myself.

"But now she had more sinister plans. She's been lying in wait, building her power. She is going to break through a weak spot and infest a human willing to become her host. If she succeeds, she'll traverse between the worlds and feast off the souls of the living. But they need a final piece to bind them together. A living ulma."

"Me," Atra whispered. "Because I'm a medical experiment."

A *mew!* from behind as Oriens came waltzing across the table. He leapt into Lex's lap, his orange-tipped fur blending in seamlessly with the ends of Lex's hair. The two of them stared at Atra with identical green eyes.

"I knew the only way to overpower the Queen was if I got to you first," Lex continued. "Being comatose meant I couldn't communicate through normal means. I found ways to manipulate the world of the living." She gestured to the cat in her lap. "I could keep tabs on the Queen's host. I could guide you to where I needed you to go."

Atra recalled the first time she'd seen Oriens, in an ash-filled hallway of the asylum. Without the cat, she would've never escaped the burning building.

"The fire at the asylum wasn't an accident, was it?"

Lex licked her dry lips, giving a half-nod.

"Since you and I are closer to death, our minds are drawn to weak spots, like this house. Where it would be easier for me to guide you into the planes."

"But why did I have to find the planes? Why couldn't you have told me this when we met?"

"You had to discover the Tentorum Plane yourself." Lex's words grew fainter. Atra leaned in closer to understand. "Just as I needed to find it to hear my father's echo, you needed to find it to hear mine."

She clutched Atra's wrist, as if fighting to stay alive.

"You may not want to, but Dread will go instinctively toward the Queen, as a flower opens to the sun."

"Because Dread can simultaneously exist in both life and death."

"Yes. Your mind couldn't cope with the dichotomy. It fractured, creating Dread as a manifestation of the part of you that belongs to death. But now that you've faced the truth, you can control Dread. Keep the Queen out. You didn't begin this war, but you will end it. Whether you want to or not." Her next words were so quiet Atra barely understood them, "It's up to us to finish what our fathers started."

Lex's head dropped to her chest as her body slumped in the chair. Oriens vanished from her lap. Atra knelt and grabbed her to make sure she didn't fall.

Lex had stopped breathing.

Atra heard how people who were dead looked peaceful, asleep. Whoever said that was full of shit.

Lex looked like she'd died before finishing what she set out to do.

Atra eased her back into the chair, then stood back up. What to do about the body?

Lex wasn't here, though, not really. Her body was in the hospital with her brother beside her. She was a projection in this house. This was her lie, like the asylum was Atra's.

But Atra was done with the asylum. She was no longer a frightened psych patient, clinging to faint hopes of a life that might never happen.

You're fake.

The voice returned.

You shouldn't exist.

"But I *do*." She silenced the voice, gritting her teeth. Now, it was up to her to get to the rift and stop the Queen.

But before she could do any of that, she had to find her way out of here.

Chapter 24

Digitalis

"This is fucking great, isn't it?"

Tom's swollen temple throbbed as he examined his wrist, zip-tied to the metal pole above his head. Getting pistol-whipped really did a number on you.

Glasser, across the greenhouse, mirrored his position.

The esteemed doctor's face had puffed up like the almost-full moon in the sky. A film of sweat clung to it. In short, he looked like shit.

Behind him, an array of bright, bell-shaped flowers blossomed. Life among death. Tom was impressed they were growing in the heart of winter.

Of course, his psychotic ex would be capable of such a feat. She knew how to make something suffer long after it was dead inside. Tom had firsthand experience.

And where did Ophelia go?

After she'd zip-tied them to her greenhouse of horrors, she disappeared. Into her hippie hideout? Unsure. She hadn't said much, looking distraught, frazzled, insane.

By comparison, Naomi was a breath of fucking fresh air.

"You have to understand I didn't mean for this to happen."

Glasser's words sounded like they were being dragged through gravel.

"Oh yeah?" Tom sneered. "And what did you mean to have happen? Because it looks to me like you're in collusion with my ex."

"If that were the case, I wouldn't be tied up with you." The undertone of Glasser's statement clearly said, *Use your fucking brain, Tom.*

"Do you want to tell me *why* she was at our motel?"

"Ophelia thought I had Atra."

"You son of a bitch." It slipped out before Tom could stop himself. "You said you weren't bringing Atra into this."

"Shut up and listen. I don't know how long we have until Ophelia comes back."

Tom clenched his teeth. That officially marked the first time Glasser sounded genuine about anything.

"I was trying to keep Atra out of this. I knew the rift was going to form before it did. There was unusual seismic activity between the worlds. When I went to track down its point of origin, I found your ex-wife.

"Ophelia means to open another portal. Merge her consciousness with a creature from the Otherside. But she needs a living ulma to do so."

Tom's stomach plummeted.

"You mean ..."

"Yes. Atra. I had to get her out of Vanishing Plains before Ophelia got to her. I would have done it myself, but I had my hands tied with you."

"So, who got her?" Tom wasn't sure he wanted to know the answer.

"When my body started to fail, I enlisted test subjects. People needing to pay bills, unbury themselves from debt, I didn't care."

"Sounds familiar."

Glasser cracked a dry smile.

"I paid one of them to disguise himself as a doctor to get Atra out of the mental institution. We were all to meet at the motel."

"Who the hell is this guy?"

Glasser shrugged. "The only name he gave was Creeley."

Tom's eyes twitched, as if something was clamping onto his optic nerves. "Now my daughter is at the mercy of some low-life who would kidnap a psych patient for *money*? Where the hell did he take her?"

"I'm still trying to figure that out. I believe something went wrong during my experiments on Creeley's shadow DNA. With the worlds coming together closer than they should, there's a chance his soul is being corrupted. Changing into an ulma, or something resembling it. Turning him, unnaturally, into a by-product of both worlds."

"And that means?" The squeezing sensation intensified as Tom's eyes threatened to explode out of his skull.

"The portal at Polaris formed where it did because of a weakening of the membrane between worlds. I think the rift is putting more strain on that membrane, making those already weak spots thinner. Since he's being affected by the Otherside, he may have been drawn to the thin spot at Polaris. Or he may have been drawn to—"

"*Fuck you.*" The squeezing sensation moved to Tom's throat. "All of this could have been prevented if you had gone to get Atra yourself. If you let me and the rift go. If you weren't so engrossed with saving yourself."

"I'm sorry, Tom. I never meant for Atra—"

Footsteps crunched on the snow outside. They both snapped their attention to the greenhouse entrance.

There stood Ophelia in all her glory, gun in hand. The way she awkwardly clutched it reminded Tom of how a nonsmoker held a cigarette.

Speaking of which, he could fucking use one.

"All right, where is she?" Ophelia's voice vibrated with hysteria. "One of you knows."

Her eyes darted between the men, the glistening irises too large. They reminded Tom of fish eyes. Unnerving.

Neither Tom nor Glasser answered.

"Where is she? I'm not asking again."

She held the gun out, not pointing it at anything in particular. Ridiculous woman.

"Or what, you'll shoot us? Either way, you won't get an answer."

Ophelia swivelled to Tom.

"Put the gun down." A nagging at the back of Tom's mind told him to stop egging her on, but he couldn't. "You look stupid."

Her face turned an unusual shade of puce. Confirmation Tom still knew what buttons to push.

Her wavering hand focused the gun on him. Tom's body tensed, waiting for the bullet.

"This is your fault! You saddled me with your brat and jumped ship. Do you know the hell I lived, stuck with a child who wasn't mine? I *hate* her." She let out a mirthless giggle.

Tom wasn't sure if he loathed himself or Ophelia more in that moment. The little girl in his wallet deserved better than either of them.

"How did you find us?" The question popped into his head unprovoked. Anything to distract the unhinged bitch from pulling the trigger.

"I can see everyone. Even if they're hiding in the farthest corner of the earth, I can find them."

And Tom believed her, with those creepy fish eyes. What had she done to herself?

"Or almost all. Everyone except *you* Tom, and your brat."

Because of our shadow DNA, Tom surmised.

Glasser let out a long, hacking cough. He doubled over, body wracked with spasms.

Ophelia rounded on Glasser. A new victim to torture. "But you, Dr. Glasser, you tried to hide from me, and I still found you."

He dry heaved in response.

"Not feeling well, *Doctor*?"

"Leave him alone," Tom interjected.

"Shut up. You'll want to watch this."

Glasser keeled over. If the zip tie hadn't been holding him up he would have collapsed to the greenhouse floor.

It was awful to watch, yet Tom couldn't look away. Glasser clutched his chest, fingers bunching the fabric of his no-longer-crisp business shirt.

"Are your heart problems acting up?" Ophelia's voice dripped with disdain. "Maybe you should take some more medicine."

She towered over him as he continued to struggle. His restraints forced him upright and, goddammit, Tom felt sorry for the bastard.

"Stop it. Leave him alone."

Ophelia didn't answer, engrossed in Glasser's suffering. She gestured with the gun to the bell-shaped flowers behind him.

"Foxglove. When consumed in large quantities, it can cause digoxin toxicity."

The wheezing coming from Glasser's throat was akin to nails on a chalkboard.

"Notice anything *off* lately? Have you been tired, confused? How's the heartbeat? A little ... *irregular*? For someone who thinks he's so clever, you should have seen the symptoms of digoxin toxicity. Especially since the final symptoms can be deadly disturbances of the heart."

Glasser was sick, as Tom knew, but not from his experiments. Crazy bitch was fucking poisoning him.

Tom recalled the pill bottle with the ripped-off label he'd discovered in Glasser's briefcase. Ophelia must've found a way to switch out the heart medication inside with this foxglove shit.

Glasser's eyes bulged out of their sockets, filled with the fear of knowing his poisoned heart was giving out.

Tom turned his head away. It was too brutal to witness.

Half buried in the soil behind him was a pair of gardening shears.

Surely this was a trick? Ophelia wouldn't be so careless as to leave a weapon in his reach.

Or would she? The woman was unhinged, in more than one way.

Tom shifted toward the shears, keeping his stare glued to her. She paid him no attention, fixed on Glasser like a spider about to devour its mate.

"Where is she?" she screamed into Glasser's face.

Tom inched closer to the shears. Any second, she'd notice him moving.

But she didn't. Instead, she grabbed Glasser by the chin, forcing him to look at her while she shrieked, "What did you do with her?!"

Glasser's lips moved, but instead of words, a trickle of bile came out.

Ophelia leaned in closer, cocking her ear in the direction of his mouth. Tom lunged for the shears the moment she turned. With his one free hand, he plucked them from the soil and hid them behind his back, hands trembling.

Glasser's lips moved again.

"Po ... pol ..."

Don't you dare say it.

"Po ... lar ... is."

Ophelia's face broke into a grin, skin pulling taut against her skull. She let go of Glasser. His chin dropped to his unmoving chest.

Ophelia spun on her heel, exiting the greenhouse without a glance back.

Shit. Even if Tom escaped and found a ride to Polaris, she'd beat him to it.

She had to go.

"Ophelia."

She ignored him.

"Hey, Ophelia!"

Louder this time, as if that would do anything. She continued onward, undeterred.

"What makes you think Atra's gonna come without a fight?"

Tom had no idea what he was talking about; he just needed *something* to keep her in here.

Ophelia paused in the doorway.

"What makes you think she *can* put up a fight?"

She didn't turn around, but Tom imagined her face contorted in disgust at the mention of her stepdaughter.

"Why won't you say her name?"

"Whose?"

The tendons in the back of her neck tensed.

"Don't play dumb, Ophelia. You know who." Tom gripped the shears behind him. "She's so important to your plan, but why won't you say her name?"

Ophelia rounded on him, fire in her eyes. Tom immediately regretted his decision.

"Her name is irrelevant."

"Too afraid to admit she's more important than you are?" He surprised himself at how steady his voice was.

The vein forking down her forehead pulsated.

"She's a means to an end, nothing more."

"Say her name!" It took everything Tom had not to shrink away as Ophelia raised her hands, ready to snap his neck.

She was still too far away. Dammit. One of them was going down. It was only a matter of who got to who first.

"Say Atra's name!" Tom shouted, as Ophelia lunged for him.

That's all he needed—the split second of hesitation from her hearing the name. He brought up the shears and plunged them into her neck to the hilt.

Time froze. Ophelia's arms remained outstretched.

Then, an inhuman cry of needles against razor wire. She clamped a hand over her neck, but it did nothing to prevent the crimson spouting from it.

Holy shit. Holy shit. Holy shit.

She keeled over sideways, dropping against Tom's legs. He squeezed his eyes shut, nausea twisting his esophagus, the air thick with the stench of iron and blood.

A viscous bubbling came from her—mouth? neck?—as her long fingernails clawed the dirt. He didn't think anything could be worse than Glasser's prolonged death rattle, but he was gravely mistaken.

Finally, the greenhouse went silent. He cracked his eyes open. The scene in front of him wasn't what he'd imagined.

It was worse.

Blood. So much of it. Tom stretched for the shears buried in Ophelia's neck. They evaded his grasp.

The bitch had died two inches too far away.

A half sob, half laugh escaped his throat. It quickly turned into a dry heave. He needed out of here, out of this greenhouse of death, surrounded by blood and shit and puke.

The zip tie dug into his flesh as he reached out. Another half inch ... still too fucking far ...

The muscles in his shoulder screamed as he stretched them to their limits. He let out a strangled cry. Just a little ... bit ... more ... *aha!*

His index finger hooked around the handle of the shears.

Tom wanted to say he didn't remember the slight resistance of the blades, the wet puckering like he was removing them from a water-logged sponge. He wished he could say he couldn't recall the way his fingers grazed her neck as he sat up, or the way her still-warm skin sent a shudder down his spine.

But he did.

Now that he was looking at Ophelia, he didn't want to look away. He expected her to spring up, finish him off, but her chest remained still, glassy eyes staring into nothing.

He turned his attention to cutting himself free, but the blood was everywhere, making everything so fucking slippery. If he wasn't careful, there would be a third body in here bleeding out.

The zip tie snapped in two. His fingers turned to pins and needles as sensation flooded back into them.

Run, Tom. Run.

For once, he didn't feel guilty for doing so.

Stumbling outside, he gasped for breath from air heavy with ozone. The rift washed out the early morning sky. He brought a hand up to shield his eyes, surprised to find the handgun clutched in it. He didn't recall picking it up.

He ran into Ophelia's house, all too aware of Glasser's remarks. Atra, with one of his lab rats. A *dangerous* lab rat.

Glasser and Ophelia deserved to rot in that greenhouse together.

Car keys. Tom needed car keys. He searched the kitchen countertops, the living room, nothing.

He froze. What if they were still on Ophelia?

Nononononono.

He couldn't go back in there.

Instead, he tore the living room apart, throwing aside the cushions, rummaging through the boots beside the door, looking under the couch—

"Found you."

He snatched them up, running for the driveway. As he climbed into the car, he mapped out the route to Polaris in his head. What was the fastest way?

Down the road he went, the hum of the rift fading in the distance. The more distance he put between himself and those bodies, the more clear-headed he became.

Take Exit 5B, out of Telos. Head north on Highway—

A revelation jolted him.

"He may have been drawn to the thin spot at Polaris," Glasser had said about Creeley. *"Or he may have been drawn to—"*

But Tom had cut him off.

In hindsight, Glasser had divulged the location to Ophelia *too* easily. Why would he give it up when he had gone to such great lengths to keep Atra away from the rift?

Because Atra wasn't at Polaris. And Glasser knew that all along.

Bastard.

He said his hired lab rat was supposed to take Atra to the motel. But did the lab rat get distracted? Was there a thin spot close to the motel he'd been drawn to instead?

That would mean ... Tom should go toward the mountains.

If there *was* a thin spot there, hypothetically, he'd be able to feel it. Like he felt the portal years ago at Polaris. Like he felt the rift, stretching in the sky over Ophelia's house.

Tom slammed to a stop on the deserted road. West to the mountains, or north to Polaris?

He drummed his fingers against the steering wheel.

Glasser said Atra was in danger. Time was running out.

He had one shot.

No pressure.

At last, he cranked the wheel left and headed west. He glanced into the rear-view mirror at the rift lighting up the sky.

He hoped he'd made the right choice, for once.

Chapter 25

Get Out Alive

Atra grabbed the fire poker off the table at the same time a great *boom!* shook the house.

Earthquake was her first thought, but her instincts told her otherwise.

Another *boom!* reverberated the walls. Closer than the last one.

Not an earthquake. Something.

Someone.

Boom!

The pictures hanging on the walls rattled. She turned to Lex, but the kid was gone. For good this time.

Boom!

It sent a shudder through Atra's feet, up her spine, and into her clenched jaw. The candelabra on the table wobbled. Its flames flickered out.

She strained her ears. Nothing but a silence so oppressive it was almost a scream.

Minutes passed without a sound. She couldn't stay this way forever. Clutching the poker, she stood and moved toward the doorway.

Every picture in the hallway, large and small, had crashed off the wall, making the carpet a minefield of shattered glass and splintered frames.

The glass under her boot cracked like an ice shelf breaking away. She might as well just slap a target on her back.

Taking an L-bend that didn't exist when she first came down the hall, Atra was faced with more destruction. A long, drawn-out whistle rang across the walls, echoing off the vaulted ceiling. It came from around the corner she'd just turned. Her stomach curdled.

Without disturbing the sea of crushed glass, she extended a hand for the closest door handle. She twisted, but it didn't budge.

Fuck.

The house went silent again. She bit her lip so hard she drew blood, listening for *anything*.

Then—

The whistle. Closer? She took her chances and moved forward, hoping the whistling would drown out the crushing glass under her boots.

The whistling stopped. So did she.

She gripped the poker, the metal slipping in her sweaty palms.

Crunch, crunch, crunch.

Someone walking down the hall. A pause. Then a series of clicks. The image of a thousand beetles, rubbing their pincers together, flooded Atra's mind. She shuddered, feeling them crawling across her skin.

Crunch, crunch, crunch.

Faster now.

Atra broke into a run.

A door, at the far end of the hall. Oh please, oh please, oh please don't be locked. The footsteps behind transformed back to those *booms!* shaking the house like claps of thunder.

She reached the door, expecting it to be locked like the last one. Instead, it swung open. Racing inside, she slammed it shut. She stood inside the cramped bathroom with the dripping pipes.

The loudest *boom!* yet as the door flew off its hinges. She ducked, her hands coming up to shield her head before she could process what happened. Stumbling back, she *should* have hit a wall, but the door wasn't the only thing that had been demolished. The entire wall had collapsed too. She found herself in the living room again, with the faded couch and crackling fire.

A footstep crunched in the destruction behind her. Atra whipped around.

Dr. Creepsley stood among the rubble, his fake doctor's lab coat covered in drywall dust.

He didn't move. He didn't say anything. Instead, he let out a long, rattling breath.

His pupils were enormous, swallowing the whites. A glistening sheen coated his skin. Not sweat, but slime. Something was very wrong with his face. The bones under his skin appeared to have been broken and rearranged. His jaw jutted out oddly, his splintered cheekbones illuminated under the new shadows of the house.

Atra didn't know how long they stood there as his rattling breaths shook the space between them.

He cocked his head in an abrupt, jerking movement. A revolting clicking came from the back of his throat.

"What dwells within you?" he asked.

But it wasn't Creepsley's voice. It wasn't Creepsley at all. Something closer to Dread wore his skin, only it radiated malevolent intent.

"I need it."

Atra's teeth chattered as a tear escaped her eye. This thing was going to kill her.

His black eyes followed the tear rolling down her cheek. Then that clicking again.

"Don't cry." He cocked his head to the other side in another abrupt jerk.

She clamped her lips together, unable to contain the whimper that escaped her.

They'd been in this house together all this time. Vanishing Planes was their shared delusion. That's why he didn't disappear along with Beryl and Rei. Creepsley was as real as she was. Only this wasn't Creepsley anymore. He'd been taken over by something else.

He smiled, showing rows of needle-thin teeth.

Atra raised the poker to defend herself as he simultaneously launched himself at her.

She felt like she'd been slammed into a brick wall. A tremendous *crack!* filled her ears. Her spine or the couch frame? A weight crashed on her, accompanied by something wet dripping onto her neck.

It was over in less than three seconds.

Her dazed vision came back into focus. The poker had lodged itself in Creepsley's eye.

She was unaware of wiggling free from under him or getting to her feet. He writhed on the ground like a bug half squished and left to suffer.

Atra fled to the kitchen. A chair bumped against her leg. She tried pushing it back. Why wouldn't it budge?

Because the walls were contracting.

The countertops and table butted against one another, the gap between them gone. The ceiling closed in, inches away from her head, and the door—

The door.

She tried in vain to push the table aside. The room continued to shrink, the chairs buckling against the countertop.

A laugh hiccupped out of her. She didn't come this far to be thwarted by a fucking table. Grabbing one of its corners, she tipped it sideways, giving herself enough space to make it to the exit.

As she reached for the handle, the door burst open. Sunlight

—*real* sunlight—streamed in. She lunged for it, but a chair blocked the way. She clambered over it, getting one foot out the door, but the other foot didn't follow because it was trapped by the bottom rung of the chair.

The frosty air of the outside world danced over her face, but it didn't matter because she was going to die this way, cut in half as the house shrank out of existence.

A hand grabbed her shoulder, pulling her forward. Atra's foot ripped free and she fell through the doorway.

Something—someone—caught her fall and dragged her forward.

She stumbled, unable to get her footing as the rotting planks twisted inward behind her. She tore her eyes away from the house to see who her rescuer was, but his back was turned.

Her boots, released from the house's clutches, crunched on the snow. The porch folded into nothing. An awful sucking noise accompanied it—the opposite of the sound the rift made when it opened the sky.

And then there was nothing but a field of untouched snow. The shadows of the trees stretched out over it, black against white.

"Attie?"

Her head whipped around. The face was so familiar, but aged. Not the same face she'd seen in the Tentorum Plane.

"Dad?" she choked out.

A deluge of emotions crashed through her. Anger from him abandoning her, rage from him creating her, mixed with relief because she was no longer alone. He had finally come back for her.

Her chest was wracked with heavy sobs. A pair of arms wrapped around her, and she didn't shove them away like she imagined she would if Dad ever showed up again.

"It's gonna be okay, kiddo," she heard him say, from far away.

His words made her sob harder, because no, nothing was okay.

The *click! click! click!* of the turn signal caused Atra to stir in the passenger seat. Tom had pulled off the highway and into a gas station in the middle of nowhere. The sodium lamp in the deep blue twilight made her eyes water as she rubbed the sleep out of them.

Turning to face her father, she noticed he'd cleaned himself up while she'd been out cold. He'd rubbed away the blood splattering the side of his face, save for a large smear on his neck. He wore what looked suspiciously like a woman's peacoat. What had he been up to before he got to her?

But more importantly, how could she fall asleep at a time like this? No time to rest. She had to bring Dad up to speed. She needed his help to get to the rift.

But she didn't know where to start. They'd sat in silence as his funky-smelling car raced down the highway after he'd rescued her from the house. She'd gripped the edges of the seat, reliving the final moments in the van with Creepsley before it crashed. But she couldn't tell Dad to slow down. She couldn't tell him anything. The pathway between her brain and mouth was broken.

Eventually, Dad either slowed down or she got used to the speed because her panic gave way to bone-tired exhaustion.

She didn't remember closing her eyes.

"Hungry?" Dad broke the silence, cutting the ignition.

Atra's stomach growled in response.

He dug around the cupholders, collecting all the spare change he could find, and counted it.

"Check in the glove box for money," he said.

She obliged, finding fifty bucks folded between a spare set of keys and a sunglasses case.

"Want anything in particular?"

Atra paused. She didn't have an answer. She'd spent so many years eating whatever slop was put in front of her, she didn't know what she was craving.

She shook her head. Dammit, Atra, say *something*.

Dad stared at her awkwardly for a few moments, and she realized he didn't know what to get her either.

He stepped out of the car. The second she was alone, the interior of the car was too claustrophobic. She unbuckled herself, opening the door.

Dad stopped.

"You wanna come with, kiddo?"

She shook her head.

"I need some air," she replied, finally finding her voice. It didn't sound like hers, though. It was weak, broken.

"Okay. Don't go far."

Like she was still a seven-year-old. To him, she still was.

He shuffled into the gas station, head down, shoulders hunched. He walked like a coward.

Atra hated herself for thinking it more than she hated him in that moment.

He came back.

Did it make up for anything? No. Would it ever? She didn't know.

She stared at the lights illuminating the parking lot. The sky deepened behind them.

Free. She was free.

If only it was Seth going into the gas station, instead of old deadbeat Dad. A pang of guilt wracked through—

A sweeping shadow, like a large bird, at the top of her vision. She ducked, covering her head with her hands.

Dread?

She couldn't be sure. Dread hadn't been right, not since she left the house. No longer her shadow but no longer smoke, it had transformed into something in-between.

She and Dread both felt the tug of the rift on the horizon.

Suddenly, Atra didn't want to be outside. She ducked back into the car. She had to speak up. The second Dad came back, she needed to tell him where to go. But the pressing panic had left her, like waking up scared in the middle of the night and then not remembering why the next morning.

Dad returned to the car, his hands so full he was barely able to open the driver's side door. Saran-wrapped sandwiches, bags of chips, packages of licorice ...

Atra snatched a sandwich, unwrapped it, and shovelled it into her mouth. She couldn't eat fast enough. She only paused to open a bottle of water, before she inhaled half its contents in one go.

How many days had she been in the house? It couldn't have been more than a couple.

So many questions she'd never have answers to.

"Save one of those waters," she barely heard Dad say. "You can use it to clean that gunk off yourself."

Gunk. She guessed it sounded better than *Creepsley's blood.*

She punctured one of the many chip bags, tipped it back and funnelled the chips into her mouth. So much food. Dad bought too much. A veritable "Sorry I Abandoned You Feast" as it were.

Dad scanned a newspaper as she gorged herself. He sighed discontentedly before folding the paper and stuffing it between the seat and console.

Atra was picking chips out of her teeth, stomach swelling after being empty for so long, when she glanced at it.

"December's Cold Moon Sees Red," the headline screamed above a picture of a bloated, blood-tinged orb.

Her heart dropped as she fought the urge to regurgitate everything she'd just eaten.

The date in the top right corner confirmed her deepest fears: *December 21.*

The Cold Blood Moon, hours away. Could she still get there in time?

"Dad?" Her voice came out thick. "We have to go. *That* way." The urgency she failed to feel earlier switched back on. She pointed out the rear window at the rift. If she weren't so frantic, she'd have noticed the expression of horror that crossed his face. "I'll explain—"

"No." Flat-out.

Of all the outcomes she'd imagined, she never took into consideration being shut down immediately.

"What? No. Please drive, we have to get somewhere ... *I* have to get somewhere."

She was a fish flopping around the deck of a ship. Useless. Helpless. How was she supposed to do anything if she couldn't explain herself?

"No." Dad's face turned to stone.

"You don't get it, I've learned things—"

"So have I."

"No, not *like that.* These are weird things. You're not gonna believe me, but I'm not nuts. I'm not fucking nuts. I swear it's real."

Atra's body fluttered, as if it were about to hover off the seat. She reminded herself to breathe.

"The world is going to end—"

"I believe you."

She went silent as if he'd slapped her. She wasn't expecting *that*.

"If anyone is going to believe you, kiddo, it's me. But there are things you don't know." Dad gestured toward the rift.

"You can see it too?"

Of course, he could. He decided to create her, a fucking science experiment, and neglected to tell her. Who knew what else he'd done?

"I sure as shit can. And I can tell you—you are *not* going there."

"Fuck off, like you can tell me what—"

"—I refuse to let you get—"

"—you don't get a say. You left me!" Atra's face grew hot. "You abandoned me and left me with that awful woman. How could you leave, knowing what she was like? She threw me into a loony bin the first chance she could and you never even came looking for me. I never understood what was wrong with me, and you had the answers, but you both left me to rot."

She drew in a ragged breath. Was she crying? She didn't care.

It was Dad's turn to act like he'd been slapped. He was silent for so long she thought he was going to throw her out of the car. Which was fine by her.

He closed his eyes, pinching the bridge of his nose between his index finger and thumb.

"That's not what happened." He sounded like he'd been kicked in the nuts.

"Then what happened."

It wasn't a question.

Silence. He wouldn't look at her.

Atra's mind worked furiously. What else wasn't he telling her?

"What happened at Polaris?"

Dad blanched.

"Was *I* at Polaris?"

"Later. Right now, we—"

"Tell me or I'm leaving to deal with this myself."

"No, you won't!"

He grabbed the steering wheel, shaking it. Atra jumped.

"Goddammit, do you have any idea what I went through to get you? You are coming somewhere safe with me."

"Don't tell me what to do."

"It's your stepmother behind this. That's who you're running off to. Bet you didn't know that, huh?"

By the way Atra's eyes widened, the answer was obvious. The Queen needed a host, Lex said. Atra never considered it might be someone she knew.

"So maybe you know some stuff, but you don't know everything. And it doesn't matter because Ophelia is dead. Nothing is going to happen."

"That isn't the whole story. There's something else on the Otherside, the Queen, controlling—"

"Look, kiddo, I know I fucked up. I promise I'll tell you everything, but drop this till we get somewhere safe, okay?"

"Your solution to this is to run away again and let the world end?"

"No! Your stepmother is dead. There's no one left to open the rift. End of story."

Wrong. He was so wrong. The Queen remained, lying in wait. The rift wouldn't go away.

Dad patted his jacket pocket.

"Fuck. I forgot smokes." He opened the car door, then paused, grabbing the keys out of the ignition. "I'll be back."

Into the gas station again, leaving her simmering in her rage. Atra should've run the second she got out of the house. She hated herself for wanting to trust him again. For wanting a parent again.

If she went with him, she'd be as much a prisoner as she was in the asylum.

The moon on the newspaper mocked her. She stole a glance over her shoulder at the rift. It flickered in time to her heartbeat, calling for her, for Dread.

She couldn't ignore it. Though she didn't know its origin point, she felt if she moved toward it, it would guide her.

Something else out the rear window caught her attention. A black cat sat on the pavement behind the car. Oriens? Lex? They were one and the same.

As soon as Atra met his stare, the cat turned around and padded across the street toward the rift.

Trust the cat.

If Atra was going to chase the rift, she had to leave now. She wouldn't get another chance until it was too late.

She popped open the glove compartment, grabbing the spare set of keys she'd seen earlier. Clutching them close to her chest, she took a deep breath.

She could do this.

She owed it to Lex.

Crawling over the console, she seated herself on the driver's side. The cushion was still warm from Dad's body heat. She clasped the seatbelt with a shaking hand, extending her foot toward the gas pedal.

Too far away.

How the hell do you move the seat forward? Atra bucked her hips, as if that would do anything. The seat remained infuriatingly stationary.

What am I doing, what am I doing? I've never driven before, her mind raced, as her fingers explored around the bottom of the seat. They gripped onto a handle. She pulled and the seat jolted forward.

From over the steering wheel, she saw Dad at the till, the cashier doling out his change.

She turned the spare key in the ignition. The car headlights lit up as the engine roared, reflecting in the glass-front window of the gas station.

She threw the gearshift to R—for reverse, she hoped—and slammed her foot on the gas pedal. For a moment, the car didn't move and then it was moving too much.

Crunch, into another car it went.

Okay, less gas.

Dad noticed the car moving, his eyes bulging when he realized what she was doing. Shit. Time to go.

Atra clicked the gearshift forward, stomping on the gas. The engine revved, sounding like it wanted to explode, but the tires refused to spin.

Dad disappeared from the counter. Any second now he'd come screaming out those doors.

She glanced at the gearshift. It was on N. What the fuck was N?! She clicked it down one more. If R meant reverse, surely D meant drive?

She accelerated again, too fast. The car was going to end up through the gas station window. Cranking the wheel, the car tires bumped up onto the concrete stoop in front of the store. Containers of bright pink washer fluid flew in every direction as the hood clipped the display they sat on.

It was fucking impossible to get this car to do anything between full stop and full speed ahead.

Dad burst through the doors, sprinting after her. From the rear-view mirror, he advanced on the car, screaming her name.

Atra eased off the gas pedal; she couldn't do this to him.

Dad's eyes were frantic with horror but also steeped in betrayal, like she'd torn his heart from his chest and stomped it on the ground. A feeling she knew all too well.

You left me. Adrenaline surged through her as she changed her mind. *Now, it's my turn.*

She sped up, turning onto the road. The blare of a car horn, the flashing of lights, as another vehicle narrowly avoided her. Her arms trembled as she straightened out, the steering wheel too heavy.

Holy fuck, holy fuck, holy fuck.

Atra pushed harder on the pedal with a shaking leg. She tore herself away from the road for the briefest of moments to watch Dad running down the road after her. He'd never catch up.

Turning right, she pulled onto the highway, gathering speed. The rift sprawled out on the skyline in front of her, guiding the way.

Chapter 26

Mother of Most

Was she dead?

Ophelia cracked her eyes open. Every nerve ending screamed, on fire.

Death wouldn't be this excruciating.

She'd come close to this agony only once before, and that was when her piece-of-shit ex beat her within an inch of her life.

The bright light caused her head to churn and swell—

Oh shit.

What time was it?

She tried pulling herself up, but her arms slid out from under her. A horrible sensation radiated from the side of her neck, like a gigantic splinter had jammed itself under her skin. Maddeningly itchy, yet deeply painful.

Tom. Clutching the shears. Sinking them into her neck. The blinding pain, taking over and then ebbing as the life flowed out of her.

Had she died? Ophelia didn't think so. She was beyond death.

Yet the greenhouse smelled of it so potently she couldn't stand it. Summoning her strength, she slowly got to her feet and took inventory of the situation. Her eyes blurred over. She tried to rub away the irritation, pulling out more hairs. The greenhouse came back into focus.

Glasser's body, still in a heap in the corner. Tom's broken zip tie on the ground beside her.

Stupid, stupid, stupid.

How could she be so careless?

She patted herself down. He'd taken the gun as well.

Stepping outside, she shielded her eyes from the late-afternoon sun. Her head throbbed in time to a heart that refused to stop beating.

She was wrong earlier. This *was* the worst she'd ever felt.

Ophelia turned toward the cypress tree, the crusted blood along her neck and chest cracking like clay. Absently, she scratched at it.

Not a hint of light emanated from the tree. The Queen remained ominously silent, watching, judging.

Ignoring the pounding headache, Ophelia entered her house.

The keys. Where were the car keys?! Not on the coffee table where she usually dumped them, because she'd shattered the coffee table over Chuck's head. Instead of wasting time searching, she went to grab the spare set ...

Shit.

They were sitting in her glove box from the last time she'd locked herself out.

Fool. Utter fool.

The hairs on her nape bristled, feeling the presence of the urn behind her.

What had visited her the morning she opened the rift? Seth's ghost? A warning from the Queen herself?

Ophelia hated to admit it, but she was afraid. Seth's urn no longer provided her comfort.

Maybe hallucinating her long-dead son was her mind's way of

cutting her last human tie to this world and readying her for the next.

The silence from the cypress tree taunted her. She went out the front door, not surprised to find her car gone.

She would get another one.

"I will make this right. I will get to Polaris. There's still time."

She didn't know if she was reassuring herself or the Queen.

A dull grinding filled her ears as she marched down the road.

Stop.

The faintest of whispers, carried by the wind, but it chilled her to the marrow.

Ophelia listened intently but was met with dead air.

Had she imagined it?

Yes, my Queen? she desperately wanted to ask; but if the Queen really wanted to communicate, she wouldn't be playing this game.

Ophelia cast a glance back at the rift humming over her house.

The sun threatened to dip below the horizon. She would never make it to the closest neighbourhood at this rate.

She ran. The sudden burst of energy was akin to releasing the scream trapped beneath her rib cage. The headache was gone. The itch in her neck had healed.

Her breath came out in puffs as the sun's rays faded on her face. It was the last time she'd feel their meagre warmth as a mortal.

Although she wore no jacket, her back was sticky with sweat. She needed to slow down but couldn't. At this rate, she could run all the way to Polaris if she felt like it. And she did.

The Queen was the one who needed *her*, not the other way around.

The Queen had hunted Ophelia after Lyall was buried six feet under the garden bed.

Haunted her dreams.

Showed her a tree, a light, entwined into one being.

But there was one other thing they needed. A face, a child's face. Always the same one, with deep-set grey eyes, a smattering of freckles, and hair as dark as a raven's wing.

Find her, the Queen had commanded. *Do whatever you have to. We need her for us to be complete. To be one.*

And Ophelia had found her. In a coffee house, attached to the hip of one Thomas Hart. So, Ophelia did the one thing she swore she'd never do again. She'd married Thomas Hart to get to his child.

All for the Queen. Her precious Queen. This would only be for a while. She'd only have to pretend for a while ...

And then the while stretched into years. Every day she asked her Queen, *How long, how long must I do this until we are together?* And every day the Queen was silent.

And then Tom left, and she was stuck taking care of his brat. Reduced to nothing but a single mother of two. Surely the Queen would come forward now, reveal her true intentions, and all would be well.

But she never did.

And then the Queen abandoned her too.

After the hauntings, the nightmares, the promises. Silence. For years. Ophelia locked Atra away, so it was just her and her son again. Things should've gone back to the way they were before. But they didn't because that brat was Seth's *sister*, a sister always on his mind, one he longed to visit.

And then he died.

And then he abandoned her too.

And then she had nothing.

What was The Drove without a Queen? Meaningless.

Ophelia threw herself into her work. Saving other women from the same mistakes she'd made.

She sold her house, not wanting to be attached to its memories. She searched for a rental on the fringes of Telos, far away from the city, from everyone, from everything.

And then she saw it. A small, one-bedroom cabin a step up from a garden shed; but the house didn't matter. It was what the backyard contained. A winding, cobblestone path leading to a cypress tree.

To the field ... down the left-hand path we go ...
Hand in hand, we will never be alone.

The Queen, waiting for her all along. Ophelia just didn't know she had to be found.

The grinding roared in Ophelia's head as she gained inhuman speed running down the road.

In the distance, the yellow streetlamps of the neighbourhood blinked on as night descended.

Stop.

More than a whisper this time.

Ophelia didn't want to stop. It felt good to run. She didn't remember the last time anything felt good.

She forced herself to slow to a walk as she entered the neighbourhood. A pair of car headlights blinded her as they came up the road. The vehicle pulled in a few driveways from her.

Perfect.

A man stepped out, overcoat thrown over his business-casual slacks. He turned as she approached, wearing a placid, not-quite-there grin people reserved for strangers passing by. The smile slipped from his face as he took in her bloody clothes and matted hair.

"Ma'am, do you need help?" His hand went to his pocket to retrieve his cell, no doubt ready to call 911. What a good Samaritan.

"Yes, I do." Ophelia grabbed him by the shoulders and tossed him into the garage door.

Climbing into the still-running car, she backed away from the crushed garage door and crumpled businessman at the bottom of it.

The tires squealed on the pavement as she peeled out of the

neighbourhood before anyone noticed. Already she could feel herself growing lighter. Plenty of time left to get the situation under control.

Which led to the next snag. *Technically,* she didn't know the location of Polaris. Two hours north of Telos. That's where the extent of her knowledge ended. Would the Queen help?

Never mind her. Ophelia would do this herself.

She reached out. Tom should be hurtling down the highway, headed north.

Nothing.

She did a broader sweep of the area surrounding Telos.

Blank.

She gritted her teeth, causing a molar to crack in two.

Tom or Atra—Ophelia couldn't see either of them. Of course. Their connection to the Otherside must shield them. That was why she could see only Glasser when she'd tracked him and Tom down at the motel.

Fucking Evie. If she had done her job, Ophelia wouldn't be in this mess.

STOP.

The voice yanked her out of her thoughts, causing her to slam on the stolen car's brakes.

The whisper from earlier. Not the Queen, but her own subconscious. Because—

She wasn't supposed to be going to Polaris.

Atra would be coming here. Of course. The thing inside her, the thing Ophelia needed, wanted to go through the rift. And Atra wouldn't be able to resist.

Ophelia's hands trembled against the wheel.

Am I making the right decision? She longed to reach out to the Queen for reassurance.

But she could still feel the Queen's foreboding eye. Making sure Ophelia was the right person to join with. Making sure she could fix this mistake.

Ophelia turned the car around, glancing at the clock on the dashboard.

5:02 p.m.

If her instincts were correct, Atra would be delivering herself right to her doorstep.

All she had to do was wait.

Chapter 27

Bone to Dust

Atra stood at the end of a driveway. The rift stretched overhead like an infinite galaxy. Its uncanny hum washed over her, causing the hairs on her arms to stand on end. She wanted to reach up and touch it.

She assumed the shabby house in front of her, dwarfed beneath the rift, belonged to her stepmother.

Dad said Ophelia was dead. He was wrong. Atra sensed evil lurking; the air was heavy with it.

She glanced over her shoulder at the long, empty road. No streetlights. No houses. Only the vast stretch of the prairies beneath the eerie purple glow.

No Lex. No Oriens. They'd guided her to where she needed to go. They couldn't help her anymore.

There was nothing here but the absolute crushing terror of facing the other monster of her childhood.

Atra's grand car hijacking hadn't ended so grandly after all. Not twenty minutes into lurching down the highway did the car run out of gas. Great oversight, Dad.

Luckily, people took pity on a girl hitchhiking on the side of the road in the winter. She didn't want to get into another stranger's vehicle, remembering how that turned out last time.

But what choice did she have?

If she survived this, she was going to fucking learn how to drive.

She walked up Ophelia's driveway, stopping at the front door. Dread pulled away from her, funnelling toward the rift.

Atra resisted the tug. She had to know what was inside. She had to know how Ophelia went about her life after throwing her stepdaughter away.

She creaked the door open and crept inside. The space was cold, both sparse and cluttered. Bare walls, bare furniture, but the mantel above the dead fire was crowded with knickknacks.

She drew her arms over her chest. Every part of her screamed to get out, but something on the mantel drew her in. What was that tarnished silver thing in the middle? It reminded her of a trophy, a silver cup mounted on a wooden platform with a small plaque at the base. Atra inched closer, deeper into the house.

Seth Lampard, the plaque read. Her stomach knotted.

What was this, a trophy from school? She grabbed it. There was a lid on the top. She popped it off.

Inside was filled with dirt.

No. Not dirt.

She snapped the lid back, as if that would prevent her revelation of its contents. She tried suppressing it but—

Ashes.

A great roaring filled her ears. She grabbed the mantel for support as the living room went grey.

Grey. The same colour as those—

Ashes. Seth's ashes.

What the fuck?

Seth, visiting her all those years. Seth, saying he was going to get her out of the asylum. Seth, not doing any of that because he was too busy lying in here, too busy being—

Don't think it. Don't you dare think it.
The idea was impossible to shove away.
Rei, in the asylum, on the bed.
"You are dead and Dread is dead and Seth is dead!"
The final word reverberated through Atra's entire being.
Rei knew. And that meant Atra knew. Because Rei was a part of her subconscious.

How long had she been talking to a ghost? Only she knew in her heart it wasn't a ghost. He was a hallucination, something only she saw.

Which meant—
She *was* crazy.
Delusional.
What else did she imagine?
The house? Lex? Her dad?
Was there really a rift in the sky with an unspeakable evil lurking behind it? Was this really her stepmother's home?
Or was she some psych patient who'd broken into a stranger's house, overtaken by a delusional fantasy?

A deep groan came from somewhere behind her. She almost dropped Seth's urn.
Urn.
A sob rose in her throat as she placed it back on the mantel and faced the noise.

Another groan, accompanied by nails scraping against the wood floor. It came from the dark hall beyond the living room.
The muscles in her neck tensed.
More scraping.
Something grabbed her ankle.
Atra shrieked. Her first thought was that she'd been grabbed by an actual dead, reanimated corpse. The whites of its—*his*—eyes shone like two moons inside a skeletal face. Something was caked around his mouth, dribbling down the front of his suit. Blood?

The man's grip eased. She jumped back as he flopped over. His chest fluttered, breaths coming out in broken wheezes. Crouching over him, she extended a hand, then retracted it. She didn't know how she could help.

"Mmm ..."

Now Atra was closer, she could see the stuff around his mouth wasn't blood. It was something dark, mixed with his spit. Dirt, or charcoal.

He raised a hand, an old man on his deathbed seeking comfort. She took it.

"Molly?" he finally gasped.

His voice jogged something in her memory. She'd heard it before, but where?

"I'm so happy ... to see you again."

It clicked. He was from the Tentorum Plane. The other person in Polaris with Tom.

Her co-creator.

"Who are you?" Atra found her voice, wrenching her hand free.

"It's me ..." His empty hand clawed for her. "*It's me,* your—"

But whatever he was, she'd never find out.

Light filtered in through the gap in the curtains, accompanied by the unmistakable crunch of tires on gravel.

She turned back to the man on the ground.

"Run."

She didn't need to be told twice. She darted into a narrow kitchen and through the backdoor.

In the backyard stood a dead tree. Its skeletal limbs reached for the rift. Or was the rift twisting toward it? They were one and the same.

Atra didn't realize she'd been moving closer until her boots sank into the ground. Warmth radiated from the earth in sharp contrast to the frigid night above.

A ring of melted snow extended from the tree all the way to the house. A tingling sensation spread through her toes and up her ankles. The soil undulated underneath her feet like waves at sea.

Run, Atra. Run while you still can.

Something moved by the tree, snapping her back to her senses. It reminded her of some predatory bird getting to its feet.

Atra would've recognized the swooping silhouette of her stepmother anywhere.

Ophelia paused before moving toward the house at a preternatural speed.

Atra's nerve broke. She ducked, wedging into the tiny gap between the greenhouse and house. Suddenly, she was just a little kid again and doing what she did best when her stepmother came around: hiding. How could she have thought she was ready to face Ophelia again?

Had she been spotted? Straining her ears, she listened for Ophelia, but the soft ground muffled any footsteps.

She glanced at her footprints. They led right to her hiding spot. The rippling ground had nearly etched them away, but not enough.

Please, please, please.

How far away was Ophelia?

A pointed boot stamped into the ground in front of her. She waited, petrified, expecting the boot to turn, for Ophelia to find her.

Atra's gaze darted up.

Ophelia stood in front of the door. The muscles around her jaw rippled, giving the illusion of them sitting over rather than under the skin.

As bizarre as it had been to see Dad after his extended absence, seeing her stepmother was far worse. At least Dad still looked human.

Ophelia turned. Their eyes met.

Atra's body pulsed with shock as Ophelia lunged for her. A cry escaped her as sharp nails punctured her jacket, piercing her skin.

Impossibly strong hands dragged her from her hiding spot. She cried out, struggling to break free of her stepmother's merciless clutches as she was dragged toward the cypress tree.

Atra's face was mashed into the ground. She tried spitting out a mouthful of dirt, but the gag got in the way. Too tight, like the restraints Ophelia was currently wrapping around her wrists and ankles. A tear leaked from the corner of her eye, mixing with the gritty earth.

Ophelia pulled the restraints taut, jostling Atra back and forth. Overhead, the clouds parted to reveal the moon. The faintest sliver of white crested its outer edge as the lunar eclipse neared totality.

Red rays spilled through the branches, the same colour as the blood that would be spilled from Atra shortly. At least, that's what she presumed by the dagger her stepmother had clutched between her teeth.

The luminous core of the tree flared, spilling light from the Otherside into this world.

Ophelia finished with the rope.

"You thought you could ruin my life and get away with it, huh?" The sharp blade pressed against Atra's throat.

She squeezed her eyes shut. She'd been in this position before when Creepsley tried to lobotomize her. But why couldn't she get her mind to unfocus this time so she could escape into the planes again?

"You're finally going to serve your purpose, you little bitch."

Atra's breath hitched as her stepmother's hand knotted in her hair. It was too hard, trying to travel to the planes with Dread pulling her to the rift. Ever since she'd arrived here, she fought to keep Dread tethered to her, afraid it would give itself to the rift and leave her behind.

But Lex said she couldn't destroy it. It couldn't be without her, nor her without it. It couldn't leave unless she went too.

"You thought you could take everything away from me." Ophelia's breath fell against her ear as she leaned close. "But now, I'm going to take something away from *you*."

"Fuck. You." Atra hissed as the pressure of the blade increased.

Ophelia already had taken everything away from her. Her childhood, her freedom, her brother. She wasn't going to kill her now. She wasn't going to win again.

Atra gave into Dread, letting go, flowing into it. And just as the sun, moon, and Earth aligned above in perfect syzygy, her body, soul, and ulma did the same within. But she wasn't moving toward the rift.

The sensation of the knife puckering against her skin, on the verge of slashing it open, disappeared. Ophelia wouldn't get rid of her so easily this time.

Atra had entered the Tentorum Plane again.

Chapter 28

Twin Skeletons

Tom shot up the driveway. He slammed on the brakes, the tires skipping over the sheet of ice.

Crunch! went the truck's bumper into the side of Ophelia's house.

The brakes on this vehicle were shit. He couldn't complain; he'd stolen it right from a gas pump as it was being filled. It was a miracle he'd made it to Telos without getting arrested. But what was a little grand theft auto on top of fraud and attempted murder?

Tom cut the ignition, grabbed the handgun he'd taken off Ophelia, and clambered out of the truck. A high, almost imperceptible whine—like a radio broadcasting dead air—filled his ears. The light of the rift reminded him of those neon signs in the casino he frequented to escape Naomi. That was a lifetime ago; the memory didn't feel real anymore.

Where was Ophelia's car?

Tom's stomach lurched. Maybe Atra never made it. It certainly didn't *seem* like she could drive. And when would she have learned? Between morning meds and psychoanalysis in the loony bin? Of course, she couldn't.

But there had been no wreckage, no evidence of a crash. What if she was headed in another direction?

He went cold. Atra knew as much about getting here as she did about driving. She could've crashed anywhere, lying injured, trapped, slowly dying—

None of this would have happened if you didn't go back for your fucking smokes.

The front door to the house gaped open. Atra must be inside. Unless—

Tom balked at the thought of checking the greenhouse for Ophelia's corpse. He couldn't face those glassy eyes, forever staring at nothing.

And what would he do if she wasn't in there at all?

No. *No.* She was dead, he decided as he entered the house in search of Atra.

If he believed it, why was he so afraid of someone else hearing him call his daughter's name?

"Tom."

It was the closest he'd ever come to shitting himself.

He didn't think he screamed. In fact, he didn't think he did anything but nearly pass out from shock.

"Is that you?"

Glasser.

The man was a cockroach.

"I'm so glad you're here," Glasser said, sounding like he was talking from a mouth shot full of novocaine.

"How in the fuck are you still alive?" Tom's voice shook as much as his body did.

"Activated charcoal. Slows the ... poison ..." He went silent, then gasped, as if shocked back to life. "Tom! Molly's here!"

"Atra? Do you mean Atra?"

Before Glasser could answer, a haunting wail filled the night.

It didn't sound human. And what was the closest thing to not-human around here?

Ophelia.

Glasser wasn't lying dead in the greenhouse, and neither was she.

"Glasser." Tom grabbed his shirt and gave him a shake. "Answer me, dammit! Is Atra here?"

But Glasser had slipped back into his poisoned delirium. Tom dropped him to the ground. His head hit the floor with a thud.

Tom gripped the gun. He could shoot Ophelia, but what would bullets do if a pair of shears to the jugular didn't stop her?

Maybe he didn't need to stop her. Maybe he just needed to close the rift.

Leaving Glasser to die, Tom bolted outside.

Ophelia was standing in a clearing between the house and a dead tree.

Where was Atra?

He scoured the area, searching around the tree, around the—

In the seconds he'd taken to look around, Ophelia had disappeared.

He charged forward.

Where did she go?!

He reached the tree. Nothing here but some rope and a—

Oh shit.

He picked up the dagger, the edge red. He touched it; the blood was still warm.

"Atra!" he bellowed, into the cold night. "Where are you?"

Atra had entered the house in the forest. Its familiar wooden cupboards lined the kitchen walls.

This wasn't right. She was supposed to be done with this place.

"Lex?"

The kid's back was to Atra, two bright orange braids trailing down it. She stood on a wooden stool in front of the sink. The water running from the tap swirled steam into the air.

Lex didn't acknowledge her as she plopped a plate still dripping with soap bubbles into the dish rack.

Atra stepped closer, hesitant to leave the doorway lest it disappear and trap her here again.

"It's my brother's turn to do the dishes." *Clink!* "But he's not here anymore."

"You mean you're not here anymore."

Lex turned, all grown up.

"You can come with me," she offered. "When you're finished with the Queen. You have as much a right to be over here as there." A pause. "You can join *us*."

The banging of palms against the window above the sink. Seth stood on the other side. He pointed to something behind Atra, and although she couldn't hear him, he was shouting her name.

She stumbled, hitting the kitchen table. She didn't want to, but she forced herself to look out the window again. Nothing out there but the forest.

"No, I can't come with you," she told Lex. "I have to stop living with the dead."

Lex nodded, understanding.

The door behind Atra swung open, hinges creaking. Spilling across the floor and onto the table was the shadow of a robed figure. It wore a crown that resembled a pair of horns.

The Queen.

Atra ran across the kitchen and bolted up the stairs.

There was a single, narrow hallway on this landing, leading into a bedroom. She recognized the grey carpet immediately.

The bedroom from her childhood. She wasn't done with it.

Control Dread. Keep the Queen out.

The only way she could do that was if she faced the thing under the bed again.

Something dark darted across the bedroom carpet. A shadow with pointed horns flooded the hall.

Ophelia stepped into the doorway. Atra's veins turned to ice.

"The police are on their way," Ophelia threatened.

Atra recognized the yellow-handled screwdriver in her clutches.

A memory, just a memory.

This was Dread, throwing obstacles in her way because it knew she was coming.

"They'll lock you up for violence against your own stepmother."

Ophelia wasn't real. So, why was she so hard to ignore? Although the words were only an echo from the past, the threat behind them had been real once.

The screwdriver hovered over Ophelia's thigh in the terrible moment *before*, the triumph plastered across her face—

Atra ran forward before Ophelia could go through with it.

She can't hurt me, she's not real—

Ophelia grinned. That wasn't part of the memory. The purple-grey veins trailing from her temples down to her jaw pulsed under her skin.

Atra didn't remember turning. She didn't remember running down the stairs or bursting outside. She was suddenly on the front lawn of her old house, legs pumping as hard as they could, but still not fast enough. The yard was so big ... or was she small? Was she a child again?

She dove into the hedges lining the front of the property, squeezing her eyes shut as the tangle of branches scraped against her face. How did Ophelia get here?

Ophelia stalked across the lawn, sweeping her head from side to side. Something resembling a thick artery protruded from her stomach.

Atra leaned forward, trying to make sense of it. The cord—tube?—attached to Ophelia extended beyond the lawn, as far as the eye could see. Did it extend beyond the planes? Ophelia seemed unaware of it.

A branch snapped under Atra's foot. Ophelia swivelled around. Atra let out a silent hiss; how was she ever going to get around Ophelia and back into the house? She needed to get to her bedroom.

The planes heard her desperate thoughts. A doorway appeared in the middle of the lawn.

Ophelia noticed it too.

"What do we have—?" Her mocking tone broke off, as her gaze landed on the grey carpet.

Atra saw it click in her mind.

Ophelia rushed for the door.

No, no, no.

Atra scrambled to her feet, running after her stepmother. Her chest hiccupped in panic as Ophelia disappeared through the door that led to the bed and Dread under it.

Atra followed. Catching up, she slammed into Ophelia with all the force she had. They both went sprawling. Atra's shoulder hit the ground hard, but she ignored the pain and pulled herself toward the bed. At least, she hoped; the room had been turned upside down in the collision.

Ophelia grabbed at her sweatpants, but Atra was quick enough to jerk away. She heaved herself forward, out of Ophelia's grasp. Every ounce of her concentration was on the bed. The gaping blackness underneath grew closer, something shining within.

Dread's eyes?

The fingers locked around her leg again, crushing her ankle. Atra clawed at the carpet, nails catching the fibres as Ophelia dragged her back.

A weight landed on her. A sharp pain shot through her kidneys as something bony dug into them—a kneecap. Ophelia was crawling over her, pinning her down, inching closer to the bed.

It couldn't end like this, face smashed into the carpet, forced to watch as her stepmother wrenched Dread away from her.

The crushing heaviness abated, weightlessness taking its place.

Atra looked down. She felt the carpet under her hands but had a clear view through the floor. What was supporting her?

Her stepmother was in the bedroom below her, sprawled out on the floor with the bed in front of her.

But Atra was *also* in the bedroom with the bed in front of her.

Which version of the room was true?

Ophelia pushed her hand under the bed, coming up empty.

The lie was down there.

A hand seized Atra's wrist, yanking her forward. For a split second, she thought Ophelia had found her, but those putrefied fingers were too familiar.

Dread.

Terror gripped her as she braced her free hand against the bed.

Push and pull.

Black and white.

The end for one of them. But which one would consume the other?

Atra dug her boots into the carpet, pushing against the bed frame. She and Dread were deadlocked, both only as strong as the other.

She let out a cry, tapping into the deepest reserves of her strength. Her shoulder threatened to pop out of its socket from the force as she drew Dread out.

Dread emerged like a deep-sea creature exposed to light for the first time. Atra's first reaction was utter disgust.

It was grey, dead, withered, its milky eyes fixed on her. Atra fought back her revulsion as she pinned it to the floor. Dread's face contorted, twisted mouth showing rotten stumps. An odour wafted from it like something left underwater to decay.

Neglected.

And whose fault was that?

What would it look like if Atra hadn't spent her life trying to drown it out? It thrashed, desperately trying to break her grip.

"Where is she?" Ophelia screamed from below.

Dread momentarily ceased its struggle. Atra couldn't read the expression on its face. If Dread was her, then it should feel the same resentment and hatred toward Ophelia as she did.

But Dread was also different; it didn't belong to the world of the living. It wanted to go to the Otherside. And their stepmother was the perfect vessel to hitch a ride on.

Dread writhed again. Atra couldn't stand its leathery flesh under her fingers, but she held on. This was *her*. She shouldn't be disgusted.

"Atra!"

A voice rang through her head. Dad. She instantly recognized it.

So did Dread. It stopped moving, eyes narrowed, suspicious.

"Attie?"

Where was Dad coming from?

Trick or truth?

One way to find out.

"Dad?"

She sensed him breathe a sigh of relief.

"Where are you? Are you safe?" The confusion in his voice mirrored the confusion she felt.

He wasn't in the planes, that she was sure of; but how was he listening in? How were they speaking?

"Yeah, I'm safe." Atra's voice cracked with the lie.

"Good." Dad sounded distracted. "Look, kiddo, I don't know how we're doing this. But we both know how this ended the last time I closed the portal. If we don't talk again, I want you to—"

He was saying goodbye. The realization of what he intended to do dawned on her.

Everything fell into place. Atra now understood what the

strange cord protruding from Ophelia was—a feeding tube. One end was attached to her, and the other attached to the Queen.

Keep the Queen out, Lex had warned.

"DON'T CLOSE THE RIFT YET!"

That caught Dread's attention. It bucked her off, wresting itself free. Atra flew back as Dread sprang onto the bed.

"What? Why?" Dad asked.

Dread stared her down, its muscles tensed, a wild animal out of its cage.

"I don't have time to explain, but I think Ophelia is connected to the Otherside through the rift. The rift won't close until her connection is severed."

"How—"

"You have to trust me, Dad. Please."

"I don't know where Ophelia is." Dad's voice was filled with desperation, verging on giving up.

"I do. I'm with her now."

"WHAT?!"

"I've got this."

"I thought you said you were safe!"

"Wait for me, Dad. *I'm* not saying goodbye."

She broke the link between them. A new idea flooded in as she turned her attention to Dread.

"That was our dad." She then nodded to the ground below. "But down there? That's not our mom. She'll never be our mom. She doesn't want you because she loves you."

Dread blinked.

"She'll only take what she needs from you. Because that's what she does. She takes. She'll never give you what you need."

Atra choked up. She wasn't just telling Dread this; she was telling herself. How strange it was to have this revelation while confronting the thing she'd been hiding from her entire life.

Beneath Dread's milky eyes, her own were staring back, scared and confused. Atra's disgust for it was fading.

"We need to stop her."

Dread didn't respond. Was it understanding her?

"I think we need to cut that cord before Dad can close the rift."

Dread cocked its head.

A flutter of something between excitement and triumph caught in Atra's chest. Maybe she was getting through.

Without warning, Dread bolted. It scampered past. Before Atra had a chance to react, it was through the door and out of sight.

Chapter 29

Blackout

Ophelia's boots echoed off the linoleum as she crossed the stark white hall. A sharp, clinical odour stung her nostrils.

Although she had never stepped foot in it, this was the nuthouse she'd thrown her stepdaughter into. Where she should've been left to rot as far as Ophelia was concerned.

She sensed the lunar eclipse shift overhead—or wherever it was, up or down didn't exist in here—reaching totality. The barriers would never be this thin again. She needed to merge with the Queen *now*, before the window closed.

Where was Atra?

They'd worked so hard. Sacrificed so much. From building The Drove to burying the crooked cop under the tree.

One little brat in hiding wasn't about to ruin that. Ophelia would prevail.

She stepped through a doorway at the end of the hall, the shadow of the Queen's horned crown cast across the floor in front of her.

The bedroom she entered was as stark as the rest of this place. And there, standing between the metal-framed twin beds: Atra. She faced away, unaware of Ophelia's presence.

Not her, though. Ophelia observed the spill of matted black hair, the grey flesh.

The other half. The half the Queen needed.

It turned and faced her.

"Do you know what you are?" Ophelia asked, as she advanced.

The thing stared at her. It didn't run. It didn't hide.

"I can make you whole. You don't have to be half of anything if you come with me."

With each step closer, the bond between her and the Queen solidified. All her life, she'd lusted after the feeling of being powerful. Of being complete.

That feeling was within reach.

"I can take you to where you belong."

She stopped in front of it. It continued to stare at her with its clouded eyes.

Ophelia reached out, wrapping her fingers around its neck.

Atra emerged from the bathroom. Ophelia, fixated on Dread, didn't notice.

A profound agony spread through her as Ophelia siphoned off Dread. Atra moved too slowly, as if wading through a bog. This was a mistake; Ophelia was going to deplete Dread before Atra could reach her.

No.

She pressed ahead, through the bog, willing her feet to move faster.

Almost there, almost there.

Ophelia still hadn't noticed her.

Atra reached out and grabbed the cord connecting Ophelia to the Queen. Its slippery, tough texture reminded her of a giant exposed artery.

Ophelia spun around, mouth agape. Her face mirrored the deep ache that gnawed at Atra's stomach.

Dread slipped out of Ophelia's weakened clutches. It wrapped its decaying fingers around the cord as well.

A crease of confusion and pain formed between Ophelia's brows as she lurched forward. She clutched at her midsection, realizing what was happening. Her gaze flicked between Atra and Dread. She snarled, trying to take a step toward them, but the tension on the cord kept her locked in place.

The cord pulsed under Atra's palms. Her eyes watered under the fluorescent lights.

How many times would she keep coming back to this asylum?

Enough of her life had already been wasted in it. All because of the vile woman in front of her. Ophelia had robbed her of her childhood, robbed her of her teenage years, and now she was trying to rob her of half her being.

Atra let out a cry, her pent-up rage the final push she needed. With a tremendous tug, the cord ripped in two.

She stumbled back. The cord turned to ash as it disintegrated in her hands.

Ophelia stared at the severed stump, appearing oddly naked. Then—

Her face contorted, reflecting the furious storm inside her, ready to destroy anything in its path. Atra braced herself for the wrath, but Ophelia didn't take two steps before suffering the same fate as the cord.

She crumbled into nothing.

Did Atra kill her? Or had Ophelia merely returned to her mortal body?

Atra and Dread were left alone. The rise and fall of Atra's chest matched Dread's own.

Lex was right; she couldn't destroy it. It was a part of her.

Dread knew it too. Because these weren't Atra's thoughts anymore; they had merged with Dread's.

She held up her arms, fingers spread out, palms turned out. Dread mirrored her movements as they stood, facing one another.

No more fearing it. No more hiding from it.

Atra's hands trembled as she moved toward Dread.

Tom stood halfway between the clearing and the greenhouse. He turned, not knowing which direction Atra—or Ophelia, for that matter—might come from.

The moon was a blood-red eye, challenging him: *The rift, Tom. Close it.*

And he could.

But where was Atra? If she didn't show herself before the eclipse waned, he'd have to—

Movement in the clearing. Shit. Ophelia. He fumbled, nearly dropping the handgun. Where the fuck had she come from?

She stepped toward the tree, then sank to her knees. Something was wrong. The corners of her eye sockets and mouth drooped, like a jack-o-lantern left on a porch to rot.

Where was Atra?

"My Queen!" Ophelia's harrowing cry echoed through the night. "Come back to me!"

She reached for the trunk, still glowing with the power of the rift, then jerked her hands away. Tom smelled seared flesh.

"My Queen!" Ophelia knelt in front of the tree. She held out her scorched palms, crippled body wracked with sobs. "Let me in, wait for me, *I beg* ..."

Tom aimed the barrel at her with shaking hands. He'd never fired a gun in his life.

A rustling; the faint snap of a twig. He jerked around, expecting Glasser to be lurking about, but nothing. He turned back to the tree.

Two people in front of it now.

He was in time to witness Ophelia deliver a blow to the side of Atra's head.

"You little bitch!" she shrieked, as Atra crumpled to the ground.

Ophelia pounced, wrapping her fingers around Atra's throat, squeezing. Her now-white hair fell over her rapidly aging face.

Atra struggled, legs kicking, hands grabbing at Ophelia, but she sank farther into the soft earth as Ophelia pinned her down.

Tom pulled the trigger. The kickback and resulting *boom!* caused him to flinch. Holy shit this thing had power.

He fired again, and again, and again, and again, ignoring the rattling shocks vibrating down his elbow and up into his shoulder blade. The gunshots did nothing to deter Ophelia; she was hellbent on one thing and one thing alone.

Tom ran for them. Why was it taking so goddamn long to—

His shoulder smashed into the ground as his legs went out from under him. Had he bashed into something, or had something run into him?

Through his dazed double vision, he made out the silhouette of Glasser stumbling toward the tree.

So Glasser was going to get through to the Otherside after all.

That didn't matter. What mattered was saving Atra.

But then ... Glasser stopped. He seized Ophelia by the shoulders and pulled her off Atra.

Tom thought he was going to escort her through the tree—maybe *they had* been working together all along. Glasser grasped her temple with one hand and cradled her chin with the other. He pulled her close, as if ready to embrace her.

A vicious *crack!* echoed through the night as he twisted her head to the side. Ophelia's final breath expelled in a puff of white. She fell toward the tree, face frozen in surprise. The whites of her eyes reflected the rift's glow.

In that moment, time slowed.

Tom didn't mean it *felt* like it slowed. It did.

A gateway opened within him. He reached for the rift, running across its edge with invisible fingers.

The same thing happened when he closed the portal all those years ago. He was going to forget this the moment it was over, wasn't he? Like last time.

He found the hinges.

Aha.

As simple as pushing a door shut.

A weight lifted as a giddiness overtook him. He felt lighter, almost joyful. As much as he had denied it, he'd felt its presence from the start.

The night plunged into darkness as the rift blinked out of existence. Glasser dove for the tree as the light went out. His outstretched palms bounced off the tree, now solid. He stared at his hands, then at the tree, as if it would make the light return.

His hands balled into fists. They shook as he rounded on Tom, nostrils flaring.

Happy? Tom thought. *I fucking closed it for you.*

He raised the gun. One bullet left.

He didn't miss.

Atra gasped for air. When had the world gone dark? An echoing *boom!* slammed through her head. She managed to lift herself off the ground, massaging her throat. It still felt like Ophelia's hands were around her neck. Had Dad pulled her off?

That sound.

A gunshot.

Dad.

Dad?!

Atra struggled to her feet, slipping and sinking into the dirt.

Did she shoot my dad?

Her vision adjusted to the night. The world hadn't gone dark; rather, the rift had gone out.

The light of the Cold Blood Moon spilled through the dead tree branches. She made out the shape of a body beside the tree trunk.

Ophelia.

Not a whole body, Atra saw as she approached. Just a pair of legs, still clothed in a long skirt and boots. The tree had sliced Ophelia neatly in half when it sealed shut.

Someone else was lying facedown beside her. Atra forced herself not to think of who it was as she scrambled toward them and rolled the dead weight over.

No, not dead weight. He's not dead, he's not fucking dead—

He wasn't her dad, either. It was the man from inside Ophelia's house.

Atra touched something warm across his front and jerked away. His hand lashed out, seizing her around the wrist.

"Atra?" Glasser's eyes flashed as if seeing her for the first time.

"Where's my dad?" She tried to yank her hand away, but his grip was unrelenting. "You were with him at Polaris. Where is Tom Hart?"

His neck muscles went slack as his head sank into the earth.

"He did it. I can't believe he did it."

Something dark trickled out of the corner of his mouth.

"He left us all to die."

She backed off as his fingers slipped off her wrist.

"All of us in Polaris, left to die ..."

His eyelids fluttered shut and his hands contorted into C-shapes over his chest. His lips moved, but no sound came out.

He left you too, she thought he mouthed.

"Atra!"

The hoarse cry of Dad's voice. Running to her. Hugging her. She wanted to throw him off, but Glasser's last words had physically winded her.

He left you too.
"Are you okay?"

Nausea twisted in her stomach.

Tom pulled away, holding her by the shoulders. She couldn't bring herself to look at him.

"Atra. Are you okay?"

Was she?

She flexed her jaw. Her temple throbbed where Ophelia smashed it, but no permanent damage had been done. Out of the corner of her eye, her shadow did the same. A perfect mirror.

"I'm not hurt."

The air was heavy with unresolved questions. Everything was too still, including inside of her. The tugging sensation that led her here abated. Because the rift had closed, or because she'd accepted Dread?

"Good ... good ..." Tom's gaze slipped over her shoulder, focus no longer on her. Typical. "Shit."

He let go, moving over to Glasser's body. He crouched beside it. Atra thought he was going to prod it, but instead wiped a metallic object off on Glasser's suit jacket. A handgun.

Atra realized who'd fired it.

"We have to get out of here, kiddo." Tom placed the gun beside Glasser. "Someone will have heard the gunshots, and this scene is fucked."

He straightened up, pushing the hair out of his eyes.

"I don't think either of us wanna be found here."

Either of us.

Whether she liked it or not, they were in this together. And they had been from the beginning.

She stared at the bottom half of Ophelia. The only evidence left that the wretched woman ever existed.

"I mean ..." Tom added almost meekly, "if you want to come with me." He seemed to be remembering her previous carjacking.

Atra paused.

Seth's urn, sitting on the mantel, leapt to mind.

No big brother. No big dream. None of that was real.

This was her reality. Her only family left was the lying coward in front of her. She could either be like him and run, or she could accept it. Deal with it.

Because they were in this together.

"Yeah, Dad." She forced herself to meet his eyes. "Let's go."

Epilogue

In the Cold Light of Morning

The grey light of impending dawn filtered through the window to Atra's right. Her fingers rested on the metal edge of the table. The smell of coffee and frying bacon filled the air.

Her stomach growled.

How different this was from the last café she'd been in, right after the fire. How different *she* was.

Instead of Dread at her side, Dad sat across the too-small table. He offered her a thin smile as he stirred sugar and ample amounts of cream into his coffee. Dark purple-grey bags hung under his weary eyes, mirroring Atra's own. Neither of them had anything left to say.

She lifted her dripping-wet hair off her shoulder, letting it fall down the back of her new T-shirt, courtesy of the gift shop connected to this truck stop diner. The stiff, scratchy fabric was still creased where it had sat folded on the shelf. She'd rinsed off in the attached showers, washing the grime and evidence of the past week down the drain.

The journey from the cypress tree was a blur of utter exhaustion, mixed with too much adrenaline. Atra still couldn't believe it was over.

They'd stopped somewhere beyond the city limits of Telos. Atra didn't know if they'd be travelling farther. Dad appeared satisfied with the distance put between them and Ophelia's house. For now, at least.

He'd taken Ophelia's wallet, draining her bank account at an ATM. He talked a lot about money, seeming very concerned by it.

He also seemed very concerned about where he was going to go. Not his apartment; from what Atra gathered, he was in a lot of trouble.

He, he, he.

He barely asked how she was doing. She was remembering what he was like. All Tom, all the time.

She didn't know where they would sleep after breakfast. That was Dad's problem. He was the parent, not the other way around. Time for him to step up for a change.

A waitress came, setting a hot chocolate in front of Atra. She took their order. Atra got the same thing as Dad—the "Breakfast Special," whatever that meant. As long as it wasn't powdered eggs, her stomach would be happy.

She took a sip of her drink. Out of the corner of her eye, her reflection did the same. So strange, after all these years, to not see her shadow moving on its own. She kept wanting to turn, to make sure Dread hadn't returned but knew the answer without looking.

For the first time in her life, she felt whole. Anxiety no longer buzzed through her, putting her on edge, questioning her own mind.

Atra finally got her greatest wish: her demonic shadow had been banished. A girl divided she was no longer.

She thought once that was solved, she'd be happy. The pieces would fall into place; she'd have it figured out.

The opposite could not be more true.

Seth was dead. Her dream of living with him was over before it began. All she had was a father who lied to her. Who—

The squeak of Dad's chair against the floor.

"Going to the bathroom," he muttered, standing.
She nodded.
He left you too.
Glasser's last words tormented her.

Was she there, at Polaris, when Dad shut the portal? Lex never specified. And Atra, with her fractured childhood memories, couldn't recall.

What could she do?

Hey Dad, before we eat, quick question: did you leave me for dead before you ran away?

He'd deny it either way.

Was this how she was going to start her life anew?

No, she didn't want this—some sad gas station truck stop with a sad breakfast and a sad excuse for a father.

Though she was free of the asylum and the shadow that landed her there, she still didn't belong anywhere. Maybe she should've gone with Lex, further into the planes, to the Otherside.

Dad's wallet sat tucked between the napkin holder and the window. Bulging with all that cash. She had already left him once, yet he trusted her with this. That meant something.

Or was it an oversight? Was he too absorbed in himself to pay attention?

Atra's bet was on the latter.

Her hand moved for the wallet.

She could leave. But the real world was a vast ocean and she was adrift in the middle of it. How would she get a job, get a house, *live* like a normal person? She couldn't exist in that ocean without an anchor. And, as much as she hated it, that anchor was her father.

She froze, her hand outstretched. Something caught the corner of her eye. A sharp blade of terror pierced her. Dread?

Her head whipped around.

On the concrete pad in front of the gas pumps sat a bushy

black cat. The orange tips of his fur were bleached white in the cold light of morning.

Atra retracted her hand, leaving the wallet be. Leaning back in the chair, she grabbed her mug and took another drink. She hadn't tasted anything this good in ... well, she couldn't remember.

The hinges squeaked as the bathroom door opened. Footsteps approached the table.

Through the window, Oriens stared at her with his bright green eyes, unblinking.

No, she wasn't alone after all.

Thank you for reading

If you enjoyed this book, please consider leaving a review. Reviews are the lifeblood for indie authors. Even if you write "I liked this book" it means a lot. In fact, you could even leave an incoherent keyboard smash. A review that says ";ksjdVHUwr" still helps immensely.

AMAZON  GOODREADS

And if you really, really enjoyed this book, consider subscribing to my newsletter for exclusive short stories and publishing updates.

Acknowledgments

First and foremost, the biggest of thanks to Chris, Claudia, and Kerri for not only being awesome beta readers but for also being awesome friends. (And for answering all my stupid questions many times over because I kept forgetting what you said.)

Thank you so much to Little Red Herring Editing for the proofreads. And for dealing with my problem with hyphens and unspaced ellipses.

Thanks to my family for everything. I'm not going to write a long, mushy post because, quite frankly, it would make us all gag.

Big thanks to Ian for dealing with all the mental breakdowns that came with this story and still, for some miraculous reason, wanting to be around me.

Finally, thanks to my cat for existing. Because you don't do much else and you don't need to.

About the Author

Sam was named after a dog, a fact her mother disputes to this day.

While she's terrible at writing "About Me"s about her, she's been told she's great at writing about what fictional people do. The more miserable she can make them, the better.

Her love of horror films from the 80s, sci-fi shows from the 90s, and alternative music from the 00s have inspired her to write what she's calling "Weird Sci-fi Horror" although she's kind of making that up as she goes along.

When she's not ready to pull her hair out after discovering another plot hole she's created, she goes camping with her husband as far away from society as possible. So far, this tactic has been mostly successful and she's only had to physically converse with a grand total of nine people this year. Next year, she hopes to get that number down to six.

http://authorsamweiss.com/

 instagram.com/samwisestrange

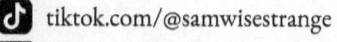 tiktok.com/@samwisestrange

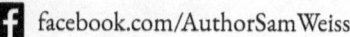 facebook.com/AuthorSamWeiss

www.ingramcontent.com/pod-product-compliance
Lightning Source LLC
LaVergne TN
LVHW091531060526
838200LV00036B/563